MINNOW TRAP

Brian Horeck

ISBN 1-55383-078-4

Printed and bound in Canada by Friesens

Thank you to:

My loving and patient wife, Shirley

Sean Costello, author

Ministry of Natural Resources
Blind River Office

Dr. John Gunn
Laurentian University
Sudbury, Ontario

Embassy of the Russian Federation in Ottawa

Sault Ste. Marie Armoury

Arnold Schwarzenegger

Stacey Clark, History Teacher
W. C. Eaket Secondary School
Blind River, Ontario

Lindsay Killen, History Teacher
Elliot Lake Secondary School
Elliot Lake, Ontario

Front cover art by Gerry Dunphy
Copy editing by Catherine Lake
Book design by Kim Diamond

Author's Note

Some people experience an event in their lives that greatly changes the way they look at things. We learn to appreciate life and to not just take it for granted, especially when it comes to family, friends and all of God's beautiful creation around us.

My story represents that vision — to help us see how small we really are in this vast universe and yet what an important role each of us plays with our fellow man.

chapter 1

retirement

It was mid-June, on a sunny afternoon in Northern Ontario. Steve and his wife Mary were in Sudbury at a motorcycle dealership shopping for a new four-wheeler. Steve, at age fifty-five, had just recently sold his business. They had both decided that because of his heart problems, he should retire.

"I think I'm going to keep the old bike as back up," he said. "It's still in good shape." He saw Mary in the corner of his eye, nodding in agreement.

"Well Steve, I think you've made the right choice," replied Eric, the salesman. "This Honda has all the power you'll need for hauling those heavy loads on hunting and fishing trips. It can really handle those rugged, twisted trails you were talking about."

Steve was already sold on the model. "Now that I have more time, I'm really looking forward to this. Check this out Mary! It has a built-in GPS."

"Whatever dear," she responded with little interest in the bike's options. She stood back and observed him sitting high on the bike with an ear-to-ear smile, like a kid on one of those coin-operated rocking horses.

"It's a global positioning system that works off a satellite. I'll be able to log key hunting and fishing areas. So Eric, how soon can you have her ready?"

"It'll take us about ten minutes for the paperwork. She's already been serviced. You can back your truck up to the showroom doors and load'er up."

"Well, go ahead and get started then!" he said anxiously. "Mary, remind me to call Mike or Bob. We'll need to use their pontoon boat to bring it across the lake."

"Sure dear." She was happy to see his excitement.

Thirty minutes later, Steve and Mary

were traveling west on the Trans-Canada Highway, singing along to a rock and roll classic on the radio.

"You wanted to make that call," she reminded him, cutting into his song.

"Thanks." Turning the volume down, he dialed his cell phone. After a cheerful conversation he laid his cell phone on the dash and smiled. "Well Mary, I have horseshoes up my ass! Mike and Bob were just heading out fishing. Carol caught them as they were untying the boat. Bob said they would meet us at the public dock in about an hour with something cold to drink. Oh yes. Remind me to pick up some minnows for Bob."

"Sure Steve. That's the least you can do. It's nice that you guys are always there for each other."

Steve had grown up on Birch Lake with his fishing and hunting buddies, Mike and Bob. The brothers had cottages side by side, at the north end of the lake. Steve and Mary's cottage was at the opposite end.

Forty-five minutes later, Steve and Mary turned off the highway onto an old back country gravel road, just north of the

Town of Webbwood. The area has a high summer population of cottagers who travel from as far away as Chicago and Detroit just to, as they say, get a taste of God's country.

During this part of their trip, Steve enjoyed the ritual of rolling down his window and deeply inhaling the countryside air like his father and mother did in their time. The fragrance was a blend of newly flowered white Ontario trilliums along with other fresh growths of wildflowers. Every mile or so, an old farmhouse would appear. Cows and horses could always be seen standing with their offspring alongside rustic, snake-rail fencing that had somehow stood the test of time. Now and then, the road crossed over a small meandering creek, which was often occupied with a mother mallard and her ducklings. Then the farmland feathered out into a denser bush line of pine and hardwoods that suddenly became dominated with aggressive terrain. And one would be more apt to see deer, moose or a black bear crossing the road.

"I'm sure glad you didn't trade in our

old dependable bike," Mary said, leaning over to turn off the radio.

"Yeah, tell me about it! We would've taken too much of a loss."

"It'll make for a good backup at times, and Sarah will sure be happy to know she won't have to double-up anymore. Remember Steve, one of the first things I want to do when we settle in, is to dig up some of those large ferns. Like how your sister transplanted some along that back trail behind the cottage. We can plant some ferns around the rock garden. I also want to bring a few clumps home. They would really compliment the flowers in our backyard." Mary looked over at Steve. He was pre-occupied, checking out his new bike in his rearview mirror. "Did you even hear a word I said?"

"Oh yes, Mary. We'll make it top priority!" he replied while still checking out his new ATV. "I can hardly wait to try'er out."

Mary snuggled up close to him, like when they were first courting. Happy for his excitement over his new toy, she said, "Well dear, it's time you start having more R & R."

They drove down a steep incline where they could see the lake and boat-launch area. Bob and Mike were standing on the dock beside the pontoon boat, each with a beer in hand.

Steve turned his truck around, and backed down to line up with Bob's boat. Mike directed him with hand signals. He held his left hand out flat like a traffic cop, still holding his beer casually in his right hand. "Okay stop. You're good right there," said Mike.

Steve no sooner got out of his truck when Bob and Mike began to congratulate him with strong handshakes on his retirement. "So how is Mr. Easy Street doing this afternoon?" asked Bob.

"I don't know yet. But I'm sure glad you guys could make it to help us take this bike across!"

Bob responded. "The pleasure is ours!"

"Hope you guys weren't waiting long,"

"No. Just two beers. So is this part of your retirement package?" added Mike, checking out Steve's new bike.

"Yes," said Mary. "And it better last him for the rest of eternity!"

"Oh shit. Is this the new Canadian trail

edition with the built in GPS?"

"That's right Bob," Steve replied as he started releasing it from the truck.

"You really went all out with this one!" said Mike.

"I had to! You heard my boss. So I got the Cadillac."

"That you did!" responded Mike, still eyeing the bike. He helped Steve unfasten the remaining hold-down straps. Meanwhile, Bob lowered the truck's tail-gate, and proceeded to set up the ramps.

"Let's see if I still remember how to start this thing," said Steve, as he climbed up onto the bike.

"And don't forget to turn the side fuel lever on," suggested Bob.

"Well I guess it would sure help," he smiled. "Pull out the choke. Okay, here's the start button." He compressed it, and the engine started up. "Next, take the choke off. All right now. Let's try'er in reverse. Stand back. Here goes nothing." He squeezed the throttle a little, with a confused look on his face. "What's wrong? It won't move!"

"You're right about here goes nothing," commented Mary, walking by Steve carrying a cooler down to the boat, with a smirk on her face. Steve was nervous enough trying to familiarize himself with the vehicle, he didn't need any smart remarks. Bob and Mike knew how hyper Steve could get under pressure. They wouldn't dare make any wise cracks towards him. Only Mary could get away with that. And she played it all the way to the bank when she had her chance.

"Maybe try taking the park brake off!" said Mike with a smile.

"Holy shit. You guys know more about my bike than I do. Okay. Here we go again!" He backed down the ramp onto Bob's pontoon boat. "That went on like a piece of cake," Steve said as he turned the engine off.

"Now remember to put your parking brake on. Or it'll sink to the bottom of the lake, like a lead balloon!" said Bob, trying to be casual. They continued to unload luggage from his truck onto the boat.

"Now just give me two minutes to park my truck, funny boy. Then I'll be ready to go!" He briskly walked toward his truck, being anxious to get out onto the lake.

Mary shouted. "Now slow yourself

down dear. Or you'll have to give your-self a shot of nitro," quite concerned over his aggressiveness.

"Oh, come on now Mary. As if." Looking back at her, he felt embarrassed from her remarks in front of his best friends.

"He really hasn't been feeling too good lately," said Mary to Bob and Mike. "Hopefully his new medication is going to help."

"I'm glad you told us that Mary," said Bob. "We all know how stubborn he can be at times."

"He still thinks he's twenty-five!" she said shaking her head.

"A toast to Steve's retirement," said Mike, handing Steve and Mary each a can of beer.

"And let's not forget our new hunting partner!" Steve clanged his beer can against his new bike, with rest of them following suit. Departing from the dock in Bob's pontoon boat, Steve sat on his bike, playing with the GPS buttons impressed with his bike's technology. "Holy shit! It has the whole North

American map downloaded in it."

"I don't know why you need all that fancy-ass stuff! You've never got lost before," remarked Mike, looking over Steve's shoulder.

"That's because everyone always told him where to go," said Bob.

Everyone was having a good laugh. Halfway across the lake, they came across a pontoon boat cruising slowly with an attractive, middle-aged, well-tanned brunet. She was wearing a small green bikini and dark sunglasses. She managed to navigate with a book in one hand and a cocktail in the other. Bob slowed down as he approached, and pulled up alongside her boat.

"I can't understand why you're not dragging a fishing line behind your boat. Especially when the lake trout are up high this time of year," shouted Steve so he could be heard over the sound of Bob's motor.

"Steve, all I want is the sun, a good book, my cocktail and a quiet, relaxing boat cruise. Which I was having 'til you rudely interrupted me!" she replied, as they all started laughing.

"Brenda sure told you!" said Mike.

"Okay, okay! Don't be a stranger. And drop in for a cold one! We're up all week," said Steve. "Better yet, come over tomorrow afternoon for a barbecue."

"Make it around six, for a before-dinner cocktail," said Mary.

"Sure Mary. What can I bring?"

"Just your appetite. Steve is doing his ribs."

"I'll be there. And by the way, I like Steve's new boat seat. It looks like it has lots of options. I'll have to check it out tomorrow."

"We'll catch you later. And don't catch too many. I mean too many sunrays," said Steve.

"Ha!" she replied with a smile as they departed.

"I still can't believe that Bill isn't with us anymore. But he's looking down at her right now, proud to see how well she's adjusting out here," said Bob.

"I hope someday she'll meet the right guy," said Mary.

"You mean to help her get out of that cocoon of anxiety," remarked Steve, feeling bitter over Brenda's snappy response to his gesture. He knew full well that Brenda would be fishing if Bill was still around.

"Well I'm sorry Steve, but I don't believe that at all. She's doing quite well for herself," said Mary.

At this point, Steve realized he hadn't said the right thing. "Well to fill Bill's shoes, you have to be over six feet tall, love the outdoors and have a great sense of humor!" said Steve.

"And don't forget the beer!" replied Mike.

"Here's to you Bill!" said Steve, raising his beer can and looking up to the sky, with the rest of the crew doing the same.

"When you were razzing Brenda for not trolling, it reminded me, did you buy some minnows?" asked Bob.

"Ah shit!" replied Steve with a disappointed look, shaking his head in disgust.

"Ever since we left the shop, the only thing he could think of, was to get that bike on the trail," said Mary.

Steve was upset for letting Bob down. "I'm really sorry guys. But I think that the large pond at the end of our trail should have minnows in it." He was trying hard to compensate for his forgetfulness.

"We've never seen any fish ducks in that old, abandoned beaver pond," said Mike.

"That doesn't mean anything. I'll set a minnow trap in there before dark."

"I'll make sure of that Mike," said Mary. "Because I'll go along as well so he doesn't forget my ferns either!"

"Damn! Now I have my wife in my face as well."

"Well, I'm sure glad your head is screwed on," remarked Bob.

"Yep, or I'd forget that too," replied Steve shaking his head from side to side, while rolling his eyes back.

"Looks like Steve won't be breaking-in his new toy today," said Mike, looking up at the dark clouds that were quickly moving in from the west end of the lake.

They arrived at Steve and Mary's cottage, pulling up alongside a dock which extended out from a natural white sandy beach. A patio stone ramp led up to their cottage making it easy for them to bring up supplies in a trailer hitched to their ATV. They didn't waste any time unloading the bike and supplies.

"Don't forget to tell the girls about the barbecue tomorrow afternoon," said Mary, while untying the bow rope.

"My name isn't Steve," replied Mike with a big grin on his face. "What can we bring?"

"Extra ice. And, for being such a smart ass Mike, a couple bottles of your great wine," replied Steve. He started his bike, "Thanks again for your help guys."

"Don't think we're letting you off that easy," said Bob as he started his outboard. "I'll just put the ride on your tab."

"Go ahead!" shouted Steve, as they departed from the dock.

"Let's get this stuff up to the cottage, before we get dumped on," urged Mary.

That night it was cool, dark and rainy. Mike and his wife Carol were entertaining Bob and Janis at their cottage. As the two couples sat comfortably in front of the fireplace sipping Spanish coffees, the sound of heavy rain could be heard falling on the roof.

"Mike, that dinner should keep me full for the next week. Carol, your apple pie sure was great!" said Bob. "Thank God for sweatpants! That reminds me, Steve and Mary want us over for a barbecue tomorrow."

"Sounds good. That'll be two days without cooking dinner," said Janis. "Bob and I will have to entertain soon."

Just then, a bright light flashed across the lake startling Mike and Carol. "What the hell!" said Mike jumping to his feet and running to his telescope at his front window.

"What's going on?" asked Bob, walking towards him.

"It was a bright beam of light coming from the top of that high rock bluff, across the lake!" said Mike peering through his telescope.

"And what in the hell do you expect to see through that thing on a dark, rainy night like this?" asked Bob with confusion.

"Nothing. Unless that light reappears. Then I'll be able to take a heading on it. I hope it's not Steve up there on his bike! That pond where he wants to set his minnow trap is just on the other side of that ridge. And his trail follows to that very spot."

"It was probably lighting" said Bob.

"No. It wasn't a lightning bolt. It was a straight beam of light."

"I saw it too," remarked Carol. "It wasn't lightening because we're not hearing thunder."

"True enough," replied Bob with a concerned look, nodding his head.

"Steve's not that desperate for minnows to be out on a night like this," exclaimed Janis.

"Steve was so excited over his new toy that he forgot to buy Bob some minnows at the bait shop. He mentioned he'd try to trap some in the pond behind that high bluff."

"Isn't it dangerous to be up there on a dark, rainy night like tonight?" asked Janis.

"Let's just give Steve and Mary a call on their cell," said Bob.

"No, let's not bother them. If he's crazy enough to be out there on a night like this, and doesn't make it back to Mary by a certain time, she'll be calling us," remarked Mike.

"That's right Mike," said Bob, as they

both went back and joined their wives by the fireplace.

Mike shook his head and muttered to himself, while taking his place on the couch beside Carol. "I know freakin' well it wasn't lighting…We didn't hear any thunder!"

Steve and Mary were relaxing in front of their fireplace, listening to some jazz music. "One more for the road." He topped off her wine glass, not giving her time to respond.

"Are you trying to take advantage of me?"

"That's the plan honey-pot," he replied with a slightly intoxicated smile.

"Well here's a toast to your retirement dear and to more R & R!"

"And more hanky-panky!" he said with his wine glass still high in the air.

"Hanky-panky my ass," Mary retorted, realizing that he was always a little frisky under the influence.

"That's exactly what I mean." He smiled seductively.

"Well, I'm ready to call it a night." As she rose from the comfort of the couch,

Steve slid his hand under her robe. "Forget it Dear. I want you to save your energy for digging up those ferns tomorrow morning."

"Okay sweetheart but I'll be back for my rain check then."

"That depends on how many ferns we bring back."

"Hmmm, now that sounds to me like a real challenge dear. And you know full well how I like a challenge. In that case I'll bring a big shovel and the trailer. Lots of ferns equal lots of hanky-panky!" He gently patted her behind and followed her closely while they proceeded up the stairway to their bedroom.

chapter 2

fern excursion

Early the next morning, Mary walked up to the woodshed with two mugs of coffee. Unlike most woodsheds, this one was quite unique. At 512 square feet, it had three large stalls for wood storage and an open area with a workbench and plenty of tools. Two large openings through the middle, Steve called it his drive through. It was convenient for parking their bikes or hauling firewood. Mary entered and found him listening to a local radio station while sharpening his chainsaw on his workbench.

"Thanks for the coffee dear. I could smell it brewing all the way up here."

"Do you plan on cutting firewood

today?" she asked with a curious look on her face.

"No. But I thought we'd bring it along in case of any fallen trees obstructing the trail. After all, we've had some high winds in the last few weeks. Will you be ready to leave soon?"

"Yeah. In about ten minutes. I packed us a lunch for the lookout. Maybe I can work on my tan and have a picnic at the same time."

"Sounds good to me baby!" he said with a flirty smile. "Will you be riding the old bike Mary?"

"No. I'll just be your passenger today." She returned a sexy smile.

"Just remember. None of my passengers ride for free."

"I won't forget big boy." She walked back to the cottage wiggling her ass, trying to arouse him in a fun way.

Mary returned with a cooler in one hand, and a small over-night bag in the other.

"You'd think that we're going for the week."

"Not a long time. But we're going for a good time. And I like your fancy customized shovel holder," she nodded towards the shovel placed in his bike's gun rack.

"I don't want it bouncing around in the trailer. The noise would drive us nuts."

"And I see you didn't forget the minnow trap."

"The guys would never let me hear the end of it. Well, climb aboard." He made sure she was comfortable. "How are the foot pegs? Are they at the right height?"

"They're quite comfortable," she said after resting her feet on them.

"You know, they can also be used as stirrups, if we get bored back there."

"Is that all you think about?"

"No, I wouldn't say that. Sometimes it's fishing, hunting, or my Blue Jays."

"Enough, enough. You men are all alike! Let's get going."

They drove along the picturesque trail, passing through high and low areas, with different trees growing throughout. Steve took them down to a large low-lying area dominated by cedars. Growing amongst them were large dark green ferns. He slowly brought the bike to a stop.

"Oh Steve. How did you ever find a spot like this?"

"This is one of the places we hunt on windy days."

Stepping down from the bike, she gave him a big kiss, reached for the shovel and handed it to him. "Now get to work big boy," she said in a sexy voice. "And should you have the slightest pain in your chest, I brought this." Mary held his nitro spray. "Now remember what your doctor said, don't be afraid to use it. I'll keep it handy." She tucked it into her cut-off jeans pocket. "Now I don't have to worry about you getting a little too physical!"

"Yes ma'am." He winked, slightly aroused over her comment. Just as soon as he would dig up a clump of ferns, she would load them into the trailer, while picking out the next bunch for him. The morning was far along, as Mary dropped another clump in the trailer.

"That trailer sure makes this job easy," she remarked.

"Seems to me, that how many ferns we bring back, the greater that some reward is going to be."

"I find it strange how you have a good

memory for some things." She walked over to him while undoing two of her top shirt buttons, exposing a lot of cleavage. "Can I interest you in a little treat right now… big boy?"

"Sure baby!" Steve planted his shovel into the ground, and wiped some sweat off his forehead.

Mary reached into the cooler and pulled out six cold beers on a plastic web. "So how would you like to grab one of these cans then?" she said, dangling the beer in front of his face. He realized that he'd been had. She was just teasing him.

"Sure. A cold one will do for now. But those other cans look more inviting." He yanked one from the pack.

"The next time you see these cans, they'll have tanning lotion on them."

Steve watched her button up and then pack the beer back into the cooler. "If that's not enough incentive for me to get these ferns loaded, nothing is. If all bosses were like you Mary, the Teamsters Union would be obsolete." He set his beer down on the bike, and started loading more ferns.

An hour later, the trailer was completely filled with ferns. "I sure hope this will keep you busy at the cottage for awhile."

"We can keep them in the trailer in the shade of the woodshed. And I can water them 'til they're transplanted. So, would you be up for a picnic?"

"Would I be? Are you kidding? I'm still up from that beer break." He placed the shovel back into the gun rack, while rubbing his crotch up against her hip. "This puppy is oversexed and undernourished!"

Mary climbed onto the passenger seat. "It sounds like I'll have to do something about that, won't I?" She patted his ass as he was taking his place on the bike.

"Well hold on. The lookout is just up over that ridge."

Parked at the highest elevation on a flat, bedrock plateau, they could see their friends' cottages down across the lake. Behind them, to the far south, they had a breathtaking view of the La Cloche Mountain Range. Just to the west lay the stunning landscape of Manitoulin Island out on Lake Huron.

"Every time I come up here, I can't get

over this view," said Steve. "Just think, a
hundred years ago they logged this
whole area out. Every spring during the
runoff, lumberjacks would float logs
down through those narrows, connecting
into the Spanish River which empties into
Lake Huron at the town of Spanish."

"Thanks for the history lesson sweetheart," said Mary getting down from the
bike. "Can you help me with this cooler?"

"Guess I got carried away," said Steve
unloading the cooler from the bike.

"Not really. It's good to remember all
the history that took place in this area."

"Some of my old scuba buddies did
shipwreck research on the north shore
region, at the archives in Ottawa. We
were surprised that one of the first
Hudson's Bay trading posts was estab-
lished in the town of Blind River—just
west of Spanish."

"This is a great spot, overlooking the
lake." They sat down to relax and enjoy
the view. "I've had a lot of coffee breaks
up here during hunting season." For a
few minutes, Steve was pre-occupied,
gazing out, not noticing Mary.

"Well then, if you want to see more,

you'll have to help me with this lotion."
To his surprise, she had already stripped
down to her thong and was laying face
down on a beach towel taking sun.

"Oh yes. I'll gladly help you with that
lotion. If you turn over," he said, hoping
she would give into him.

"Sorry. This body only turns over every
ten minutes. You snooze, you lose. But
you can do my back for now." She handed him the lotion.

"I guess that's a good start. I see Bob's
boat didn't leave his dock." Steve was
looking down across the bay while applying the lotion on her. "He really is stubborn at times."

"What do you mean?" asked Mary still
facing down on the blanket.

"You can still go fishing without live
bait. I've caught all kinds of trout and
bass on lures. I guess he's hooked on minnows only."

"Great lunch Mary," Steve said, taking
out a roll of toilet paper from the bike's
storage compartment. "But nature calls.
I'm just going up a little higher in that
bush line on this plateau."

"Hurry back! I'll need some more suntan lotion on other areas."

As he was returning to Mary, Steve came to a sudden stop. He looked down at the ground. Mary watched him staring intently. He dropped down on one knee and rubbed his hand on the rock surface. She became curious as to what was distracting him from applying suntan lotion to her front.

"What is it?" she hollered out impatiently.

"I don't know!"

"You don't know?" she inquired with surprise. Mary knew that he was very knowledgeable concerning the outdoors. And that it would take something very odd to stump him. Her mind was in a whirl as she got up from her comfortable blanket. Intrigued, she walked over to him.

From across the bay, Mike had been observing Steve and Mary. "It's really nice to see you enjoying your Father's Day gift," said Carol, who was doing dishes across the room from Mike and his telescope.

"Yeah, the scenery really makes it." He kept the telescope fixed on Steve and Mary high up on the plateau. Mike was curious and confused as to what was going on up there. "What the..." he muttered out loud.

"What's going on?" asked Carol, walking over to him.

"It's Steve and Mary up there on the lookout. Steve's seen something on the ground that's interesting enough for Mary to take a break from her tanning."

"Her tanning?" She nudged Mike to the side to look into the telescope, which was focused on Mary's backside. She was up on the plateau standing in front of Steve. "Is this what you meant by good scenery?" asked Carol angrily.

"No freakin' way! First, I was curious to see what was in Steve's trailer. Then I wanted to see what is on the ground. It's not like I haven't seen tits before!"

"I hope you're not using that thing to invade other people's privacy," Carol responded, still doubting Mike's story.

"I'm shocked that you would even think that of me," he said in an upset tone. He looked back into the telescope, leaving her wondering.

Mary was standing beside Steve as they both looked down at a flat bedrock surface. They were consumed with curiosity as to the origin of three large and mysterious ring engravings.

"What on earth could have made those marks in the rock?"

"You've really got me there Mary. Maybe it's some kind of Indian markings from hundreds of years ago. The three overlapping rings could represent the sun, the moon and the earth. But then, to make engravings like these, you'd need some heavy sandblasting equipment or impact tools. And no one could lug that all the way up here. And check out the outer ring Mary. Notice how the moss hasn't grown over it?"

"So?"

"Well, that tells us that nature didn't make these rings. What I mean is, that they aren't natural." He started walking back to his bike.

"What are you doing?"

"I'm going to drive the bike back to this spot. So I can log this into the GPS."

"Lets pack up our stuff first. We need to start heading back."

"Right. And I still want to set the min-now trap in that pond. Don't worry. I'm not letting you off that easy. I'll take my rain check later!" He gazed at her body glistening in the sun then kissed her while gently massaging her buttocks with both hands.

Minutes later, they were on the bike, parked over the strange rings on the flat bedrock. Steve logged the location into a pocket book with Mary looking over his shoulder. He pointed down to his GPS.

"That pond we are driving to is only one hundred yards due south from our position." He pointed to a steep rock cut. "We'll take our trail. The longer, but easi-er way."

They drove down a steep ridge that opened at the entrance of a large pond. About the size of a football field, its perimeter was high rocky bluffs. A large, old beaver dam held back the pond water from a river below. Many old trees lay crisscrossed and partially submerged.

Others still stood out from the water with their dried branches. Out in the center of the pond remained an old and abandoned beaver house. Steve brought the bike to a stop at the edge of the pond. "This looks like a good spot," he said and unfastened the trap from the bike's front rack. "That's just great," he commented with disgust.

"What's wrong?"

"I forgot bread to bait the minnow trap."

"I still have half of my ham sandwich from our picnic."

"That will do just fine. Would you mind breaking it up and stuff it into one of those holes while I look for a cord to tie to the trap?"

"Sure sweetheart."

After rummaging around in the tool chest of the bike, he found a long green cord. "Oh no," he groaned, looking back at Mary.

"What's wrong now?"

"I only wanted bread in the trap. Not the ham too!"

"Sorry, but your instructions were to tear up the sandwich and poke the pieces in."

"You got me there." Steve picked up the trap and made his way to the edge of the pond. He began slowly walking atop a fallen and partially submerged tree. He held onto a large extended branch for balance and shuffled his feet along the tree, being careful not to fall in. He glanced back at Mary, who was watching him from the comfort of the bike, grinning. "It looks like you're just waiting for me to slip into this loon shit."

"I didn't say a thing dear."

"You didn't have to. That big smirk of yours gave your thoughts away!" He tossed the trap out into the water, then fastened the other end of the cord to a branch and cautiously made his way back to safe ground. Suddenly, a loud but deep and long moaning echoed around the pond and it's rocky bluffs.

Steve froze in his tracks, trying to get a bearing on the location of that strange sound. After about fifty seconds of standing motionless, he walked over to Mary. "I never heard a sound like that before. Probably a cow moose calling her calf."

"It sure as hell sounded spooky to me!

And it's time we get back to the cottage. I have some things to do before our company arrives."

"Sure Mary. Or is it that you don't fancy this spot anymore?" he remarked with a smirk.

"That sound was so eerie. I just can't describe it."

"Let's go. I don't want you to hear that spooky sound again. You might drop something in your sexy thong and I'd have to smell you all the way back to the cottage!"

"Funny boy!" She elbowed him in the ribs, as he climbed onto the bike.

chapter 3

back to the cottage

Back at the cottage, Steve and Mary unhitched the trailer in a shady corner of the woodshed. "Thanks for helping me get those ferns."

"The pleasure was all mine. What d'ya say we have a little tug to a successful fern hunt?" He grabbed a bottle of vodka off his workbench and pulled two Dixie cups out of a dispenser.

"I hope you're not over-doing it with the drinking dear."

"Are you kidding? This cup is only half full." "So here's to our great day. And to many more!"

"And many more!" responded Mary as they touched Dixie cups.

Later back in the cottage, they were busy preparing for their guests. "Where did the time go?" said Mary. "Our company should be arriving soon."

"No problem Mary. The ribs are marinated. Potatoes are washed and wrapped. The bruschetta is ready for the oven. And your Caesar dressing is made.

"Sweetheart, you always make everything seem so easy-speak of the devil, I think I hear them coming." Mary glanced through the kitchen window. "Yup, that's them all right."

They made it down to the dock, just as Bob's pontoon boat pulled up. Mike was standing on the bow, with rope in hand.

"Here easy street, catch," said Mike in a slurred tone. He threw Steve the bow rope, which fell short of the dock. Steve and Mary couldn't help but notice that Mike was quite intoxicated.

"Easy street?" replied Steve with a smile, going down on his hands and knees to retrieve the rope in the water. "It looks to me like you have a good head start on the crew."

Carol scoffed, "I wonder why?"

"Just because I'm retired, doesn't mean

I'm living on easy street. My new boss has a honey-do list a mile long."

"What the hell is a honey-do list?" inquired Mike, as he slowly stepped from the boat to the dock without stumbling.

"It's honey do this. And honey do that!" replied Steve, watching over him.

"I call that pussy whipped," mocked Mike sarcastically, as he always did after a few too many drinks. Everyone knew he didn't mean any harm with his remarks.

"You're lucky Steve doesn't throw your ass into the lake for talking like that," said Carol.

"No way," replied Steve, "I don't want his wet butt on my patio cushions." He put his arm around Mike. Patting him lightly on the back, helping him up the high ramp walkway towards the cottage.

"Now, how does a batch of Caesars sound?" suggested Steve to his guests who were now comfortably seated in the upper deck gazebo.

"Sounds good," replied Janis and Bob.

"Me too," said Carol, "but make Mike's a virgin."

"I can't remember the last time I had one of those," responded Mike, still slurring his words.

"Ha, ha!" gestured Carol. She stared back at him with the same disgusted look, as the rest had a little chuckle at Mike's humor.

"I'll make him a weak one Carol. After all, he's not driving."

"You guys always stick up for each other!" Carol mocked back to Steve.

"I notice that too," said Janis. "They'll make fun of or bitch at each other but still back each other up in the end."

"Yeah. And we stick together like shit to a blanket!" said Bob.

"Just like brothers," replied Steve.

"All right. No more than two fingers," Carol urged Steve. "But you better coast with it."

"Sure sweetheart," Mike replied like a spoiled little boy who always ends up getting his way.

Steve returned with the drinks, only to find Bob and Mike alone in the gazebo. "Have the girls left us?" asked Steve.

"We're not that lucky," replied Bob. "Mary took them up to the woodshed to show them some ferns and your new toy.

So how does your new bike perform Steve?"

"Talk about suspension—it made those rough spots near the plateau feel as smooth as a baby's butt," replied Steve.

"Nice retirement gift you've got up there Steve," said Janis as she and the girls entered the gazebo. "And those ferns are something else."

"I'll say. There wasn't any extra room in that trailer for a straw." slurred Mike.

"Well, how would you know smart ass?" mocked Steve.

"When you and Mary had your picnic up on the lookout Mike could see you two quite well through his new telescope," said Carol.

"So much for privacy," replied Steve, with a timid smile. Not knowing how much Mike really saw.

"Oh, were you guys having a little fun up there?" inquired Janis with a smirk.

"Unfortunately, not this time. I used all my energy digging up those ferns. Too bad for Mike. He could use some love-making tips," blurted out Steve, as they all laughed.

"Just one thing got my curiosity today,"

said Mike, still speaking a little slow.

"Just one thing?" he responded with a canny smile. Steve figured that Mike had seen Mary topless.

"What in the hell were you two staring at on the ground? Up there on the plateau. I know for sure it wasn't deer shit."

"No," he answered, laughing. "Now that you ruled out deer shit—and I know how good you know your shit—I'm sure glad you mentioned it. You guys have to see this." Taking his glass he lifted it up and down on the table, leaving three wet rings that overlapped. "This is what is engraved up on that plateau. I logged the location with the GPS on my bike. And all three rings were exactly the same size, each measuring twelve feet across."

"Sure, sure," responded Bob, in a negative tone.

"Oh yes," said Mary, in a serious voice. "Remember Mike, I saw it too." She also realized that Mike had seen her topless.

"Steve, you've played too many pranks on us in the past. Like the time you put that telephone booth out on Bear Island. And remember when you let those wild turkeys loose on Jim's island. And what about your fake mongoose that you used to scare the shit out of everyone with!"

"Okay, okay Bob," smiled Steve, with everyone laughing. "Sure, I played some pranks in the past, but Mary and I just arrived at our cottage. Mike's our witness—he saw us through his telescope when we were looking down at those rings. Would you girls mind if we just go for a quick bike ride for about an hour, so I can put this to sleep."

"As long as Mike doesn't drive," urged Carol.

"He can hop on with me then," agreed Steve.

"We'll help Mary with dinner," said Janis.

"Medium heat only for the ribs," suggested Steve. He sprung up from his chair and headed out the gazebo with the guys close behind him.

"Don't worry Steve, we'll have everything under control," said Janis, waving goodbye to the guys as they made their way up to the woodshed.

Not even thirty minutes had passed and

the guys were parking their bikes at the top of the plateau. "Well what do you think?" asked Steve, crouching down beside the ring engravings in the bedrock.

"Son of a bitch," replied Bob. Going down on one knee, he put his hand onto the groove of one impression. "This has got to be some kind of old Native engraving. Or some spiritual sun god or something like that, from a tribe that lived here hundreds of years ago!" exclaimed Bob with a curious expression.

"I had the same thought. Remember that old trapper who found a perfectly round hole in a large rock twenty minutes from here, just outside of the Town of Massey? As it turned out, it was in fact from an old Indian village. And that hole in the rock was used for grinding down grain for bannock," said Steve.

"What the hell is bannock?" inquired Mike.

"It's a type of bread they cook on a stick. Over an open fire."

"So much for your history lesson," said Mike, now sobering up. "If I recall, that area's been restricted. Ten square miles. And the government only lets in university students."

"You mean for archaeology?" asked Bob.

"Yes," replied Steve.

"All we need," said Bob, "is for the fuckin' government, or Laurentian University to get wind of this. Say good-bye to all our hunting, hiking or riding anywhere near this place.

"So Mike, from where your cottage is, can you see this area good?" asked Steve.

"I can see it real good," he said with a mischievous grin. "I've ordered a digital camera that should be in by tomorrow. It'll mount to my telescope and then I'll really be able to monitor this whole area. I plan to set it on time-lapse twenty-four seven to be able to review it in sixty seconds. Then download it on a disc. Or even email any or all activity anywhere in minutes."

"Huh. And I thought my bike was high tech."

"That was going to be my surprise for you guys," said Mike.

Steve snorted. "What surprise? Seeing my wife and I on the internet sun bathing, or something else."

"No, no," he laughed nervously. "I hoped it would be that ten point buck, you missed up here last fall."

"You mean to tell me, your getting all this equipment just to monitor deer movement?" said Steve sarcastically.

"You mean more like string bikini movement on the decks of boats driving by his dock," jested Bob, nudging Mike.

"All kidding aside," said Steve, "we should cover the ring engravings with those logs over there. It would be just our luck that some berry picker or someone on the water saw us up here. You never know. Someone just might follow our trail to this spot."

"Maybe you could drag a few of those old logs over here with your bike Steve," suggested Bob.

Fifteen minutes later, they had a huge pile of logs covering up the circles. "Good work guys," said Steve. "That should do it for now."

"So, what should we tell the girls?" asked Mike. "You know just as well as I do, that when we get back, they're sure as hell are going to question us."

"Ahh shit! We'll just tell them it's wear

and tear marks in the rock from logging equipment years ago," mocked Bob.

"Do you think they'll eat that up?" asked Mike.

"Sure, why not?" replied Bob. "What do they know about early logging in this area?"

"Yeah you're right," said Mike. "We can feed those girls anything."

"What's the time look like?" asked Steve.

"We only have twenty minutes," replied Bob.

"Do you two really think the girls are waiting on pins and needles for us drunks to get back to them?"

"Speak for yourself Mike. But why don't we make a pass down to the pond and check out that minnow trap I set earlier."

"I'm for that. Then we might finally get some fishing in tomorrow morning."

"I guess majority rules," said Steve. He started up his bike with Mike already seated behind him.

They found themselves driving down a steep part of the trail, as Steve led them to the entrance of the pond. "This is the spot guys. I'll only be a few minutes. If you look into that compartment under you right arm Mike, you'll find a cold beer for you and Bob in a cooler bag. I forgot them there from today's picnic."

"Take your time," said Mike. "It's quite comfortable up here, sitting in this passenger seat. Trapping minnows could make for a great spectator sport, especially with a cold beer. Hell Steve, I'll be your passenger anytime."

Bob and Mike watched Steve as he carefully walked across the half-submerged tree holding onto its dried branches for balance. He then slowly crouched down and grabbed a green cord and pulled the trap up out of the water.

"Any luck?" called out Bob.

Steve was disoriented. He stared at strange looking creatures crawling around making high-pitched screeching sounds. Olive green, they had large, disproportionate, crab claws and scorpion tails. He didn't answer Bob, but instead opened the trap and poured the freaky creatures back into the pond. He then slowly turned around and headed back, carrying the minnow trap at his side. "It's a no go for minnows."

"What in the hell did you empty out of your trap then?" asked Bob.

"I don't know. They looked like cray-fish but had a tail like a scorpion."

"You mean like the one you have cling-ing on there?" asked Mike, pointing down at the minnow trap as he took another swig of beer.

"That's one of them."

"Wow! I see what you mean," exclaimed Bob with a startled look.

"Mike, grab me that wide-mouthed water bottle in the left compartment," he asked in a hyper tone, as he studied the creature. Mike threw it over to him. Steve caged-in the creature then headed to the edge of the pond to put some water into the container.

"Now that's some strange and freaky-looking thing!" blurted Mike, quickly sobering up.

"You've got that right!" he replied, returning with the bottle half full of water. "Bob, if you can hold the trap open, we should be able to free it." Steve tried prying and tapping it with a stick. It squirmed. Then it let out a high-pitched screech like a bat and loosened its grip, falling right into the water bottle.

"He's one hell of a frisky, freaky little thing isn't he?" exclaimed Mike.

"Sure is!" exhorted Steve. "I just want to know what on earth they are. And how did they get in this pond?"

"Let me see it again," said Bob peering in, as he studied the creature closer. "It's got a tail like a scorpion with a dorsal fin at the end of it. Those huge, mean-looking claws are really something else. Not to mention those rows of needle-sharp teeth! Hmm, it's too bad you didn't keep the rest of them. They might be good boiled and served with garlic butter."

"That's a good one," smirked Steve.

"I'm serious," said Bob.

"They made that weird screeching noise when I pulled them out of the water. That's why I dumped them back in. But as for this one," he said holding the bottle up high, "I think I should give this one to Sarah to bring back to her university. Hopefully, they'll know something about it. She's supposed to be up here in a few days. We need to make sure that none of these things get loose in our lake. That would put an end to our late night skinny dipping with the girls!"

The guys laughed. "Seriously though, these things could start spreading like those zebra mussels that started in the St. Lawrence Seaway."

"Those little clam-like things that cling to everything and screw up our lakes?" asked Bob.

"How in the hell is that possible for them get into our inland lakes?" asked Mike.

"Sport fishermen fish in Lake Huron today for salmon and the next day in an inland lake. They empty their live wells into an inland lake releasing all those microscopic mussels in their early stages — traces that you can't even see. The rest is history. But for now, I'm really curious as to how these creatures got into this pond," replied Steve.

"Maybe a flock of Canada Geese on their way back from Mexico landed here, and had a dump. You don't know what in the hell they ate over there!" blurted Bob.

The boys laughed hysterically.

"Maybe it's the water they drank," said

Steve.

"Oh yeah, don't drink the water either!" jested Bob.

Just then, a loud moaning sound echoed throughout the whole area. The three men looked at each other, remaining motionless and silent, trying to hear it one more time so to know what it was and where it was coming from.

"What in the hell was that?" said Bob.

What they didn't realize is that the sound they all heard was a warning. A warning from a creature of another world that even their worst nightmares could not prepare them for. They had stumbled into the wrong place at the wrong time. The creature was using the old abandoned beaver house in the middle of the pond as a shield. With its large body submerged, only its dark, crocodile eyes protruded from its head, just enough to break the water's surface. While honing in on its prey, it traveled through the water like a torpedo heading straight for its target, creating a small wake on the calm pond. The men just stood, there curious as to what they just heard.

"Mary and I heard that same freaky

sound here earlier today, when we set the trap. At first. I thought it could be a cow moose calling its calf."

"You've gotta be kidding me!" said Mike, still a bit light-headed. "A cow moose wouldn't make that loud or that low of a sound."

"Whatever it is, it's spooky," exhorted Bob.

"Now you're sounding like Mary," said Steve, chuckling.

"Now that Steve mentioned it, that cow moose we were tracking two years ago let out a bellow similar to that one when we got up close to her ass," gestured Mike.

"Yeah," mocked Steve, "it was Bob's aftershave that was turning her on."

"That's right Bob, there was a little romance going on."

"What in the hell do you mean by that Mike?" questioned Bob.

"I remember you crying out afterwards that she had a great ass."

"You guys are nuts," said Bob shaking his head with a smirk.

"Drink up boys. We have ribs waiting for us," said Steve.

"Hey, the last time we were late, they

made us do the dishes," said Bob.

The creature was advancing across the pond as they joked.

"I talked her into paper plates this time."

"Paper plates eh? I'm glad your wife isn't one of those tree huggers."

"Tree huggers," said Steve, "tell me about them. If they're so much against paper products, they should try wiping their ass with plastic!"

"Right on!" laughed Bob.

"I'll have to remember that one. Let's get back to the cottage guys, I'm dying for Steve's ribs," urged Mike, fastening the minnow trap to the bike. Steve climbed on, squeezing between Mike and the handlebars. Within seconds they were driving away, as the creature emerged from the water only a few feet from where they'd parked.

When the guys arrived back at the woodshed, they could see the girls down at the cottage deck preparing dinner. Listening to pop music, they were having a great time laughing and carrying on like teenage girls at a sleepover.

"We don't want to crash that party just yet," suggested Steve, looking toward his tool bench. "Besides, I have that lonely bottle of vodka on my workbench. What d'ya say we have a quick tug?" He sat the water container down next to the vodka. Then he set up three Dixie cups and filled them with vodka. They each grabbed a cup and raised it high in the air, as was their custom. "A toast to our discoveries and secrets!" said Steve.

"To discoveries and secrets," repeated Bob and Mike, looking at the water bottle on the workbench. They drank up.

"Now pour us another one Bob while I log in these coordinates." The guys watched him as he jotted down all points of interest on his hunting and trail map, which was fastened just above his tool bench. "Now we have a true picture of the hunting area. And I can hardly wait to find out the deer movement patterns up there on that lookout."

"Just give me ten days. And I'll tell you how those deer like their toast in the morning," added Mike.

"It's just where in hell they hide their toaster that gets me," jested Steve.

"Let's toast to finding the toaster then," added Bob.

The guys were now sitting down with the girls enjoying their barbecue. "More wine?" Steve asked, hunched over the table topping off Mary's glass.

"Sure," said Bob.

"So what did you guys think of those strange engravings on the lookout?" inquired Mary.

"They look like wear and tear marks. From some early logging equipment, like a pulley block. Or steel chain abrasions used on a pulley system. Or something along that line," replied Mike, while looking at Steve from the corner of his eye.

"That's good to know," said Mary. "Steve thought it could be some kind of Indian markings."

"I did, 'til we took a better look. But Mike's theory holds more water."

"It's nice to see you guys all agreeing to something for a change," said Carol.

"I'll toast to that," said Steve trying to change the subject.

"And cheers to the girls for a great dinner," said Bob.

Just then, they saw an aluminum boat with two people approaching the dock. "Oh!" said Mary. "It's probably Brenda with a friend. I'm glad she made it out." As the boat pulled up a little closer to the dock, Mary could see that it wasn't Brenda at all. It was her daughter Sarah, who hadn't been due to arrive until midweek. "Oh Steve, it's Sarah. And she's with a friend."

"She's in a little early," he said with concern. He stood up from his chair to have a better look down at the dock. Minutes later, Sarah and her friend joined them in the gazebo, exchanging hugs with everyone. "What a surprise! We weren't expecting you 'til Friday afternoon."

"I really pushed it Dad and finished my assignment two days ahead of schedule."

"Just like her father," said Mary, "giving it her all."

"Great, That gives us two extra days together," said Steve.

"And will we ever be introduced to your company?" asked Mary looking eye to eye at a tall and slender young man.

"Oh, I'm sorry. This is my friend Tom.

He's majoring in science at the university."

"Well Tom," said Steve, giving him a strong handshake. "You just might be able to help us out with a little mystery here," as he looked back at Bob and Mike.

"Sure sir. In whatever way I can," he replied.

"Well not now," Steve said. "It's pleasure time. And at Birch Lake we don't mix business with pleasure."

"Unless pleasure is your business!" said Bob laughing out loud.

"Don't mind him!"

"Oh Dad, it's okay. I gave Tom a briefing on this lake and on how we carry on."

"That's why I'm here," he said. "You folks sound like fun."

"Well Sarah, grab a couple of beer from that cooler and load up on some ribs!"

"That's my Dad—always cooking for an army. Are you enjoying your retirement Dad?" she asked, opening two cans of beer.

"Maybe later. If I can take an axe to your mother's honey-do list," he chuckled.

"Axe, my ass," replied Mary.

"Hell no. I wouldn't do that," he said as he patted her behind, being a little light-headed. "She still has a few good miles in her yet."

"Dad! You're embarrassing me!" Sarah cringed as everyone laughed.

"You should know your father by now," said Carol.

"You know what I call it?" blurted Mike in a slurred voice.

"Hey Mike, remember, we can't go there," teased Steve, with everyone enjoying the humor.

"Let's toast to Tom's first Birch Lake weekend. And to good fishing!" said Steve, as everyone raised their drinks.

"Cool," Tom responded.

"Tom, while you're up here, get Steve to show you where he catches all those lunker smallmouth bass. Mike and I have been trying to pry it out of him for the last five years. Maybe you're in a better scoring position, being with Sarah, if you know what I mean," urged Bob.

"Oh, I'm not so sure about that," responded Sarah, as she reached into the cooler for a couple of more beer.

"Wow. That was a quick one!" remarked Mary, surprised at how fast they'd drank.

"Oh don't mind that Mary. Being one of Steve's offspring automatically gives her a genetic predisposition," jested Bob.

"Now that's a good one Bob! I'd like to use it if you don't mind," laughed Sarah.

"Go ahead Sarah. It's all yours."

"You bugger! I'll get you for that one!" said Steve. "Just for that smart ass remark, you'll have to wait five more years before I show you guys my hot spot. Come to think of it, maybe I can use this as leverage to find out where you catch your lake trout Bob."

chapter 4

later that evening

Steve and Mary were seeing their guests off, down at the dock. "Just look at that sky," said Mary.

"It's the northern lights," exclaimed Janis. Everyone witnessed a spectacular display of long vertical beams of light flickering and shooting upward, along with bright shining stars over the northern horizon.

"You can't put this on your Visa!" said Bob.

Steve scoffed, "But it's just a matter of time until our government finds a way to tax us on this too."

"What causes that?" asked Janis.

"Scientists say it's a reflection of the

sun off the polar ice caps," replied Bob, starting up the outboard motor.

"Thanks again for a great dinner and evening. Hey—come for dinner at our place tomorrow," Carol shouted over the sound of the outboard as they departed from the dock. "And that means Sarah and her friend too!"

"We'll be there," Sarah shouted back, waving from the doorway of the gazebo.

Steve and Mary remained standing on the dock, still watching the northern lights as they heard the distant cry of a loon. "What a breathtaking setting Mary."

"Yes sweetheart. What we have on our doorstep makes tourists drive hundreds of miles. Let's join Sarah and Tom for a nightcap," she said as they walked back up to the cottage.

"Speaking of that, what are the sleeping arrangements?" asked Steve.

"Our daughter is a grown woman now. She's twenty-one, and has been sharing an apartment with Tom for the last three months. I think they'll want the guest camp."

"You know how I feel about this," Steve replied.

"Sorry dear. But it's time you let go. Remember when I was eighteen in high school—or is that different."

"Let's not go there now."

"You're Sarah's overprotective father who judges all other men like himself."

"Okay, end of conversation," said Steve in a quiet voice, fearing that Sarah might overhear them, as they were getting closer to the gazebo.

"I've got a little cleaning up to do in the kitchen. I'll join you guys later," said Mary.

"Can I grab you two another beer?" asked Steve, standing beside the cooler.

"No thanks Dad, I'll pass. Remember, you're responsible for my predisposition," said Sarah smiling.

"Bob won't get off easy for that one," he teased with a chuckle.

"I'm going to help Mom clean up a little in the kitchen. You and Tom can enjoy one together." Sarah felt that this was a good time for them to get acquainted.

"That reminds me," he said, grabbing two beers from the cooler, "so Tom, you're majoring in science?"

"Yes sir. Three years now at Laurentian

in freshwater biology."

"Just call me Steve. Tom, I've been on this lake for over fifty years now. And I've hunted and fished every square inch of this area. Well, today I caught the strangest looking creatures that I or even my buddies have ever seen in our lives," he exclaimed.

"So how and where did you catch this thing sir? I mean Steve."

"In my minnow trap in a remote old beaver pond. I have one in a wide mouth water bottle up there in the woodshed. It looks like a crayfish, but somewhat different."

"Oh, it must be a rusty crayfish," he replied.

"A rusty crayfish?"

"Yes. They're invasive crustaceans, spreading to lakes, rivers, and streams in several areas of North America. And they're more aggressive than other native crayfish."

"Aggressive?" he inquired.

"Yes sir. It's better equipped to avoid fish predation like a smallmouth bass. And can harm native fish populations by eating their eggs and young. They can displace native crayfish, hybridize with them, and they can eliminate aquatic plants."

"Holy shit. They sure are destructive."

"That, they are Steve. In fact, the natural resources ministry has a handout on them at all their offices, warning about them. I think it's called Rusty Crayfish Watch. Laurentian and the University of Minnesota are doing some work on them."

"Those critters sure as hell have big clippers!"

"I think they call them claws Steve," he said with a straight face, respecting his ignorance on the subject. "The movable claw has a S-shape to it," to demonstrate, Tom pinched his thumb and forefinger together, " each with a black tip on the end."

"No," Steve replied with a puzzled look. "They sure as hell are big. And they have a flat face with lots of needle-like teeth. A turned-up tail like a scorpion. And they put out one hell of a screech when you take them out of water!"

Tom just sat there in total confusion, playing the details over in his head.

Nothing he ever imagined could even come close to the description that Steve gave him.

"Care for a little peek? I was going to let Sarah bring it back to the university. But if you could tell us what the hell it is, you might put this mystery to sleep. I'd sure appreciate it Tom."

Tom's curiosity was accelerating. "Sure Steve, I'd like to see this so called thing you're talking about. You've sure got my brains smokin' on this one!"

"Well, there's no time like the present is there?" Steve stood up from his comfortable chair, making his way out of the gazebo with Tom anxiously following.

"I'm right behind you sir. I mean Steve."

As the two men entered the woodshed, a florescent light was hanging over the tool bench, attracting moths. About a dozen were fluttering about the light, some landing on the tool bench.

"What the heck!" said Steve as he approached the workbench, finding the container on its side. "Frisky little bugger, isn't he?" he remarked with Tom now at his side, "I'd left that upright." He grasped the bottle and started to slowly unscrew the top off. Tom watched anxiously. The cover came off with a bit of water spilling on the bench top. Suddenly, an olive color set of claws appeared attached to the scorpion body. It let out a little screech as Tom jolted back.

"My God. This is a strange type of crustacean," he said, totally amazed.

They watched the creature slowly crawl along the workbench. Its scorpion tail was swaying from side to side like an attentive cat. It came to a full stop, observing some moths fluttering on the workbench. Suddenly it lunged after the moths, tearing them apart as it fed its wide mouth with their shredded pieces. It became motionless, waiting patiently for its next prey. With a loud clang of a coffee can, it was now out of commission. "Time out for now, you frisky little creature," said Steve as he slid the coffee can to the edge of the workbench. He let it fall back into the water bottle and quickly screwed the lid back on. He handed it over to Tom, "What do you think?"

Still in shock at what he saw, Tom held

up the container to the light. "We can rule out mollusk. A mollusk is a snail-type animal. This creature here is way too freakin' fast for that category." They laughed out loud together. "Steve, you're right. It sure is a strange water creature! And amphibious since it handles itself quite well out of water though it probably favors water to keep its shell moist. I can hardly wait to get this back to the lab. My professor is really gonna shit when he sees this!"

"All right then, let's get back to the gazebo and celebrate this find. But first you'll have to do me a favor Tom," he said looking directly into his eyes. "Just promise me that you won't open it until you get back to the university."

Tom sensed Steve's concern for Sarah's safety. "You have my word on that Steve."

"I also don't want the girls to get spooked by this. If you know what I mean."

"I'll take good care of it Steve. And I'll let you know, when I find out from my professor just what the hell it is!"

"I appreciate that Tom," he said, patting him on the back. "Cheers," said Steve and they clanged their beer cans together like two old friends. "Now let's get back down there and join the girls."

The guys entered the gazebo and Sarah noticed the water bottle in Tom's hand. "You switched from beer to water?" Sarah chuckled.

"Sarah, this could be a discovery of a new type of crustacean. I'm bringing it back to the lab. We'll get to the origin of this thing in a matter of days."

Sarah turned and looked at her father. "Where did you find that thing?"

"In that remote pond. At the end of our trail, just south of that lookout area."

"Oh yes," she remarked. "That's a large pond. I've always had a weird feeling whenever you took me close to it."

"Like mother, like daughter!"

"Are there anymore of these in the pond?" asked Tom.

"How many pounds do you want?" Steve replied.

"Well that's good to know," as he still gripped the bottle with a hand on each side, as though afraid to part with it.

"Can I have a look?"

"Sorry Sarah, but it's a little too frisky to be let out," warned Steve.

"Oh come on," urged Mary with a smile. "It can't be that fast."

"Oh yes Mrs. Gorman. Believe me, it's not something that you would bring to a show and tell," Tom insisted.

"Mom, I think those two are playing a good one on us!"

"You can't make us believe there's a dangerous creature in that bottle," Mary snorted. "We're not taking the bait, dear."

"Yeah, we heard you two laughing it up earlier in the woodshed. So there!"

"Well then, in that case, we won't have to worry about it getting loose, will we?" said Steve, looking at Tom and feeling good about their gestures. "I don't have night hawk blood like you kids do. So this old man is calling it a night." He leaned over to Sarah with open arms and gave her a big hug and kiss. "It's nice to see you two made it up here sweetheart. I'll see you both at breakfast."

"Sure Dad. Maybe after breakfast you can introduce me to our new family addition in the woodshed."

"Mary, I was hoping to surprise her in

the morning," Steve said with a disappointed look.

"Sorry...We can all go for a ride after breakfast to the lookout," she suggested.

"That sounds like fun," said Sarah.

"It's been nice meeting you," Tom said shaking Steve's hand.

"And that goes for me too," he said as he left the gazebo.

"I'm right behind you dear."

"Dad seems more relaxed."

"Oh yes. He's not talking on his cell phone half the time he used to. Or following up on proof-work from the shop. But he still gets up early. Now he'll be fishing and trail riding or in the woodshed puttering around. He'll also be spending more time with Mike and Bob."

"They've been good friends for many years now. And you get along great with their wives. The two of you have something really good here. I'm happy to see that."

"Between the house and the cottage, I think we're doing just fine. It's been a long day," Mary yawned, "I'm calling it a night." She gave Sarah a big hug and kiss goodnight.

"And goodnight to you Tom. I'll wake you two up just before breakfast, okay?"

"Sure Mom. That sounds great. Goodnight."

"You have super parents, Sarah. And your dad is really cool. He knows how to have fun. Lots of middle-aged men would love to have his lifestyle—living on a lake in a remote cottage like this. And such privacy with no neighbors on either side. This sure makes for great skinny-dipping! And it sure beats living in the city with all that noise, hustle and bustle."

"It took them years of planning and work to set this stage. I guess it all boils down to choices and sacrifices we have to make in life. Like you and I going to university."

"That's true enough Sarah."

"Well Tom. Should we call it a night?"

"Let's," he replied with the water bottle still in his hand. "Skinny-dipping tomorrow night instead?"

"You're on," she replied, as they exited the gazebo.

Upon entering the guest camp, he

stood the water bottle on the window ledge. "That's good," she responded, while taking off her clothes. "I thought for a minute you were going to take that thing to bed with us."

"Well, it's a real exciting find."

"Yeah," she remarked, now under the covers. "I'll bet that you can discover more exciting finds under these covers, than in that bottle."

"I won't argue with that," he said, as crawling under the sheets beside her.

"Now do you really think my dad discovered a different type of water animal?" she asked, with a curious look on her face.

"Oh yes! Big time!"

"I could really feel your enthusiasm."

"This find can help kick start my biology career. My whole thesis will ride on this find. Studying their habitat and origin. Maybe I can spend the rest of the summer here to study them. Of course with your parent's permission."

"Sounds good to me. We could link up a web on a laptop to the university satellite. And then I'd be able to finish my term here as well. I know my parents would be in favor of that. If it means seeing more of me. And you'd be able to use the old bike to access the pond."

"Everything you said sounds good Sarah. But there's only one thing," he said with a troubled look. He stared at the ceiling while twiddling his thumbs on his chest. "Remember earlier in the gazebo, when you said that it's choices and sacrifices we have to make in life, to get where we want to be? In order to do this, my professor would first have to see that animal before approving any remote field study. He'll only be in the lab tomorrow morning. Then he leaves at noon for a one-week international science think tank in Ottawa. We can head out first thing in the morning and get there in plenty of time."

"Well, let's go for it then!"

"Thanks Sarah, I was worried about cutting your holiday short."

"Are you kidding me? If this goes the way you said, we'll have all summer here, working out of our swimsuits!"

"That sounds great to me." Tom gave her a big hug and kiss. Then he turned his head and looked at the water bottle on the

window ledge. "We won't let the professor down, will we, you feisty thing? He's
going to shit when he meets you!"

chapter 5

in latvia

It was six o'clock on a clear sunrise morning. Two Russian soldiers up on a hill, dressed in camouflage fatigues, were in a prone position, hidden behind some old fallen trees. They were scanning over a large pond area through their binoculars. "Oh shit Nicholas! It's the size of a car. That must be like the head NYANYA, the one that got Yacocheve. It's one hell of an ugly fucker! I can pop it off right now and serve it up at the base with garlic butter tomorrow." jested Alex. "It's been at least three weeks since that last UFO spotting. If I had my way, I would nuke this whole fucking area!" snorted Alex. He shook his head, clenching his teeth angrily.

"Just tell that to the general," responded Nicholas. "We know that whatever is in that pond, is not of this world. And our hands are tied until we receive further instructions from the Federation. If we play our cards right, we just might get the chance to try one of them with garlic butter."

"Yeah sure, and watch them kill another one of our comrades!" he exclaimed.

"Ah fuck Alex, how do you think I feel? I was on over thirty assignments with Yacocheve. We were like brothers. And you know as well as I do, he got too close and broke direct orders," he whispered. Nicholas, a former Russian special task force officer at age fifty-five, was on his last assignment and due to retire in a month.

"I still liked it better in the army. At least you knew who your enemies were. Instead, they have us babysitting these big fuckin' lobster things. And their little babies!" exclaimed Alex.

"Well until we or the Federation can figure out what those aliens are up to, we'll just have to wait this one out," said Nicholas, trying to calm his partner.

"Sure." Alex blurted, impatiently. "Wait... Wait...Wait...!"

Steve was filling a thermos with coffee, when Mary walked into the kitchen rubbing her eyes. "Where are you off to so early with coffee to go?"

"I thought I would put a few clicks on my bike this morning by grooming the trail. I plan to be back for breakfast around nineish. I took one communicator and left you a note on your dresser mirror to call me later."

She picked up a note that she spotted on the kitchen table. "It seems that Sarah and her friend are early birds too. They're already heading back to Sudbury."

"What?" he asked with a surprised look while adding creamer to his thermos.

"Apparently, they have to get that thing you caught over to some professor at Laurentian University before he leaves this afternoon. Tom is trying to get the right to pursue a field study on that water animal here at the cottage for his thesis. Sarah will be able to do her work through the same remote link from here as well.

Whatever that means," said Mary with a yawn.

"So much for our summer retreat," gestured Steve, rolling back his eyes.

"Oh honey, they can stay in the guest cottage. And we'll still have our own space. Besides, it'll give you more time to bond with Tom."

"Like I'm so looking forward to bonding with him..." he responded. "As long as he doesn't bring some research team here, I guess it should be okay."

"At least we'll get to see more of Sarah. They hope to get approval by mid-week. And she'll be calling us at eight tonight. So remember to keep your cell on. She ends the letter with, 'P.S. don't catch any more strange animals. Love Sarah.' And I didn't even get a chance to see it. Steve, I can tell you're very nervous about this situation by the way you scratch your chin. So what the heck do you mean by 'a little frisky'?"

"When I showed Tom that creature up in the woodshed last night, you should have seen how it attacked some moths that landed on the tool bench. It tore them up and consumed them in a matter of seconds. And the thing that really shocked Tom was how well it could maneuver out of water. I was lucky to catch it and put it back into the container. That's why we didn't want to show it to anyone 'til it gets to the university. When you thought we were playing a joke, we just played along so we didn't have to show it to you girls. I'm hoping I don't regret bringing that thing here," he cautioned.

"Oh darling," she said now hugging Steve with the note still in her hand. "Go for your ride and have fun. I'll call you before breakfast. I'm going to get a little more sleep and let you carry on with your thing sweetheart."

"Let's not forget about all those ferns in the woodshed that you want to transplant."

"It'll give us a chance to work off our breakfast," she urged.

"I'd like to get them in before it gets too freakin' hot out. You know I can't take that heat much anymore," he remarked.

"That reminds me," she said, grabbing Steve's bottle of nitro spray off the window ledge and handing it to him. "Have a safe and fun ride. I'll call you just before breakfast."

"Thanks." He left the cottage and walked up towards the woodshed with the thermos swinging from his index finger. He wondered how Mary could interpret dragging a large tire behind an ATV as being fun. Within minutes, Steve drove off pulling a fifteen-foot chain with a three hundred pound tractor tire dragging behind it. Like a pendulum, it swung from side to side, grounding the trail behind him. Uprooting small bushes and ferns, he always repeated this procedure a few times a year.

Tom and Sarah were traveling down the highway with the radio cranked to a hip hop song. His left hand was on the car roof with the fingers of his right hand taping on top of the steering wheel to the beat, still in heavy thought over the find.

Sarah was in the groove as well. With her dark sunglasses and bare feet up on the dash. Glancing down between the bucket seats right beside the stick shift, she noticed that the bottle was shaking a little. Intrigued over it, she slid her glasses up to her forehead and slowly reached over and turned the radio down. "Tom, I could've sworn I saw the bottle rocking," she said turning the volume back up. The bottle started to rock again. When she turned the music down, it stopped. Tom and Sarah found this to be quite comical, both laughing hysterically. "Well Tom. I guess your friend likes hip hop!"

"Sure looks that way!" he said still laughing.

"Sarah leaned over with her left hand on the lid. "I'd like to see this cool dude."

Tom's right hand fell hard on top of hers, pinning the bottle down as the mood suddenly changed. "I'm sorry Sarah, but you'll have to wait," he said in a defensive, yet stern voice trying to detour her.

"Wait my ass!" she said sharply. "If it wasn't for me bringing you to my cottage, you would've never laid eyes on that thing," she said sounding like a spoiled brat.

Tom had not seen this side of her before. He realized that he had to stay calm, not wanting to jeopardize his chance to go back to her cottage for further studies. This could be the chance of a lifetime. He waited a minute or so, for her to cool down before he spoke. "Sarah, it's just that I promised your dad that I wouldn't open this container until we got it to the lab."

"What the fuck is this, our first lover's quarrel? My dad won't know if I get a little preview," she said, now somewhat calmer. "All right then," she said, slowly unbuttoning her shirt and speaking in a soft, sexy voice. "Let's play you show me a little, and I'll show you a little..."

Tom was now in a very uncomfortable dilemma. Either play along with her and have fun or give in just enough to keep the peace. "Just a peek then," he said.

"Well, the same goes for you," she replied. She undid another button, now with her cleavage starting to show.

He lifted his right hand off of hers, "Now just hold it right there tightly at the base, while I do the unscrewing." As she watched with curious anticipation, putting her feet back on the floor, he began unscrewing the lid. "Okay. You show me a little," he urged, glancing at her cleavage while trying to watch the road and the bottle. Tom now felt no more thread resistance at the bottleneck. "Let's see," he said, glancing over at Sarah. At the same time, she leaned ahead in her seat, staring at the bottle while undoing another button. He slowly slid the bottle top to the right until it was halfway across the top. "Now it's your turn." She slowly opened her shirt up, exposing her round breasts to him. "Oh yeah," he said fully aroused with a content smile as she slid off her top a little more. "Ahhh...!" Tom screamed out at the top of his lungs.

Sarah saw a lobster-like claw cutting through his thumb, with blood squirting out and landing on the dashboard. She let out a piercing scream.

Looking up at the road, Tom saw his car was on the wrong side of the road and about to collide with an oncoming transport. With the razor-sharp claw cutting through his right thumb, he quickly turned the steering wheel hard with his left hand. With a loud blast of an air horn, the transport just missed his front bumper. He found himself over-steering, tires screeching with his foot on the brake. His car went into a 360-degree spin in the middle of the highway, missing an oncoming car, finally coming to rest in the parking lot of a truck stop. Looking down at the container, he was surprised to see that through all the chaos, Sarah still managed to hold onto the bottle with both hands. He pried his right hand free. She was trembling, as he quickly screwed the top back on to the bottle.

"Oh my God! What the fuck is it?" she shouted hysterically.

"That's why we're going back to the university," he exhorted, while grasping his thumb and applying pressure to stop the bleeding.

"Let's change seats. I'm driving," she said packing a wad of tissue around Tom's thumb. "Now just hold this firm. It looks like you're going to need stitches."

"Oh no!" he replied in an angry tone. "You had your fuckin' way earlier. We're gonna get this freakin' thing to the lab first. Then we'll go to the hospital. You know how long they can keep you waiting in an emergency room."

"Okay," she said, feeling responsible for the incident, as she ran around the car and exchanged seats. She quickly drove off with Tom staring at the water bottle.

"We'll get to the bottom of this fuckin' shit soon enough!" He was clenching his teeth, and grasping his thumb, which helped him bear the pain.

Steve drove down a low incline where the trail followed the edge of the pond for about two hundred yards, close to where he'd set his minnow trap the day before.

Shutting off his bike, he slowly looked around the pond, which was as calm as glass, hoping to see some wild life. Grabbing his thermos, he unscrewed the cup and set it just in front of him on the bike's seat. He began pouring his coffee while enjoying the serenity of this peaceful place.

Suddenly, he heard that same weird moaning sound again. He quickly scanned the pond area, trying to pinpoint the origin of the spooky sound. Now in an angry state of mind, he muttered out loud, "Well screw you!" as he finished pouring his coffee. He slowly screwed the top back on, still scanning the pond, unaware that not even one hundred yards away, lurking behind the beaver house, was a much larger version of the creature he'd caught in his minnow trap the day before. With a set of claws each three feet long, the creature was six feet wide and sixteen feet to the end of its scorpion tail. In the middle of the pond, the old abandoned beaver house made a good observation point for the creature to watch over the area with its crocodile eyes. With the ability to detect any movement in a 360-degree radius, it was the perfect killing machine. It quickly submerged itself under water then headed straight towards Steve.

As Steve sat drinking his coffee and enjoying nature, less than fifty yards to his left, a mother deer walked out to the edge of the pond. Steve saw her and didn't move a muscle. Within seconds, her fawn accompanied her. Unaware that he was being stalked by the creature, Steve watched as the doe and her fawn walked into two feet of water. They began to nibble on a few lily pads, while advancing a little deeper into the pond. Suddenly, the water started to boil up all around them. The doe let out a shrilling cry and tried to jump to shore but the two quickly disappeared into the blood red water.

Steve sat on his bike in shock. This was the most horrifying scene that he had ever witnessed. He had seen something like this before on a television show about piranhas in South America. But Northern Ontario? This just couldn't be happening here, he thought to himself. He sat there in a daze while the creature climbed onto land just thirty feet behind him. It suddenly hit him that the horror show he'd just witnessed, must be related to the same creatures that he caught in his minnow trap. "My God!" he cried out to himself, spilling hot coffee on his lap. He bore the pain of the burn and quickly threw his cup and thermos into the storage compartment, and started up his bike.

With the creature approaching the tractor tire, he shifted into drive. The creature grabbed the tractor tire with its claws. Steve felt resistance on the bike. Thinking that the tire was caught-up, he shifted into four-wheel low range for maximum torque. "Okay," he mumbled, "show me your balls," and squeezed the throttle down with a hard jolt. The tire tore away from the creature's claws, leaving two huge cuts into the tire.

The creature realized that the tire was some kind of lure. This aggravated it, wanting its prey even more as it tried to dodge the tire like a cat and mouse game going on behind Steve's back. With the tire acting as his safety net, Steve continued to drive, unaware that the creature was still in pursuit. The creature grew angrier at the elusive prey.

As Steve proceeded up a steep part of the trail, the tire struck a tree on the right side, causing it to swing way to the left. Steve was now an open target, with the creature closing in right behind him ready to strike. The tire deflected off a large boulder sending it right into the creature's path, knocking it off the trail. The force sent it tumbling down the side of the high bluffs. Its back landed on sharp jagged rocks cracking the creature open like an egg. Dark green goo oozed from its body. With the rising and falling of one claw, its nerves finally came to rest.

Steve reached the high lookout area, where he brought his bike to a stop and turned it off. Reaching into his pocket he pulled out his walk-and-talk. Sitting motionless, thinking of what to tell Mary.

After taking two large breaths, he compressed the radio call button.

"Hi darling," Mary responded joyfully. "Ready for a nice relaxing breakfast?"

"Yes," he said in a flat tone, still very troubled over the horrifying incident.

"Is everything all right dear?" she asked, sensing something was wrong.

"Oh everything is great and I'm very happy with the bike's performance," he said, picking up his tempo. "I'm up at the lookout. I'll be back in thirty minutes or so."

"Okay dear. Breakfast will be ready. Over and out."

"Over and out."

Putting the radio back into his pocket, still in shock over this hellish incident, Steve was afraid. He was extremely troubled as to what to say to Mary or his friends about his bizarre encounter. Looking up, he began to pray for wisdom and protection. Feeling relieved, he started up his bike and headed back to the cottage.

Arriving at the back of the woodshed, Steve unhitched the tow chain from his bike then tossed it onto the tire. Failing to see the two large battle scars on the opposite side of the tire. "I could smell the bacon from up at the woodshed" he said, entering the cottage.

"I cooked a few extra strips for you dear. I know how you like to put them between your toast."

"Thanks. I'll work them off transplanting those ferns." He pulled a chair out from the table, trying hard to conceal his emotions.

"Had a little accident?" she asked looking at the wet stain on Steve's crouch.

"Oh, I spilt my coffee."

"That must of felt hot."

"Yeah. It's the hottest thing I've had down there for a while. But still not as hot as you dear," he joked with a smile.

"Oh, before I forget.... Sarah called us."

"She did?" he said with concern.

"Yes. She said that they got that thing over to the lab and Tom gave it to his friend to put it into a large aquarium with other water animals. The professor will be checking it out within an hour. In the meantime, Sarah took Tom into emerg to get some stitches on his thumb. They'll be returning to the university, to see the professor."

Steve knew that Tom's stitches had to have been related to the dangerous creature. "Why in the hell couldn't they have kept it in the bottle?" he said, showing Mary real concern.

"Holy shit Steve, take a pill. Tom and Sarah are adults. I'm sure it's in good hands with the professor," she said, sensing a lot of nervous tension from Steve. "Is there something more to this thing that I don't know about?"

"No... No, you're right. They're adults. I have to learn to put my end of the log down, and let them carry on and learn for themselves."

"Now that's the Steve I know," she said in a calm loving voice, while filling his coffee cup.

Sarah and Tom were getting out of his car in the university parking lot, "Great!" he said looking down at his right thumb, all bandaged up. "That's just great. I won't be able to swim for at least two weeks. Can I get an extension on that skinny dip?"

"Sure," she said. "I still can't believe that bullshit line you gave that nurse. About falling on a piece of broken glass."

"So if I'd told her that it was from a crayfish she'd have believed me?"

"I get the point," she said as they walked into the science building.

They just entered the doorway when down the hall, a tall blond young man shouted out, "Tom, where in the hell were you? Everyone's been looking for you," speaking in a frantic voice.

"Slow down! Slow down Duncan. This is Sarah..."

"Hi Sarah, just call me Dunc," he said, still excited.

"You knew I had to leave to get some stitches. So, did the professor have a chance to see my specimen?"

"Oh yeah. Big time." he replied, with an ear-to-ear smile. "Big fuckin' time!" he repeated, as he high-fived Tom.

"What's happening?" asked Tom with a curious look and smiled at Duncan's enthusiasm.

"Right now, as we speak, your little friend is on his way to Ottawa with the professor."

"No way!"

"Way!"

"He took my specimen?"

"Yes Tom. It really impressed him."

"Did you put it into the aquarium?"

"Sure did. And that's where your little friend scored you all those brownie points with the professor."

"What exactly do you mean?"

"Well, you two really have to see this." Duncan led them to a freshwater observatory with a large aquarium. Tom stopped dead in his tracks, with his eyes and mouth wide open. "Holy fuck!"

"Holy fuck is right!" replied Duncan. "That thing wasn't even in there for five minutes."

"That's so fucking gross!" exclaimed Sarah, looking at all the diced fish floating around the aquarium.

"Can you believe it!" said Duncan chuckling. "The professor went through three nets trying to scoop that thing out of there. He was so excited that we thought he was going to have a heart attack. This is his cell number and where he will be staying in Ottawa," he said, handing Tom a small white note. "He wants you to call him tonight. He's really curious as to where you found it Tom. Personally, I think you have the good professor by the balls with this one big time!"

"Well Tom. Do you still think the field study will fly?" asked Sarah, looking him right in the eyes.

Tom gave it a few seconds, and replied, "Yes...big time!" as all three of them laughed at his mockery of Duncan.

The soldiers were back on their top-secret stakeout, with the sun shining bright.

"That was some storm we had last night. Between the storm and Vicky on my son's case over him joining the army, it made for a long night," said Alex, looking through his binoculars.

"Paul joined?"

"Yes Nick. I couldn't talk to him. Like father, like son."

"Tell me about it. Well between that thunder and lightning, I also lost a few hours sleep," said Nicholas yawning. He scanned the pond and avoided commenting on Alex's son joining the army.

"They let Ketchnee and Merkimoff stay home last night," said Alex. "With that storm, they didn't expect any activity. We have nice weather for today's watch. Thank God for that." Nick's lack of sleep was quite noticeable to Alex. "If you need to take a few minutes of sleep Nick. Go ahead. I'll cover for you."

"I just might take you up on that one a little later." He saw a brief flash like a small mirror reflecting light. "Alex, eleven o'clock. Do you see something?"

Alex quickly scanned to that same area. "Yes," he replied. "A small light like a reflection of some kind. Is that the area where they found Yacocheve's body parts?"

"Yes. It still makes me sick. Seeing those pictures of him with his limbs cut off from that fuckin' lobster thing. That was before they shot it from the chopper. Some good that did. The aliens replaced it with this one the same night."

"When you said pictures Nicholas, did they ever say anything about recovering Yacocheve's camera?"

"Not to my knowledge," he replied as he lowered the binoculars from his eyes and looked over at Alex. "Now that you mention it, there was nothing in the report about any camera. We are the only two officers he was ever staked out with. And he always took his camera with him on every assignment."

"Just before this mission, he mentioned something about a computer camera."

"Digital, Alex."

"That was it," Alex said, putting his binoculars back up to his eyes, both men looking at the same spot. "Are you thinking what I'm thinking?"

"Yes. That reflection is probably from Yacocheve's camera lens."

"If you cover me, I can crawl over that ridge and be back here within twenty minutes," said Alex.

"I'm sure that you can handle that maneuver with ease. You're the best we have. But we have standing orders right from the general not to even shit without his say so. I'll make a note of the light reflection from across the pond. We shouldn't have a problem getting clearance later."

"On how to handle it by tomorrow? Oh great! Like we need back up," Alex urged.

"Alex, we don't know what we're dealing with here," he said understanding his partner's intentions, but not wanting to jeopardize his retirement.

"It's sure nice getting this first batch of ferns in," said Mary, as she touched them while following Steve down to the dock.

"First batch?" he asked with a surprised look on his face.

"I'd like some to take home as well. They'll really enhance our rock garden."

"I like the way you said 'our' rock garden."

"I did remind you on our way in the other day."

"You're right," he replied. "Did you remember to pack the cell phone?"

"My name isn't Steve," she said, tapping a straw bag she was carrying beside her. "It's here along with the wine and flashlight."

"Sometimes you scare me Mary. I was just thinking of Sarah calling us at eight."

"You remembered that? Well then, you scare me too." she exclaimed.

"Funny girl!" he said holding her hand, as she stepped into the boat. He was really concerned about the creature at the university.

"We're not going to stay too late at the barbecue," she said, as he was untying the boat.

"What d'ya say we play it by ear. And we'll see how we feel later?"

"Sounds good to me," she replied as he started the motor.

chapter 6

the barbecue

It was early evening, and Steve and Mary were having dinner with their friends around a large table on Mike and Carol's deck. "That was great chicken!" said Steve, as he laid down a bone in his plate. "And you got that recipe from the liquor store?"

"Yes," replied Carol. "Each month they have a different book. With all kinds of recipes from liqueur desserts to real rum cake."

"Oh, that would go over real good. Officer, I only had two pieces of cake," jested Steve, as everyone chuckled.

"Right!" said Bob. "That's all we need. They'll start up a campaign against eating, and driving."

The phone rang and Mike reached into the patio door to answer it. "Hello. No excuses," said Mike. "Sure, another time. Okay then," he said handing Steve a cordless phone. "It's for you."

Wondering who would be calling him here, he answered it with a surprised look on his face. "Hello. Oh Sarah, it's you." After a few seconds into the conversation, he stepped into the entrance of Mike's cottage for a more private conversation. About four minutes later, Steve returned to the table. "Well, I guess it would help if you turn on our phone," he said, looking at Mary with a big grin on his face.

"Oh! I'm sorry Mike."

"That's okay," smiled Mike. "You're just saving on your air time, aren't you?"

Steve laughed. "Well the good news is that the science professor took a big interest in that water thing that we caught. So much so, that he took it with him to an international science conference in Ottawa. He won't let Tom do any research on it 'til he gets back to him. So Sarah and Tom will just stay put in Sudbury until then. Apparently, one of Tom's friends had put it into a large aquarium with other fish. That little creature had them sliced and diced in five minutes. So I can see why that professor has so much interest in it."

"Holy shit!" remarked Bob with a serious look on his face.

"They could have come back here until they knew more from the professor," suggested Mary.

"No, I told them it would be best to follow the professor's instructions. They could end up running back and forth from the lake to Sudbury," he replied, still thinking about his freaky incident back at the pond.

"So what in the hell kind of water thing are you talking about?" asked Janis.

"Oh," said Bob. "When we went out on that little excursion with the bikes yesterday, Steve stopped at a large beaver pond where he'd set his minnow trap. He checked it and found these crayfish-like creatures in it and brought back one of them in a water bottle."

"So I showed it to Tom and he took it to the university and now it's in Ottawa," Steve interrupted. "The professor's going to contact Tom every day."

"Oh, I could have had a look at it," responded Janis.

"Me too," added Mary, "but Steve and Tom said it was too frisky for us to see."

"Too frisky?" asked Mike with a puzzled look on his face.

Steve cautioned with a smile, keeping the deer incident to himself, fearing it might cause chaos amongst his friends. "Yeah, we thought the girls would be scared of how it looked. And you know how you have those crazy nightmares Mary."

"Oh sure," replied Mary sarcastically, slightly upset that Steve would reveal that about her.

"At first, Tom thought it was a rusty crayfish which is somewhat different from ours. Like those zebra mussels, they're also starting to infest inland lakes and rivers of North America. We should know the origin of that thing within the next day or two," informed Steve. "By the way Mike, I couldn't help but notice your new telescope, when I was on your phone."

"And did you notice the camera

attached to it Steve. That little thing smiling back at you?"

"That little four hundred dollar thing!" blurted Carol. "Just to monitor some deer on that ridge across the lake. Or to watch girls in their dental floss bikinis. He calls it checking out the scenery. I still think it should have been a new dishwasher instead!" remarked Carol in a bitter tone. This was common with her after she'd had a few glasses of wine.

"Oh Carol. I'm sure that Mike has a plan to make this up to you," encouraged Steve. Hugging her, trying his best to butter her up.

"He'd better!" responded Carol, now with a smile.

"Hey guys. The sauna should be really hot by now," said Mike.

"Sauna?" asked Steve.

"I thought of lighting it for this evening," remarked Mike.

"We have extra swimsuits I'm sure will fit you and Mary," replied Carol.

"Why not eh?" responded Mary. "The lake looks so inviting."

"Why don't you guys go on ahead of us. While we help Carol clean up. And we'll join you shortly," said Janis. "Oh Steve, there's one thing that really confuses me."

"And what would that be?" he asked.

"Why did you want minnows? When you never go fishing."

"I think Janis has got you this time!" said Bob, with everyone laughing.

"Well Janis. It just so happens that I found this great recipe, in the liquor store of all places. For something called minnowstrone soup," jested Steve.

"Janis, you can't get up early enough to catch Steve!" said Mike.

"Tell me about it! She'd lose sleep trying to catch me sleeping," responded Steve. "Now let's catch that sauna guys."

"So I heard that this might be your last assignment," said Alex, scanning over the pond. "Well Nicholas?" He lowered his binoculars and looked over at him only to find him in a deep sleep. His chin was resting on his left arm on top of a tree stump, binoculars hanging down from his neck. Alex scanned the reflection across the pond then looked again at Nicholas, pondering if he wanted to make a run. The combination of a lack of patience and his curiosity got the best of him–thinking it ws now or never. Slowly, he set his binoculars down, keeping his eyes glued on Nicholas. Picking up his rifle, he quietly slipped away. Making a quick dash just inside the tree line, following the contour of the large pond.

A pesky fly landed on Nicholas's nose, waking him. He slapped it off, noticing that Alex and his rifle were gone. Only his binoculars remained, a bad sign. They never parted with their field glasses. Not even to go for a leak. Nick knew that this could only mean one thing. Alex didn't want anything bulky to slow him down or hinder his stalking skills. "You son of a bitch!" he muttered to himself. He put his binoculars up to his eyes in the direction of where they saw the reflection earlier. He feared the danger that Alex might encounter. Not knowing how long that he had slept only added worry.

All of a sudden, he noticed movement in a tree top about fifty yards away from the destination spot. Then another one, a little closer. He quickly exchanged his binoculars for his rifle and scope, being ready for anything. Just then, the familiar low moaning sound echoed throughout the pond. Nick took the safety off his rifle and put his index finger inside the trigger guard. Keeping the crosshairs of his scope fixed, he was ready to open fire at any time. He picked up some movement just inside the tree line. It was Alex, half crouched and moving ever so cautiously. He was looking from side to side, carrying his high-powered rifle in a ready position, and scanning the ground for the camera. "Come on, come on. Get the hell out of there!" Nick muttered.

Then out from nowhere, one of the creatures appeared directly behind Alex. Nicholas's saw Alex in his crosshairs and only a twenty percent visual of the creature. His mind was racing. Should he tip off Alex with a warning shot just to the right of him? Nick watched as the creature raised a pair of large claws, ready to strike. As Alex bent over quickly, he heard a large slapping noise behind him. Alex spun around. A rifle boom echoed and the head of the creature was cracked wide open with dark green goo draining out from it. It slowly toppled over on it's back. A relieved Alex waved thanks to Nicholas across the pond, while showing off the camera high in the air.

With all this chaos going on, Alex failed to see that another creature was lurking in the tall grass. Nicholas spotted it just as Alex was putting his rifle to his shoulder. This time it was too late. The creature clamped down on Alex's left arm with one of its claws and shook him viciously, high in the air like a rag doll, as he screamed in pain. All Nicholas could do was keep his finger on the trigger and wait. The razor-sharp claw sheared off his left arm, just below his shoulder and Alex fell to the ground. Alex desperately tried to crawl towards his rifle, extending his right arm. With every heartbeat, spurts of blood shot out from his stub. The creature pounced on him like a cat with a wounded mouse. All that he could feel was one set of claws clamping down on his upper left leg. Suddenly, a loud shrieking sound came from the creature. It became motionless, pinning Alex to the ground.

Alex knew that Nicholas's marksmanship had bought him another life. In excruciating pain, he reached down to his waist, and quickly unfastened his belt. Then he slung it around the stub of his left arm, to stop the blood flow. He suddenly felt weak and bewildered from the large amount of blood he'd already lost. Shock was setting in. He didn't have an ounce of strength in him to free his leg from the huge ugly creature pinning him down. He just lay there motionless, thinking, "I cannot die here like this. My wife and son need me." Then he passed out.

Nicholas was now standing up with a radio in one hand, looking through his binoculars with his other "Code red! Request back up!"

"What the hell is going on there, Nicholas?" blurted a loud voice over the radio.

"No time to explain. Alex needs help on the other side of the pond. I'm heading out there right now! Over and out!"

"You stay right there until backup arrives!" commanded a voice over the radio.

"Sorry. Moving out now. Over and out!" he answered. He grabbed his rifle, and started running around the pond, in fear of what had happened to his partner.

He realized that every wasted second could mean the difference between life and death.

Nicholas arrived at the scene and walked cautiously along the tree line, ready for anything. Then he spotted the creatures lying there with their heads cracked open. One had Alex's left leg clamped down like a vise in its claw, pinning him under its massive body. Crouching down for a better look, Nick noticed the belt tourniquet, and knew that Alex had not passed out for long, he was in shock. Alex started to moan in pain as he regained consciousness.

"Stay still," he urged, as he covered Alex with his camo army jacket to keep him warm. "I radioed for back up."

"Back up? It's all done," he replied with a half smile, while gritting his teeth in pain. "You took care of these freaks. From about four hundred yards away!"

"Thanks to that new explosive tip ammo!"

"You saved my ass!"

"Did I? Now both of our asses are in a fuckin' sling, for not following orders!"

"What do you mean us?" he asked with a painful expression. "It was me that didn't follow orders."

"And it was me that fell asleep on duty, allowing this to happen."

"No. I told you I was going for a shit. And I didn't return." He reached out to Nicholas with a camera in his hand. "Take this. I'm sure there's enough good evidence here to earn us both brownie points."

"I'm sure there is," he replied, taking it from Alex laughing.

"What's so funny?" he asked in a low tone, trying to bear the pain.

"How you managed to hang onto it through that wrestling match! At least you'll get to satisfy your vengeful craving," encouraged Nicholas. Still glancing around the whole area.

"What do you mean?"

"To finally boil it up, and try it with garlic butter," he mocked. Kicking the other claw on the ground, as the two men laughed together. Just then, a bright pencil beam of light surrounded Nicholas where he stood. He vanished into thin air, right in front of Alex. The light beam was still visible. Five seconds later, the light beam disappeared.

Alex felt totally useless, pinned down underneath the creature. He thought that it was the only reason why he wasn't also abducted. A distant sound of choppers could be heard. All Alex could do was try to make sense of what had happened and prepare himself for all the shit that the general would throw at him, over this whole ordeal.

Nicholas slowly awakened to a low pulsating sound, like a distant transport truck gearing down. Lying down on his back in total darkness, he wondered, "Where am I? Is this a dream? What is that sound?"

Raising his left arm up, Nick touched his face with his hand, but couldn't see it in front of him. He felt something rectangular in his right hand. "The camera that Alex handed me. Where am I now? Am I blind?" Nicholas brought the camera up on his chest and started to play with different buttons, relieved to see a red flash indicator light. He sat up and felt for the shutter button. Without warning, the camera flashed and he pushed the review button. A small view screen lit up, with a picture of the large pond that they'd been staking out.

He pushed the button beside the screen to advance to the next picture. It showed one of the creatures coming out of the water. He then advanced to the next one, "Oh my God!" he exclaimed to himself, horrified over the picture of a strange human-like figure standing beside two of the creatures outside an oval-shaped spaceship. "This must be the one that they'd had a distant sighting on," he concluded, advancing to the next frame to see one of the creatures very close-up...too close. "Is this the one that caught Yacocheve off guard? Is this the one that did him in?"

Advancing to the next frame he muttered, "This is one freaky picture." It looked like aliens, standing in one big circle in a big igloo-like ship, surrounding Yacocheve. "How was it possible for Yacocheve to discard his camera after being abducted, then later killed?" he thought, switching to the next frame. "No picture. Next frame then. No picture." He reversed back to the last frame showing with the aliens surrounding Yacocheve. "Hold on here. I took that last frame," he thought.

He felt the hair rise up on the back of his neck after suddenly realizing that aliens were surrounding him. He sat there motionless, trying to make sense of the scenario and wondering what to do next.

Suddenly, the low pulsating sounds faded out. The lighting in the craft started to dimly appear, becoming slightly brighter. When he looked up, he could now clearly see the aliens, standing about seven feet tall all around him. They looked down at him with large, yellow eyes mounted in their oval-shaped heads, wearing grayish-colored body suits. Slowly turning his head to the left, he could see that he was surrounded by about ten of them. Feeling helpless, he stayed sitting on the floor, not making any sudden movements, looking up at them while trying not to stare at any one alien.

In the low-light, he brought the camera up to his eye to take another picture. The flash went off and the aliens reacted, briefly closing their eyes. "Are those large yellow eyes light sensitive?" he wondered. "Maybe I should call it quits with the photo session. It wasn't his place to tick-off any of these big guys," he thought, remembering that he was on their turf.

The vessel began to slightly tilt. Moaning sounds started coming out from various aliens, as if they were disturbed about something. The shifting of the vessel got more progressive and their communicating sounds became more intense. The aliens started having trouble keeping their balance. Sitting on the floor gave Nick a much lower centre of gravity. He wasn't hampered as much, as the unstable jerky motions continued to increase.

Just then, a vertical opening in the wall of the craft appeared right behind the aliens. Then it closed, like an elevator door. The unstable motions of the craft and the aliens' moaning continued to excel. The door opened again. This time, a large foreign object fell into the entrance. It looked like a log. "Is this ship on the ground?" muttered Nicholas to himself.

"Is that log keeping that doorway ajar? This is my chance to make a go for it." The aliens still had their eyes on him yet were still struggling to keep their balance. They didn't seem to notice the opening, or even care about the obstruction in it.

At this point, Nicholas was now determined. He slowly got himself up in a starting position, like that of a sprinter. With his right hand he raised the camera, "On your mark, get set, go!" As he lunged towards the door, he hit the camera's shutter button and the flash went off. He knew that this would only buy him a few seconds. With his head down like a football linebacker, he plowed between two aliens and made it to the exit. Turning sideways, he squeezed his left shoulder through, and slid down the log, helping to free it from the doorway. Running away, he glanced back to see the door closed behind him.

He found himself on a high, rocky plateau. "Am I still on planet earth?" he thought to himself. "But where?" All that concerned him right now was putting distance between him and those aliens. Stumbling through the rugged terrain, his eyes gradually became a little more adjusted to the darkness. He was now able to maneuver with more control and noticed that he was following some kind of trail along a high ridge.

Stopping for a moment to read the compass on the handle of his army knife, he noted that the trail was heading in a westerly direction. To his right, he saw bright vertical light rays flickering through the night sky. "Can this be the northern lights?" he muttered.

He heard the cry of a common loon. Seconds later, another one cried out from a different direction. Still unsure of his location, he continued along the starlit trail, which began descending into a heavily wooded area. Mature oak trees dominated the landscape, their large branches acting like a canopy and blocking out much of the starlight, which had been helping guide his way.

Minutes later, he stumbled upon a ladder made of large tree limbs. Looking up, he could vaguely make out some kind of structure, about twenty feet off the ground. "This must be some kind of tree house, or hunting blind," he thought as he cautiously climbed up the log ladder. He was just about to grab the top rung, when a screech and a large dark object shot out towards him. He jerked his head sideways feeling it whisk the side of his face. He glanced back at a dark silhouette gliding away, his heart pounding, realizing he had spooked an owl off of its perch. Reaching the top, he felt a hasp with an open padlock hitched through it. He slid the padlock off and opened the door.

In the faint moonlight, he could make out a bench seat that folded from the wall and was surrounded by sliding windows with screens. "This is probably a hunting tree blind!" he thought. Along one wall was a shelf. Feeling around, he grabbed a lighter. After playing with the childproof mechanism for a few seconds, he had it lit. Nick spotted a candle sitting on the window ledge to light up the room. He then discovered a plastic bin under the bench. He popped open the lid to find candy bars, brandy, toilet paper, a flashlight and a few magazines. He shined the flashlight on Playboy magazines.

"Well I guess I'm in America," he

thought to himself. As he looked over the centerfold, taking a tug from the bottle of brandy. Munching on a candy bar, he felt a little more at ease. Nick shut off the flashlight and lay back on the foam bench, gazing at the stars. While listening to the hooting of the owl that had frightened him earlier, he replayed the day's events in his mind, then slowly fell asleep.

"I think I'm ready for a dip," said Mike, with beads of sweat rolling down his forehead. "Just one more dipper on the rocks. And we'll all go in, right?"

"Sure Mike. But throw that one on me first. Oh, that felt good," said Steve. He enjoyed the cool water running down his body, not being quite used to the sauna heat as Mike and Bob were. Trying hard to cope with the next dipper of water, that Mike was pouring over the hot sauna rocks, he held a cold wet face towel over his face to help him endure the hot steam.

"Well I'm ready to slide in," said Bob, knowing Steve couldn't take too much more steam.

"I'm right behind you," said Steve. With that, Steve went running out the door and jumped onto the waterslide. He plunged feet first into the cool night water, followed by Bob right behind him. "Oh yeah. This feels great!" he said, treading water beside Bob. As the two waited for Mike to join them, "Oh my God — they're out again tonight!" he exclaimed.

"Right on," replied Bob, looking into the northern sky above Mike's boathouse. Long vertical flickering rays of light danced throughout the star-filled northern night sky.

"Now this is the life!" said Steve.

"This is what they call a natural high!" sighed Bob.

"I wonder how many people ever get a chance to experience this in their lifetime?"

"Well Steve. I think part of it is the lifestyle we choose. Some like the big city in the fast lane. Their background sounds are squealing tires and sirens. Our sounds are the cry of loon, or the distant howl of a wolf. That's why they make Lincolns and Volkswagens."

"Yeah. Let's keep this a secret from them city slickers. And act like we are rednecks. Hey, come on in Mike. The water's great," encouraged Steve, as Mike approached the top of the waterslide.

"Sure it is! Your voice sounds a little high to me. Are you sure your balls didn't shrink up and crawl inside you?"

"No. Not at all," mimicked Steve in a high girlish voice.

"Sorry for taking so long. I just made sure that there's enough water for the girls," shouted Mike, as he sat down on the waterslide.

"You won't believe the view of the northern lights from here Mike!" exclaimed Steve.

Mike started sliding down the slide. Behind Steve and Bob, he suddenly saw a beam of light. "Holy fuck!" he exclaimed, as he went underwater. Mike surfaced beside them. "I saw it again!" he cried out, pointing south.

Steve and Bob quickly looked behind them and couldn't see what had Mike's attention. "Saw what?" asked Steve.

"That light over the plateau. It seemed to come from that pond area. If there's any activity at all, it'll be recorded on my digital," said Mike.

"Good call," confirmed Steve. "We'll have a lot of time to check it out while the girls are drying their hair."

"Right on Steve. Shit! That'll give us time to drink a whole case of beer!" said Bob, as they watched the girls enter the sauna.

"No shit Bob. That light was in the same location as the other night," concluded Mike, still looking in that direction. He was anticipating seeing it again, along with the guys, as they remained treading water.

"Holy frig!" shrieked Carol as she ran out the sauna door with Janis and Mary right behind her. "You really fired it up in there Mike."

"I think he likes to see women in heat!" jested Steve.

"Well, that's just too bad for that pervert! We're cooling off now," teased Carol. She jumped on the waterslide with the other girls right behind her, all holding their noses as they slid down together.

Later that night, the guys were in Mike's cottage standing in front of the computer screen, each holding a beer. "Now we'll see how crazy I am," said Mike, as he played back the data. A large beam of light appeared on the screen. "Well guys. I'm not nuts after all!"

"Holy shit!" said Bob. "It lasted for over a minute!"

"Close," agreed Mike. "The time counter on the top right of the screen indicated that it appeared at ten forty-eight. And it disappeared a little over a minute later. And is located almost due south of us. Right in line with your pond Steve. How could you not notice it?"

"We were checking out the northern lights at that time," said Bob, as they looked up at Steve with a puzzled look.

"And this is the exact same place you say it was two nights ago?" asked Steve.

"Right on," replied Mike. "Right from that couch with Carol."

"Well Mike, if you can take that same reading from that location and continue on due south on a map, I'm sure we'll find an open gravel pit operation or something along that line. Just a few miles past that pond."

"I hope you're right Steve because this

freaky shit has got me worried if you know what I mean. And it just so happens to be in line with those rings we covered up!"

"I'll take a ride over there first thing in the morning. And I'll let you guys know if I see anything," answered Steve. "But what if it's little green women?"

"Then we can keep them in my sauna to scrub our backs," replied Mike.

"Not a good idea. Our wives won't go along with that," said Bob.

"Well, maybe I'll find them some little green men," said Steve.

"That way, they'll appreciate us more," replied Bob.

"Are you sure you want to take that chance Bob? I couldn't help but notice how small your thing was when you were changing!" teased Mike, as he and Steve chuckled.

"What in the hell do you mean?" asked Bob. "With cold water like that. You have to allow for shrinkage!"

"Okay," responded Steve, as he patted Bob on the back. "We'll let you use that excuse this time!"

chapter 7

steve & mary's

Early the next morning, Steve quietly snuck out of bed, making sure not to wake Mary. He felt that it was best that she didn't know about the weird happenings. He wanted to investigate the area especially because of the deer incident, which he was keeping from Mike and Bob. While brewing coffee for his thermos, he wrote Mary a note on the kitchen counter: "Can't sleep. Gone for a bike ride. Call me when you're up. Love, your hug-a-bunch XOXO."

After driving for thirty minutes, he reached the plateau where Mike had seen the flash of light the night before. He shut his bike off, and walked around in the same area where he and Mary had had their picnic a few days earlier. Everything looked the same, so he continued on to where he discovered the rings up on the higher plateau.

As he approached the area, he was shocked to see all the large logs that they had piled to hide the rock engravings, were scattered everywhere. Some had large chunks torn out of them. It was beyond him. What could have caused this much destruction? Looking closer at the bedrock beside the rings, he noticed large chips of rock missing. As if a jackhammer had been at work here. He couldn't believe his eyes. The guys would have to see this to believe it.

Between this new destruction and those frisky crayfish-like creatures living in the pond, it was getting to be a little too much for him to handle. He now found himself in a real dilemma. Should he talk to his friends Mike and Bob about these incidences, or wait to get more information on that water creature. He also remembered that he was being monitored up here on the bluff, with the camera now running constantly. He calmly walked back to his bike, then continued driving up and around the plateau, and headed down the trail to the pond.

About halfway down, he picked up a scent like something rotting. Steve stopped to have a quick look through the bike's storage compartments, but found nothing. As he continued on down to the pond, the water was calm like glass, with a serene look. He had no reason to stop here.

What he'd seen here the day before spooked him, giving him a creepy feeling about the whole area. He was unaware that a second large creature was stalking him, and was swimming in his direction.

Attracted by the sound of the bike's motor running along the edge of the pond the creature was near Steve, just under the surface of the water. It would have been clearly visible to him, if only he would have checked out the area a little closer. It was a blessing that he kept moving, for a hellish confrontation would have resulted if he had stopped.

Steve rode just a few more minutes to his tree stand. He wanted to enjoy his coffee up in that quaint lookout, and also have better reception to call Mary on the radio. Steve parked his bike at the bottom of the tree stand. He glanced upward to the top of the ladder, and noticed a window was left wide open. "That's funny," he thought. "I'm sure that I closed it the last time I was up here." Turning off the bike, he reached for his thermos in the storage compartment.

Inside the tree house, Nicholas had awakened from a deep sleep, unaware of Steve's presence just below him. He desperately had to pee and thought that being in the middle of nowhere, with no one around, he could do his thing right through the window. Down below, with one hand on the ladder rung, Steve could now feel something hitting his right shoulder. He looked up and realized what was happening. Jumping to one side, he shouted up in a loud voice, "Hey, what the hell do you think you're doing?"

Nicholas was still half asleep, and was startled and surprised to hear a loud human voice speaking in English. "I am sorry," he answered back with a deep Russian accent. "I didn't know anyone was down there. "I'm coming down," he said, knowing he was trespassing on private property.

Steve stared up the ladder, curious to see who was occupying his tree stand, especially speaking with a foreign accent. As the stranger took the first few steps down the ladder, he could make out the man's army boots, and camo fatigues.

"I am really sorry sir," he said to Steve, now that he was in full view.

Steve looked up at this tall, muscular middle-aged man with a brush cut hairstyle, well-kept boots, and a quick apology. Despite his accent, and the mishap, he scored okay on first impressions. He was still puzzled over the stranger. "What are you doing here, and where are you from," he asked.

"Well, I got lost just before dark, and I decided to use this tree house as a refuge," he replied. "It is very nice, I might add."

"That's okay," he said, reaching out with his hand. "My name is Steve."

"Sorry again Steve. I am Nicholas," as they firmly shook hands.

"Well where did you come in from, the

lake or the highway?"

He had to come up with a quick story. So he thought that by the way he was dressed, and with his accent, he could pass for a tourist. "I am fishing here with some friends. And my motor broke down. I climbed up a ridge to see where I was, and signaled for help. Then, I saw this trail. And hoped it would lead me out to a main road somewhere."

"Oh, you must be staying at the lodge."

"That is right," he responded quickly.

"That's no problem Nicholas. I'll bring you back with me to my cottage. Then we can call the lodge to let your friends know where you are, and that you're okay."

"I can't thank you enough!"

"Don't mention it. But I have to let the cook know we need an extra plate. I'll just be a few minutes," he said as he climbed the ladder up to the tree house.

Nicholas waited patiently while he was trying to think of what other lines he could use on him until he could find out more about exactly where he was.

"You got your ears on good buddy?" All was quiet for a few seconds.

"I sure do big boy!" answered Mary.

"We have ourselves a guest for break-fast."

"Ten nine," she said, making sure to understand what he said.

"I repeat. Big boy is bringing back a guest for breakfast. Over."

"Is everything okay out there Steve?" she asked, finding it strange for him to make a call of this nature.

"Yes. I found a lost fisherman from the lodge, in case someone asks. We'll be there in twenty minutes. Over and out."

"That's a ten four," she acknowledged.

"Well, climb aboard Nicholas. I'm tak-ing you out," he said climbing down the ladder.

"Do I sit up there?" he asked. Pointing to the upper seat, not ever having been on a four-wheeler before.

"Yes," Steve answered. "And there are foot pegs on the sides." Driving back to Steve's cottage, Nick was taken by the beautiful landscape with all the different types of trees. The terrain constantly changed as they traveled along. Twenty-five minutes later, they were driving into the woodshed. Nick watched over Steve's shoulder as he turned off the bike then rolled back the bike's odometer to zero.

Nick also couldn't help notice the bike's GPS on the dash. "That is quite the guidance system this bike has!"

"Oh yeah. That was one of its selling points for me. It's great for pinpointing prime hunting or fishing areas." He climbed down from the bike with Nick right behind him. "See here Nicholas," Steve said, proudly showing him the map above the tool bench. "All these are main hunting areas marked out. For instance, that tree stand is thirty-two degrees east and twenty-one degrees west. Do you have any idea where you left your boat?"

Nick picked up a long skinny chainsaw file from the workbench, and carefully studied the map. "My guess is along this south shore around here," he pointed out with the tip of the file. He took a close look at the map, and checking out the highest contour, "I picked up your trail here. Yes, I am sure this is it," noticing fresh highlighting on the UFO site. "Why do you have this spot plotted out?"

"Oh that. I can't remember right now. One of my hunting buddies missed a big buck up around there," he replied, avoiding Nick's eyes.

With an answer like that, Nick was almost certain that he was holding something from him. But what? Was it possible that Steve knew about the aliens?

"So Nicholas, how about a little morning tug to start the day off right?" He grabbed two Dixie cups for shooter glasses and the bottle of vodka from his workbench.

"Sounds good to me," he replied just to be sociable.

After filling the cups, Steve handed him one and held his up high in the air as Nick followed suit. "To your first visit to Birch Lake!" he toasted.

"Dieboursia!" Nick said, still holding their glasses up high.

"Dieboursia?"

"Yes. That means the best of everything."

"Well Dieboursia then!" said Steve, as the two toasted together. "We'd better get down to the kitchen before the cook gets impatient."

"Yes Steve. This is a very nice place you have here!" he remarked, as they walked down to the cottage.

"Oh thank you," he said entering into the cottage. "Well sweetheart, this is Nicholas. Nicholas, this is my wife Mary."

Wiping her hands off on her apron she said, "pleased to meet you," as she shook his hand.

"I'm pleased to meet you as well," replied Nick with a thick Russian accent.

"Well Mary, Nicholas would like to rent my tree stand for the summer."

"It has no hydro or running water." They all started to laugh at his remark. "Well, have a seat. And can I pour you a coffee?"

"Thank you," he replied, as she started filling his cup.

"Excuse me for just a minute. I have to change my shirt," said Steve.

"It looks clean to me," said Mary.

"Oh, it's just a little accident," he smiled.

"So I understand you are staying at the lodge Nicholas," she said.

"Yes, I am staying with a few friends."

Being curious about his accent, she asked, "Where are you folks from then?"

"We are from Moscow, in Russia."

"Welcome to Canada!" she said.

"So that's why you were no stranger to my vodka," remarked Steve while entering the kitchen pulling a T-shirt over his head.

"You are right Steve," replied Nick with his first smile. He felt better now knowing where he was. It would only help him make up his story. "We were in Pickering working on an exchange with your government, through a nuclear power international program."

"Oh yes," said Steve. "I heard on the news that the government is wanting to get that generating station back on line. With the big demand for hydro."

"In case you are wondering, one of our friends recommended that we buy these army surplus clothes for this fishing trip," said Nick.

"Well I must admit, you sure had me curious. You fit them well. I mean you look like a soldier to me, navy seal, or something like that," Mary said with a warm smile, laying a platter on the table.

"Let's dig in," said Steve, trying to re-route the conversation.

"Sure looks good!" said Nicholas, as he took a few blueberry pancakes off the platter.

"Now don't be shy," said Steve, passing the platter of sausage to him. Just then the cell phone rang.

"I'll get it," she said. "It must be Sarah."

"Sarah's our daughter. "She attends a university, just an hour from here, in Sudbury," said Steve.

Nicholas chewed on a mouthful of pancakes while nodding his head acknowledging Steve.

"Well Steve, Sarah has so many interesting things to tell you," she said, as she handed him the cell phone. He really didn't want Nicholas to hear the conversation, but felt it would go over his head anyway. "Hello sweetheart. What is it? Sure. It's on crown land. No. No one else knows about it. Crustacean...lobster family." Now this part of the conversation really got Nicholas's attention. So much so, that he choked on his mouthful of sausage. "Well then, we should stock up on garlic butter!" he said with a chuckle. "We'll keep our phone on every morning and afternoon. Just keep us posted sweetheart. Love you too. Bye," as Steve turned off the cell phone. "It sounds like our water friend is really creating a lot of interest in Ottawa."

"Perhaps you should clue Nicholas in on the story," she said.

"I don't think he'll find it so interesting Mary," said Steve trying to divert the conversation.

"Sure Steve, go ahead. I am always interested in what interests other people, especially in a different country," responded Nick. He was really taken by what he'd heard.

"My apology then," he said. "It was just a few days ago that I set a minnow trap in this large old beaver pond we have at the end of our hunting trail. It's just about three hundred yards down past the tree stand that you spent the night in."

"Oh I am sorry Steve. But what is a minnow trap?"

"A minnow trap is a small round vertical cage we set in a creek, or pond to catch minnows in."

"Oh I see. And how far is three four hundred yards? I am sorry, we are totally metric in Russia."

"So are we," said Mary, "but Steve is

one baby boomer that never converted."

"I hope I am not out of line," said Nick, "but these things make it hard for me to understand. Go on please. Tell me about the fish trap...minnow trap," he urged, as he shook his head in embarrassment, still smiling.

"It's when my buddies and I went back to check it later that afternoon," said Steve.

"You mean after taking them to see the strange markings on the plateau?" asked Mary.

Steve now had a poker face. And didn't expect that part of the story to surface.

"Mary, are you referring to the large round grooves carved in the rock back there? We're talking about those creature things now."

Nicholas stopped eating at this point. Trying to keep focused on everything Steve was saying. Mary's comment just made it that much more interesting.

"So I picked up the trap to find about a thirty of these fuckin' strange looking creatures!" he exclaimed.

"Sweetheart!" she cautioned, as she nudged him sharply with her elbow.

He stopped talking and looked at her, "What!" he replied. With both of his hands held open in the air. He was visibly upset over of her interference.

"Should you swear in front of our guest?" she urged.

"I'm sorry Nicholas if I offended you. But these are really fuckin' freaky! Sorry sweetheart!"

Nicholas was doing his best not to laugh and offend her.

"Well, I gave one to our daughter's boyfriend and they took it to the university science department. The professor there was so intrigued by it, that he brought it with him to an international science convention in Ottawa. Now, some of the top scientists in the country and from the US are really caught up with this freaky creature."

"Sounds exciting to me," said Nicholas.

"Yes," Mary responded. "And they're really frisky."

"What do you mean?'

"Well, when they put it into an aquarium, it ended up killing all the fish and other water animals within minutes. Steve wouldn't even let me look at it. He was worried that I'd be bitten by it or something."

"No. No sweetheart. At the time I didn't want it to fall out and hurt itself," Steve protested.

"Sure, sure!"

All this information was too much for Nick to take in at one time. But it seemed to confirm the presence of alien activity in their area.

"Let's have a second cup of coffee out in the gazebo. And we'll call the lodge for you."

They heard the distant sound of a boat approaching the dock. "It sounds like we have company coming. Oh, it's Brenda," said Mary looking through the kitchen window.

"Steve, if you can go down and help her tie up, Nicholas and I will be in the gazebo."

"Sure. And I hope she has a good excuse for missing my ribs the other night," said Steve heading out the door.

Nicholas helped Mary, by carrying a platter into the gazebo. Then he sat down facing the beautiful peaceful lake. "Now I can see why they call this God's country."

"Yes. We hear that saying a lot out here."

Steve was now on the dock walking towards Brenda. "So how is our perogie princess this morning?"

"Just great Steve. I'm sorry I didn't make it over the other night. I had some old friends drop by, on their way back to the States."

"You don't have to explain," replied Steve reaching down to grab the bow rope from her pontoon boat. "This happens a lot at this time of year," Steve said as he finished tying the boat. He gave her a big hug. "Come on up. We're working on our second cup of coffee and we have a surprise guest."

"Who?" she inquired, with an inquisitive look.

"If I told you, it wouldn't be a surprise."

"Oh you!" she said, elbowing Steve in the ribs, as they headed up to the cottage. When they arrived at the gazebo, Steve opened the screen door to let Brenda enter first.

"Hi stranger!" said Mary, as the two women hugged each other. Brenda looked over Mary's shoulder and noticed a large, handsome man in combat fatigues, sitting by himself.

"Brenda, let me introduce you to Arnold Schwarzenegger!"

"That is very funny Steve!" he responded in his accent. "I am Nicholas. And my friends call me Nick," standing up to shake her hand.

"Well Nick, I think Steve has you pegged pretty good!" she said.

"Yes. I get that a lot back home."

"Nick," Steve said as he handed him his cell phone. "Just push that send button, and you'll get through to the lodge. But stand outside the gazebo. Better yet go back up there. Just behind that water tank, ten feet on the other side of it."

"There you go again Steve. You know Nick doesn't know what feet are."

"Oh shit!" he replied, as he pointed upwards. "Just around there, by that water tank."

This worked well for the privacy Nick needed. Now out of site from them he pushed cancel on the phone, and started to redial another number.

With Nick out of hearing range, Brenda

asked, "So where's the mystery man from?" with a smile.

"He's originally from Russia. Working at that nuclear generating station in Pickering, on some government exchange program. His motorboat broke down just around the bay. And he ended up spending the night in our tree house at the far end of the trail. He's staying at the lodge with some buddies on a fishing retreat."

"I'm on my way to the lodge to fuel up after this coffee. And I'd be more than glad to tow his boat back," she said smiling at Mary.

"Hmm, how convenient," responded Steve. "Well then, you should let him know. To save his friends the trouble of trying to find him."

"Sure. Excuse me for a minute," said Brenda, as she left the gazebo. Walking around the cottage, up to the water tank, she came to a sudden halt. Now standing behind Nicholas, she couldn't help but hear him speaking in Russian to someone in a high rank position. It sounded like he was trying to justify himself for his actions, talking a little louder than normal.

"Yes. I am in Northern Ontario, Canada...I was abducted by those aliens. And then escaped from them. Alex can fill you in on the rest. Yes. The same shit is happening over here in Canada. I have to speak to the general. What in the hell is he doing in Canada? Yes. I am at the place, where they found it. Yes. They are good people, and they don't know. No. There was no UFO sighting, that they spoke of. Sure. Let the general know I will be calling back tonight. And get me that Ottawa phone number. Bye for now. No. I don't need luck. I need good backup so tell Alex to get lots of rest. And I will be seeing him just as soon as we can figure out why those aliens are here in Canada. Bye for now."

Turning around to return to the gazebo, Nick was now faced with Brenda standing only a few feet from him. She was in shock and in a daze by the conversation she'd overheard, trying to keep her cool.

"I just want to tell you that I can tow you back to the lodge."

"Well, thank you. I will take you up on that. It sounds like all my buddies had too much to drink last night. And they did not even miss me."

"Some friends they are," she said to Nicholas. In a loud sarcastic voice, so loud that Steve and Mary could hear her from the gazebo.

This was not like Brenda to talk like this. They frowned at each other in wonder. Watching them walk back into the gazebo to finish their coffees, Steve asked, "Is everything okay Nicholas?" feeling bad vibes in the air.

"Well," said Nicholas to Brenda. Who was now sitting erect with her arms crossed in front of her. "I am sorry Steve. But I do not know what is wrong," he said with a long frown on his face.

"You don't know what's wrong? My ass!" she shouted out, as the drama thickened.

"Whoa, whoa Brenda," said Steve. He'd never seen this side of her before, even after being close to her and Bill for ten years.

"I'll tell you what," she said in a harsh tone, with her arms still crossed in front of her. Looking at Nicholas, straight into his eyes, she spoke loudly. To Steve and

Mary's surprise, it wasn't in English, but in some kind of foreign language. Whatever she said had a large impact on Nick. So much so that his face turned beet red. After about thirty seconds of this language, she seemed to be pushing all of his buttons, Steve had no choice but to step in.

"Okay. Okay Brenda. What's going on?"

"Well for one thing, Nicholas lied. He's not staying at the lodge. And there is freaky shit going on with him. You should call the police. He's some kind of criminal or something. And I'm worried for your lives."

With the drama now at its peak, Nicholas realized he had to come out of the closet and come clean. "I am so sorry. But I guess I have to explain what this is all about."

"Well then, go ahead. The stage is yours," said Steve.

He took a deep breath. "Well Brenda is right. I am not staying at the lodge. I am a Russian army officer."

"All right then. What the hell are you doing here?" asked Steve.

"This is the part where you guys have to listen to me very carefully because your actions can jeopardize your lives, your country, and even this planet!"

"This planet?" questioned Mary, with a big smirk.

"Give him a break Mary." Steve could sense Nick's deep emotions. Like Nick, he too had already experienced disturbing occurrences. "Time out girls. Now give him a chance to tell us his story," shouted Steve.

"Well you know those strange and freaky little creatures that you have living in that back pond. At breakfast your daughter called to inform you that the professor was really impressed. And that they had never seen anything like this on earth before..."

"Yeah," replied Steve.

"It is because they're not from earth," Nick confirmed. "We are faced with the same problem in Russia. In almost the same type of condition, in a large abandoned beaver pond."

"But that still doesn't explain how you got here Nick."

He looked at each of them for a second,

and then said, "I was abducted."

"Abducted by who?" asked Steve.

"Aliens," he said, with a poker face.

"Now that's a good one. Freaky water creatures....Now abducted by aliens. If anything, he's the freaky one and an alien to this area," exclaimed Brenda.

Steve, knowing more about all the strange occurrences going on around them, was giving him a little more rope. He wanted to know more. "Okay Brenda, when you overheard Nicholas's conversation in Russian. Did he mention anything to anyone about being abducted?"

"First off, Russian is a Slavic language. And Czechs, Poles and Ukrainians such as myself, can communicate quite well. So he can't bullshit me. And yes, he did mention being abducted. And the same shit that is going on back in Russia is happening right here. He said something about escaping and insisted on wanting to talk to some general later today."

"General?" asked Steve, looking across at Nicholas.

"Yes. He is head of our intelligence for the International Alien Watch Centre, the I.A.W. for Russia. Every country is in on it. It is kept top secret to avoid any pan-icking or rioting around the globe. It was set up almost ten years ago, when the US found a crashed UFO in some desert. It was after that incident, that the super powers realized that we all have to work together. For some strange reason, our general had to attend an emergency meet-ing over here in Ottawa with your chapter of I.A.W. and your top military aids. It so happened that these strange crustaceans, that the aliens have stocked in a pond in Latvia, have now been sighted some-where in Canada."

"Would someone please clue me in on these so called little water creatures," asked Brenda.

"Yes," said Steve. "I set a minnow trap in that large abandoned beaver pond, back on our trail. I caught a bunch of these strange looking lobster-like things, with scorpion-like tails."

"Those are the ones," said Nicholas.

"When Sarah called us this morning, she told me to stay away from that pond until further notice."

"Yes, but what makes you so sure Nick?" questioned Mary, "that our pond is the one in Canada that they're talking about?"

"Because it was brought in from that university in Sudbury," said Nick.

"Oh my God!" replied Mary, in a fearful voice.

"I am sorry Mary. What I mean is, I know for a fact that what you have back there are the same as the ones in Russia. I hope that the aliens have not stocked them anywhere else in Canada, or the world for that that matter. I will not give you false hope. We really don't know what we're dealing with."

"So, what in the hell do we do now?" asked Steve.

"Wait," Nick advised.

"Just wait?" asked Steve.

"Yes. Because when I called earlier, it was around five p.m. in Moscow time. And I didn't know that the general was over here in Canada. It is probably concerning your little creature. I will be in contact with our general in a few hours."

"Our government will be working with you as well?" asked Steve.

"Sounds to me, that they already are. After all, they did instruct you to stay away from that pond," replied Nicholas.

"Those damn little creatures!" said Steve. He hit the table with his fist, not being able to keep in his horrifying secret anymore.

"What is it Steve?" asked Brenda sensing something wrong.

"It was yesterday morning, when I had my coffee at the pond. I saw a doe and her fawn come out for a drink in that pond. They were standing in shallow water, when suddenly the water started to boil all around them. In less than sixty seconds, they were gone. The cries from those two deer are something you would never want to hear. No animal would have had any chance of survival with those creatures!"

"So that's why you weren't yourself," said Mary, knowing full well that Steve didn't need this stress on his heart.

"Steve, when I asked you why that location on the map was marked, why did you avoid it?" asked Nicholas.

"Oh, that's where I discovered those strange circles that are engraved in the rock, up on that plateau."

"That is the spot I escaped from last

night. When I first realized I was close to a lake somewhere in North America," he remarked.

"How in the hell did you know that?"

"By the calls of common loons. I heard them calling back to each other. I've studied water birds and the common loon only lives in North America."

"Was it was around eleven p.m.?" asked Steve, thinking of the night before when Mike logged in that flash of light, up on that plateau area.

"What made you come up with that time?" asked Mary.

"That's the time Mike saw a mysterious flash of light come from that direction. We checked it out on the computer," he remarked.

"Your friend monitored that event?" asked Nicholas with a surprised look.

"Yes. My buddies' cottages are across the bay from that lookout. Mike has a telescope with a digital camera mounted to it. He started monitoring that south ridge twenty-four seven on a time-lapse mode. We wanted to monitor the deer movement and keep tabs on those rings on the hill. We were afraid that some hiker or blueberry pickers might notice them. We thought all this time, that they were Indian engravings of some kind."

"Holy moley! And I thought Oprah was interesting. A lot of shit happened around here in the last three days. Sorry I'm late," responded Brenda.

"Yes," said Mary. "You know just as much as I do, and I've been here all along."

"Honey!" said Steve.

"Don't honey me! I'll never be left in the dark again. From now on, we're in this shit together!"

"So, how much do your friends across the lake know Steve?' asked Nicholas.

"It'll be too hard to keep this much from them because we see each other almost every day."

"I guess you had better have them over soon," advised Nick.

"Soon?"

"Yes Steve. Call them right now, and invite their wives too."

"Yes," said Mary, "their wives too!"

"What in the hell do I say?" he asked.

"Come on now sweetheart. You can do better than that," she said, as she handed

Steve the cell phone already dialing.

"Good morning Mike. No, I don't have a big head. But remember that flash of light you saw last night. I checked it out. You and Bob just have to see what I found. I don't know, but maybe it's a meteor, or a piece of comet. Oh yes, bring the wives too. We'll do lunch here. Yes," he said in an excited voice, "right now," then he turned off the phone.

"Now you see how good Steve can work under pressure," said Mary.

"You mean bullshit!" corrected Brenda.

"Hey, hey! Well, you guys wanted them over here pronto," Steve said. He could see Mary was still troubled over him keeping her in the dark. "Oh Mary, don't be bitter. It's just that me and the guys..."

"Save it! I'm going to put on another pot of coffee."

"Looks like it's going to be an interesting afternoon," said Steve. "Better yet, I'll bring out the hard stuff. Mike and Bob are going to want a stiff one after they hear this shit." He departed with Mary from the gazebo, leaving Nick and Brenda time to get better acquainted.

"Well Steve. I believe your story about the deer," said Bob. "But Nicholas — or Nick — you escaping from a UFO, on top of that bluff? Personally, I think it's a little far-fetched."

Steve could still feel the doubts from Mike and Bob. And he knew that it would take more to convince them. "Well fellows. He pointed out to me on my map where it took place. And oddly enough, this is the same spot we monitored last night. And you should see the destruction that spaceship did to our log pile."

"Well," said Mike, with a doubtful grin. "I'll try and work with you on this one Steve."

Nicholas knew that Steve's friends still weren't convinced as to what was going on. He then suggested, "I was hoping I would not have to do this." All eyes were now on him as he reached into his bulky leg pocket. He pulled out a digital camera, and looked everyone in the eye. "Now what is on this camera might give you nightmares for the rest of your lives. But what is in here killed a good friend of mine, and seriously injured another. You guys may as well see this now. This is what we are up against." The three men closed in around him for a close look at the camera's small screen.

"Holy shit!" said Mike. "They get that big?"

"We don't know what those are," said Nick, "but we call them NYANYAS."

"NYANYAS?" questioned Steve. "What in the hell!" said Bob with a puzzled look.

"NYANYA means babysitter in Russian, or Ukrainian," responded Brenda, in a smart-assed tone with her arms folded in front of her.

Nick looked up at her, "Very good, thank you for the interpretation," he said in a calm voice.

"But babysitter?' asked Steve.

"Yes," he confirmed. "They guard those little creatures. And you mean to tell me you have not seen one yet?"

"No," said Steve. "But we've heard some weird low moaning sounds at the pond."

"Well, that is them," he answered. "That is their warning sign," as he forwarded to the next picture.

As Bob, Steve and Mike looked up at

each other, nodding in agreement as to what Nick was telling them. "Oh my God," said Bob as he turned his head sideways squinting his eyes.

"Oh, come on now guys. The show only gets better," said Nick. "You may as well see what airline I flew with. Oh yes. Check out the flight attendants." Just by their husband's facial expressions, the girls knew that the pictures would be too hard for them to stomach.

"Okay. Okay Nick," said Mike holding up an open hand. "You made your point. So what the fuck do we do now?"

"Wait," he advised, looking up at them calmly.

"Yes," agreed Steve. "Nick will know more from the general in a few hours. Remember he's in Ottawa working with our government, in conjunction with the I.A.W. Well, if the countries can team up to help the world against UFOs and alien shit. Then we should team up to help our country as well!"

"Count me in!" said Mike.

"Me too!" said Bob.

"And you girls can help us with communication and intelligence," suggested

Nicholas.

"It took a man from another country to recognize that!" responded Mary. "Intelligent men that want to communicate are few and far between."

"So we just take a back seat and watch and wait?" asked Bob.

"Yes. Because at this point, we don't know what we are dealing with here. Remember, they are a lot more advanced than we are," advised Nick.

"How do we know that?" asked Mike.

"The fact that we cannot intercept them on our radar and yet they are here. I think that makes them superior," he cautioned.

"I believe Nick is right. We don't know what or who we're dealing with. And if we try to get physical, we might only scratch their armor. So let's not do anything to piss them off. First things first," said Steve, filling up shooter glasses with vodka. "Let's have a toast to our team. How did you say the best to us in Russian Nicholas?"

"Dieboursia!" responded Brenda with a straight face.

"Good Russian!" said Nicholas.

"Ukrainian," corrected Brenda, with a

half smile.

"Dieboursia!" said Steve as they all raised their glasses and toasted.

"I am real sorry about my sarcasm while I was previewing the pictures," remarked Nick. "I hope I didn't upset you."

"No way," replied Mike. "But it sure as hell was a eye-opener and convinced me.

"Well, you guys also had to know what you are dealing with. The big thing about dealing with the ETs between here and Russia is that they are seven hours ahead of your time. It will just make it a little harder in tracking them between both our ponds. That is, if they are not going back to their planet, before visiting another pond. Because I was abducted at around two p.m. Russian time, and I escaped over here at around eleven p.m. your time according to Mike's computer, this gives us something to work with. What I learned from you, tells me that those little creatures living in your pond are carnivorous."

"You mean like the deer incident?"

"Yes Steve."

"Well holy shit. Now that you mention

it Nick, that minnow trap was baited with a leftover ham sandwich. Mary forgot to remove the ham from the bread when she tore it up and pushed it into the minnow trap holes.

So it was really the scent from the ham that attracted them after all," remarked Steve.

"That is right Steve. And it will help us to support our theory on them as well. Now if there is any way I can get these pictures to your I.A.W. in Ottawa, it will really help your government to see what is happening here."

"No problem," said Mike. "I can download it on my computer, and email them anywhere."

"Good. Remind me to get the email address from the general, when I am talking to him. It will be great if we can take a few more pictures over there, like the landing site and pond. Oh yes Steve, I will need the heading on that pond and landing site that you took with your bike."

"You mean GPS."

"Yes. So our satellite can give us twenty-four seven vertical coverage which they will be monitoring from Washington."

"Holy shit! Our own satellite!" exclaimed Mike.

"No," said Nicholas with a chuckle. "All the countries chipped in on that one!"

"They can take great pictures of the UFOs on the ground, but the aliens somehow have a way of getting under our radar. I'm sure we'll have that part of the puzzle figured out soon enough."

"It's sure nice to now that we're running the show at this end," responded Mike.

"Now you are talking!" encouraged Nick with a big smile. He now felt a little more confident with the boys. "But remember, we are only working with the I.A.W. And they call all the shots. We can work as a team and inform them on things that could be of help to them. But remember, we cannot assume anything with these aliens. Just when you think you have them figured out, they change their minds."

"Huh, sounds like they're females to me," said Bob, as all the guys laughed.

"Funny boy," said Janis to Bob.

"Well then, it's our turn to have a barbecue. Why don't we all meet at the cottage in a few hours and continue this conversation there," suggested Bob.

"That's a good idea. We'll take you up on that before you change your mind," said Steve. "It will give Nicholas time to take a few more pictures of the area. And we'll fill you in on the phone call as well."

"Oh Steve, remember to take along your cell phone," advised Mike, "just in case anything comes up,"

"Yeah and Maggie's in the front rack of my bike," said Steve.

"Who in the hell is 'Maggie'?" asked Brenda.

"It's his 300 Magnum moose rifle," answered Mary.

"I bet you he even has a name for his dick," said Bob.

"You mean my hard drive," Steve replied.

"If we ask Mary, she'll probably say it's a floppy!" said Mike. "He'd need Viagra to make his floppy into a hard drive."

"No way, the last time Steve tried Viagra, it got stuck in is throat. He had a stiff neck for the rest of the week," said Mary.

Everyone burst out laughing except Nicholas, who couldn't quite understand. "Maggie, floppy, hard drive and Viagra," I am sure that we can use them all in Russia," said Nicholas in his accent, only making them laugh even louder.

"Sorry guys," interrupted Brenda. "But if what Nick has in that camera now is so important to the I.A.W., then why should we take any more. I mean download what we have to them now, and take more pictures later. Just in case we break or lose that camera."

"Very smart thinking. That is what I mean by teamwork!" said Nick.

"Yes," added Steve. "A bird in the hand is better than two in the bush."

"Sure. We can take more later," said Nick to Brenda, giving her the benefit of the doubt. She opened up a little, and gave him a big warm smile and a thank you.

"Well then, we'll head back and download those pictures for you Nick," said Mike.

"Yes. And it will also give me time to

prepare dinner as well," said Janis. "I don't want to be around Mike and Bob when they download those gory photos!"

"Whaddya mean? They can't be any gorier than the pictures Carol's brother took at my wedding," said Mike.

"You don't want to go there right now," said Carol, as they all chuckled.

"Nick, if you want, you can hop on with me," said Brenda. "I'm on my way to the lodge to fuel up. I can drop you of at Mike's"

"Thanks, but first I will need a little time to clean up and maybe a swim," said Nick.

"There's that private beach about halfway to the lodge Brenda. It'll give Nick a chance to get acquainted with this area a little better," said Steve.

"That's fine by me Steve. And we can pick you and Mary up on our way back to Bob's afterwards," she replied.

"Well then Nick. Let me pack you a towel and some soap. Steve also has an extra sweat shirt, and pants that should fit you."

"Oh Mary, pack those new sneakers of mine as well. They might be a little bit roomy," Steve said, as he put his foot alongside Nick's.

"You guys are too kind."

"Don't be crazy Nick."

"Those army boots just won't do it, for those casual clothes. And I can have your army clothes washed, and back to you tomorrow," said Brenda.

"Schwarzenegger goes casual. This should be fun to see," said Steve.

"Don't worry Nick. You'll have your combat fatigues in time to do more terminating," said Brenda.

"I have never seen so many clowns in one place, at one time. How do they do it? I guess it is only in Canada. Eh?" jested Nick. The gang laughed at him, for the first time seeing his sense of humor.

Steve and Mary went down at their dock to see their guests off. In the first boat it was Mike and Bob and their wives. "So we should be there around sixish," said Steve.

"Only if your captain picks you and Mary up on time. After all," said Mike. "Where the perogie princess is taking Nick, is known as Passion Bay."

"That's a good one Mike. I'll get you for that!" remarked Brenda.

"Go for it!" mocked Carol, as Mike's boat departed with everyone laughing.

"We'll see you two later," yelled Steve as Nick and Brenda departed.

"Thank you again!" shouted Nick to Steve and Mary as Brenda drove off.

Mary slapped Steve on the backside, while they were heading up to the cottage. "What was that for?" he asked.

"You're real smooth! Give Nick a chance to get acquainted with the area."

"Yeah. Well it worked didn't it?" he said with a big smirk.

"Like I said, you're smooth. I know you really meant get acquainted with Brenda," she said with a big smile, as they walked up towards the cottage hand and hand.

chapter 8

nicholas & brenda

"Well you have some great friends here Brenda," said Nicholas standing up beside her at the steering wheel.

"Yes. And they do tend to joke a lot."

"That is for sure."

"We go back a long way. My late husband Bill was best buddies with these guys, for over thirty years. I've only been here for seven. The last three by myself."

"I am so sorry to hear that."

"Don't be Nick. I'm sorry I didn't pick up on this place with Bill earlier."

"I see what you mean Brenda. I haven't even been here a full day, and I am hooked already," he remarked, as he checked out the miles of scenic shoreline.

"Look up there to your right. It is up on that ridge, where those rings in the rock are. And just over it, is that large pond. So Brenda, Mike and Bob should be on the opposite shore?"

"Yes Nick. That's their cottages over there. The one with the boathouse and waterslide is Mike and Carol's. And to the right of them is Bob and Janis's. Just around that next point to our right is where that beach is. And no, I'm not from the Ukraine," she said looking straight into his eyes.

"You mean the Russian Federation," he said.

"No, I mean the Ukraine. I was born in Canada but my family were from the Ukraine. We've never considered it part of Russia."

He felt some kind of resentment from her. And refused to tip toe around her, including any prejudices she may have against Russians. "I am sorry I had to pick Russia for my place of birth, if that helps any." His point got through to Brenda, as she sat on what he said for a few seconds and realized how much of a poor sport she must seem to be in his eyes.

"I'm so sorry. Forgive me Nick. You, like me, weren't there during those hard times. I guess if I wanted to hold grudges from histories past, then I shouldn't have bought this Honda outboard motor for my boat because the Japanese were once our enemy."

"Yes it just goes on and on," he said. Glad to see her smiling and finally coming around. He gently patted her on the shoulder in a friendly gesture.

"This is it," she said, while slowing down. She cut the motor and the boat glided towards the shore. There was a long white sandy beach with a shallow and gradual grade. "It's one of those beaches that you can walk out forever, and still be up to your waist."

"Wow. I see why Mike called this Passion Bay!"

"Yes. Most of the locals did their first skinny-dipping here as teens, along with the loss of virginity."

"By the time you see a boat heading this way, you have lots of time to get your swim suit on," he said, while looking through the bag that Mary packed for him.

"Speaking of swimsuit," she said with a big smile, "I didn't pack one. So I guess Passion Bay will have to live up to it's name." She slid off her top and shorts and jumped in totally nude.

He just stood there, stunned and surprised at what she had just done.

"Well, come on in, the water's great!"

"And it really looks inviting. I will be right in," he said with an ear-to-ear smile. Quickly untying his bootlaces behind the steering wheel console, he felt slightly intimidated by having to fully undress in front of her. Brenda waited patiently treading water.

"Yes, it sure is beautiful country around here Steve. Brenda showed me some nice views."

"Okay Nick. Lets not go there," Steve said with a little chuckle.

"So what is so funny?" he asked with his accent.

"It's okay," said Brenda. "It's Steve. His mind is in the gutter."

"What? Nick's right. There are a lot of nice scenic views around here," Steve responded while trying to sound so innocent.

"Sure there are!" said Mary, knowing full well what Steve meant.

"Here Nick, if you want to make that phone call to the general," said Steve as he handed him the phone.

"I am sure glad the general is here in Canada. I would not want to be waking him up at 1a.m."

"Oh shit. That's right. I forgot about the seven hour time difference," said Steve. "I'll fix us up a batch of margaritas. Are you girls in?"

"Sure," said Mary.

"Sounds good to me," said Brenda.

"Don't worry Nick. If you don't like them, you can always go back to vodka," he suggested.

"So Nick has been giving lessons in Russian to you, Steve?" asked Brenda.

"Yeah," he said, leaving the gazebo. "My first word was vodka!"

About ten minutes later, Nick joined them back in the gazebo. Handing the cell phone back to Steve. "Well it is like this. Your little friend from the pond is getting big ratings at that international science convention in Ottawa Let us just say that it stole the show."

"Did it?" asked Steve.

"You know that professor from your daughter's university? Well, by the time they caught up with him, he had the science community eating out of his hand. His head was so big, that he could not leave the building. They thought that his discovery was out of this world!"

"They were right on one thing," said Steve with a chuckle. "His discovery is great. That's why he doesn't want anyone else to go anywhere near that pond."

"It is not for safety sake, but his own. Thank God that the I.A.W. got to him on time!" said Nick. "And when he learned that they were not of this world, he didn't like the fact that he had no more leverage on the matter. It really blew the wind out of his sails. The I.A.W. in Canada will be in contact with us twice daily. There will be no lack of communication. Your air force as well as a US team has deployed fighter aircraft for our backup."

"That sure should gives us a little sense of security," said Steve.

"Let us hope so" replied Nick in a not so positive tone. "Like our twenty-four hour radar satellite surveillance. Some good that does. Remember, the aliens still have a way of getting under it. They also wanted to send in ground support right away. But I talked them into keeping their distance right now, until we learn more about them. If for some reason you see more boats than normal around here fishing, they are not fishermen, but secret service. Oh yes, I have that email address for Mike. It is protectingyourass@all-times.com."

"Are you bullshitting me, Nick?" Steve chuckled.

"No, in Russia, it is UFOoutofhere @Russia." Now with everyone laughing their heads off. He just smiled to be a sport, but he still didn't see the humor in it.

"Well, I think it's time we head over to Bob's, if you don't mind Nick?" Steve said. "This way you can give us all the details at one time. And I'm sure they'll get a real kick out of those email addresses."

"You still think I am bullshitting you Steve?"

"If you are, then I deserve it!" he said,

as he patted Nick on the back. "But then again, no one would ever suspect an email address like that to be real," said Steve.

"You know Steve, these margies are pretty good!" he remarked.

"That's margaritas!"

"You know, you can't make a Russian into a Mexican," said Brenda.

"Maybe after he tries Steve's nachos, he'll convert," added Mary, as they left the gazebo.

The men were all around Mike's computer, waiting patiently for him to email the latest information to the I.A.W. "It's gone, and I kept those pictures on file. Here Nick, it's a backup disc just in case," said Mike, handing it over.

"Good thinking," he responded.

"Tomorrow morning, Nick and I will be going up to the lookout and pond to explore a little more. And we'll take a few more pictures for our file. Mike, have your radio on at approximately eight a.m., so we can keep you posted on any occurrences."

"Don't worry. I'll also be watching you

guys from the comfort of my monitor," he replied.

"We can't resist the smell of that barbe-cue!" said Steve to Janis, as the men were now walking out onto Bob's deck.

"Well, your timing is good," said Janis. "Help yourself at the bar."

"Yes, we're overdue for a toast," said Steve. "And can I get you something Nick?"

"Well surprise me Mike because I am not really up on all these drinks."

"Oh, I'll surprise you all right!" he said with a big smile.

Now with everyone seated around the table, Janis said, "I think it's a good time for us to give thanks. Would you mind Steve?" Everyone bowed their heads.

"O heavenly Father, we thank you for our health, this dinner, Nick, and for wis-dom in dealing with those unearthly things around us. And we toast to you Lord, in Jesus's name, amen."

"Amen."

"Everything looks so good, I don't know where to start," said Steve.

"Well Steve, you can start by passing

me the coleslaw," said Mary.

"And Steve can you please pass me the garlic bread this way," said Bob.

"I guess sometimes, I should learn to shut up," said Steve. After realizing he was too busy talking instead of eating.

"No, no!" said Mike. "Don't be so hard on yourself Steve. And pass me the corn please," as everyone laughed.

"So how do you like that drink Nick?" asked Mike.

"It's very good," he replied.

"I knew you would."

"What is it called?"

"A Black Russian."

"A Black Russian?" he repeated.

"I was going to offer one to Brenda, but I figured she's too preoccupied with a white Russian. And, you know what they say, once you go black, you never come back," Mike said as all the others moaned.

"I am sorry. I don't understand!" said Nick.

"We'll explain that one to you later," said Bob. "It's a guy thing."

"No, I would say that it's more of a girl thing," said Brenda. With Nick now looking really puzzled and curious as to what they meant. "What they're referring to Nick, is that some girls think that size matters."

"Oh, now I get it!" he said, with a big smile.

"Sorry to change the subject. But can you pass me that platter of sausages Mike?" asked Janis. Steve watched her as she rummaged through them with tongs, finally grabbing a big one.

"I see what you mean Brenda. Janis went for the biggest one," he said, as they all started laughing.

"Okay, okay. Time out! Let's get serious now," said Carol. "So how did your conversation with the general go, Nick?"

"Well your country's officials want me to head this investigation on those ETs with you guys. It is only because I have had close encounters with them."

"Having been abducted, pretty well gives you bragging rights!" said Bob.

"Thanks," he said. "Like I wanted to be. We will also have other support."

"Other support?" asked Bob.

"Well if you notice more fishing activity around here than normal, it is because they are not really fishing."

"Oh they're working undercover?" asked Carol.

"Yes. We call them our shadows in Russia."

"And will those shadows be from Canada?'

"Yes, an all-Canadian ground crew. They are an elite force. They already know each one of you by sight, by the boat you drive, and by the cottage you occupy."

"How is that possible?" asked Mary.

"Oh, photo ID like your driver's license on the police c-pick," said Steve.

"You catch on quick. And apparently they are not too happy that a Russian is in charge of logistics."

"What in the hell is logistics?" asked Brenda.

"Oh that means the organization of troop movements," said Mike.

"Whoopee shit! That's too fuckin' bad for them. If they don't like team Canada coached by a Russian, you should remind them what the I.A.W. stands for, Nick," said Steve.

"Yes," said Bob holding his glass up to

toast. "Here's to our coach!"

"Yes," said Janis, as they all raised their glasses.

"Dieboursia!" said Steve

"Dieboursia!" said everyone, showing Nick that they were a team and completely behind him.

"Oh yes. There is one more thing," remarked Nick looking upward. "They have also deployed some air support just in case."

"Holy shit!" responded Bob, as they made out three fighter jets flying high in a tight formation.

"It's just hard to grasp all this going on here, in such a peaceful setting like this," exclaimed Mary.

"I guess this secluded spot sure looks inviting for those ETs as well," said Mike.

"Let's hope they didn't set up a universal website of the bestplanetstoinvade-inthisgalaxy.com," added Steve.

"That's almost as good as Russia's email address," responded Brenda.

"I really think Bob has a good theory on why the ETs are stalking those things around the world, here and there," said Janis.

"Not now," shrugged Bob feeling embarrassed by his wife's comment.

"No it's okay," said Steve. "I'm sure we all have our own theories. Trying to justify why they're here and what are they're up to. So go ahead Bob...the floor is yours."

"Well, I look at them as business opportunists. This might sound a little strange to you guys. But let's just say for example, that lobsters here on earth were almost non-existent. How much would someone pay for one? What I mean is supply and demand. They found a place in the galaxy that is close enough for them to transport them back to wherever their market is. So their only purpose is to produce those creatures and ship them out."

"That idea could hold some water. But why would they have those NYANYAS, I mean, babysitters guarding the ponds?" asked Nick.

"Farmers use scare crows to keep crows away from our corn crops," said Bob.

"He has a good point," said Mike. "And it's not like the ETs would contact our government for a free trade deal."

"And they probably heard of our soft-wood lumber deal, with the US making us pay an extra export tax and feel that we are once burnt, twice shy!"

"That's a good one Steve," said Mike.

"All kidding aside, is it possible that Russia and Canada have the same mineral content in the water. Or even the same ph, or something like that in common?" inquired Janis.

"The same ph!" said Steve. "Now we're getting technical."

"Well, I'm always stuck with checking the hot tub readings," she responded.

"That is good thinking," said Nick. While we are on this subject, would you mind Mike, if you could email a request for a water test back in Russia as well as some aerial photographs of both your pond and the one in Russia?"

"No problem," he replied. "I'll do that right now."

"Great. At least they will not think that I am up here on pleasure."

"You mean like, business before pleasure?" asked Steve.

"Yes."

"But up here in Canada, pleasure is our business!"

"No," said Nick. "It is more like joking around is your business!" Everyone laughed at his remark to Steve.

"He got you Steve!" said Mary.

"Mike, when you are asking them to take a water test at the pond in Russia, have them send the readings back as soon as possible," instructed Nick.

"And Janis, can I borrow that hot tub test kit of yours?"

"Sure Nick," happy to have her idea acknowledged. "I'll have Bob drop it off later tonight."

"I'll make sure you guys bring it with you tomorrow morning then," said Mary.

"That is great. I can take a sample when we do more scouting," confirmed Nick.

"Bob," said Brenda, "I'm not knocking your theory on the aliens farming those things, but why not in a more southerly region like Florida, or Cuba? They would have a longer growing season. Our pond freezes up in later November."

"That is just it," said Nick. "If the aliens are going to do anything, it will happen in a four month window, and at the same time in that part of Russia."

"Nick, you keep saying 'the pond in Russia' but where exactly is it?" said Brenda.

"In the Latvian part of the Russian Federation," Nick answered and then realized his mistake.

"In Latvia, you mean?" Brenda glared at him.

"I'm sorry Brenda. Yes, you are right. It is in Latvia. And like I said, they will drive you crazy trying to figure them out," he advised. "Because you guys are new at this, maybe you just might find the missing link. You know what they say in Russia, sometimes two heads are better than one."

"That saying is quite common in Canada too," said Carol. "Canadian women might go along with that one Nick. If only our men would think with the right one for a change!"

"Yes," agreed Carol, holding her glass up high. "Now that deserves a toast," as the girls all stood up to toast.

"I don't believe what I heard from your wife Mike," smirked Steve, shaking his head with a big grin. "All kidding aside, Bob's farming theory does hold some water. But I just can't see them as being some kind of a delicacy food source."

Steve was having a coffee in his wood-shed and listening to the news on a local radio station about scientists being alarmed after the discovery of an invasive crustacean in Northern Ontario. Laurentian University is conducting research on it. At this time, it remained in Ottawa at the international science con-ference. The mayor of Elliot Lake is requesting an explanation from the gov-ernment as to why six US F-22 Raptor fighter jets and four apache choppers are sitting at his airport fully armed. He has reason to believe the army is holding something back. "Holy shit!" he said, as Nick walked up to him in the shed. "Are they crazy putting that on the radio!"

"Yes, well I am sure that they got a lot of attention. It is the I.A.W.'s way of not trying to cover it up too quickly. Sometimes, it draws too much attention, if they drop it out of sight altogether," he replied. "And as for the airport deal, the

I.A.W. will have a way of stick handling around that mayor. Like taking candy from a baby."

"Stick handle around the mayor? What is that Nick, some kind of hockey lingo?"

"Yes, you can say that. Sorry Nick, but hockey is a Canadian thing, eh?"

"And the last time we played the Russians, we kicked their asses!"

"You are right Steve, but maybe not the next time. Your players are out of practice. They are on strike half the time."

"Well son of a bitch, you have a good point Nick," chuckled Steve. "If you snooze, you lose! I'm surprised you're up so early."

"What do you mean?"

"Well you and Brenda went on that night cruise after dropping me and Mary off. I mean she's a good friend. And a nice person, as well as good looking."

"Okay, okay Steve, I was a gentleman, if that is what you mean."

"No, no Nick. I'm not your father. What you two adults do is your business. What happens on Birch Lake stays on Birch Lake. Just be sure to get your ass to work on time," he said with a smile.

"You are right Steve. Brenda is a nice person, and she spoke highly of you guys as well."

"So, can I pour you a coffee?"

"No thanks Steve. We have to get to work. Maybe later, on the trail."

"You can ride the old bike. It's all automatic as well," he said standing over it, and pointing out all its features to Nick. "So you shift this lever, 'til a green light comes on the dash, that indicates it's in neutral. Just keep it in N for neutral, when you stop or start it. Shifting the lever ahead puts it in forward, and back is reverse. So go ahead and climb aboard."

"Are you sure?"

"Am I sure? Sure I'm sure. If Mary can drive one, anyone can!"

"I heard that," she said now standing right behind him in her housecoat. "I didn't want you to forget to take the water test kit."

"Thanks dear. What I meant is, anyone can drive a four-wheeler."

"Well then, why didn't you say that?" she remarked with a long face. She turned around and headed back to the cottage.

"I think she is holding the cards now,"

said Nick.

"Yes. But she dropped one. Me, the joker..."

"Oh come on Steve. You will have a chance to make it better."

"I sure hope so."

"Well now that I know where the gas and brake are, I am ready to go."

"Not so fast. What about our backup?" he said looking over towards the tool bench, where he had two sporting rifles standing beside it.

"I am glad you know what we are dealing with Steve."

"Are you kidding me? I saw what those small creatures are capable of doing. It had that doe and her fawn sliced and diced in a matter of seconds. And in your photos, those ninja things guarding that pond are the size of a car. What do you find so fuckin' funny?" he asked, as he could see Nick chuckling to himself.

"I am sorry Steve. But, when you said NYANYA, it sounded more like ninja. It just reminds me of a kid's cartoon I saw years ago called Ninja Turtles."

"Ha! Ha!" he said, all flustered that Nick was making fun of him. "Now who is the joker this time?"

"Relax," he said. "It just sounds so funny to hear you try to say NYANYA. When it comes out ninja. That's why I translated it to babysitter, so you would understand."

"That goes two ways. It's also funny to hear you speak English at times. But I'm sorry for reacting the way I did," he said as he handed Nick a rifle. "Are you familiar with this rifle?"

"Yes. It is a large, thirty caliber Mouser bolt-action repeater. Fine gun!"

"Yes. And that scope is on a pivot mount, allowing you to use open sights for close up shots, at one hundred yards or closer. After realizing Nick didn't understand feet and yards he said, "It's good from here to the dock. For anything further, use the scope. It's a three hundred Winchester magnum," he said as he handed him a box of ammo. "I hope these two, twenty grain puppies with power point tips, can crack through the heads of those babysitters. Because it sure as hell put that twelve hundred pound bull moose on his ass at three hundred yards, two years ago."

"Oh, I think it has more than enough. What are you using Steve?"

"A thirty odd six, with two, twenty grain shells as well."

"Steve, again. You will still have a lot of hitting power. Anything within that distance, from here to your cottage is history. You'll crack his shell and knock him on his ass! But remember, we are not lobster hunting. If we can keep our distance, there will be no sense in taking them out. We do not want to provoke the aliens to anger at this point, not being sure of what we are dealing with."

"I hear ya. So where are you headed?" he asked, as he watched Nick walk out towards the back of the woodshed.

"I guess I am just a little nervous with riding this bike for the first time," he said, now out of sight from Steve.

"If the thought of driving a four-wheeler makes you nervous enough to have to piss, then you must have shit your pants when you had that saucer ride. Even the looks of your flight attendants would have been enough. Now that I think of it, you did shit your pants. And you stunk up their saucer. That's why those ETs ditched you! Well Nick, doesn't my theory impress you?"

Minutes went by, Steve still wasn't getting an answer from Nick. Feeling eerie, he picked up his rifle, and cautiously stepped out the back way. Where he found him down on his knees, running his fingertips along the sidewall of the grooming tire.

"I am sorry Steve. But right now, this old tractor tire with these large slash marks impress me more."

"Oh that. I drag that old tractor tire behind the four-wheeler, every now and then to groom the trail."

"Well Steve. I would say you had a real fuckin' close encounter with a babysitter" Come around to the back of the tire here and check this out."

Steve stood his rifle against the woodshed and walked over to the back of the tire where Nick was kneeling, looking down at it. He couldn't believe the size of two clean but jagged cuts, halfway through the thickest part of the sidewalls. "Holy shit! What the fuck?" exclaimed Steve as he stood there in awe.

"Tell me Steve. Can you recall this

happening?"

"No!" he replied shaking his head from side to side. He had a stunned look on his face, realizing how close he came to death. "The last time I had it out was when I saw that deer and her fawn get taken by those little creatures."

"And you do not even remember feeling any resistance when pulling the tire?"

"Now that you mention it, yes. It was when I went to drive off. I felt some resistance, like the tire was caught in a piece of wood or debris. I didn't even look back to see."

"No. I was in a panic mode. I just wanted to get the hell away from that place as quickly as possible. So when I felt this resistance, I just dropped her into low four, and gunned it."

"Huh. You pulled it right out of the NYANYA'S claws. You are some lucky mother!" he said, patting him on the back. "Well if anything, you have quite the conversation piece."

"A big-time conversation piece!" he exclaimed.

"Well, we'd better make tracks Nick. I

told Mike that we would be up on that lookout plateau by eight am."

"Sure Steve. I will follow, but take it slow."

"Oh, that's right. I don't want you shitting yourself!"

"Funny boy," he said starting his bike, revving the throttle like a teenager. Then he sang out, "Born to be wild!" in his Russian accent.

Steve drove by him to lead the way and yelled out, while at the same time shaking his head, "Poor Canada!" About thirty minutes later, the bikes came to a stop up on the lookout plateau. "This is where we found those ring markings in the rock," as he pointed to a pile of logs scattered here and there. "Come on, I'll show you!"

Upon walking up to the logs, and looking down, Nick could now make out the rings in the rock. Taking the camera out from his pant leg pocket, he took a few pictures. "So why were all these logs put here?"

"It was to hide them from berry pickers, or hikers. So they wouldn't show their find of Indian art work to some archaeologist and have this place closed down by the government, as an Indian ceremonial ground or something like that."

Nick started laughing out loud. Steve was somewhat confused by this.

"What's so funny?" he asked, with a serious look. Thinking of the work that he and the boys did to keep this place a secret.

"I am sorry Steve. You are not going to believe this, but this is where I escaped from the aliens the other night. I remember their saucer having a hard time trying to stabilize. Because when the door opened, one of those logs jammed it. That was when I made my escape. You see, if you and the boys did not fuck up their landing pad, I could not have escaped!"

"Oh shit, that's funny!" said Steve.

"Yes, but not for the ETs," said Nick. "You really fucked them up with your log pile!"

They were both hunched over, laughing their heads off while Mike and Bob were watching them over the monitor. "What in the hell is so funny up there?" said Mike to Bob.

"I'm dying to find out," said Mike, as

he picked up his radio. "Come in Steve."

"Yes, go ahead Mike," said Steve, still laughing.

"Bob and I want to know what the big joke is up there. Over."

Steve had to take a deep breath to stop from laughing. "It's just how we fucked up the ETs without being aware of it. I'll explain it to you guys over at my cottage later."

"Yes Steve. I get the humor in it now!" he said.

"So Bob. What are you doing out of the fart sack so early?"

"I'm enjoying my morning coffee with Mike while being entertained by two clowns on a hill."

"I'm just surprised you're up this early. Did you shit the bed? Over!"

"Like I said. You're a real clown. Over."

"Okay we'll keep you guys posted. Over and out," he said, as he put his radio back into his pocket. He turned around to find Nick standing close to the edge of the bluff, overlooking the lake.

"It is quite the view, is it not?"

"Yes it is Nick. But if you walk up here,

just a little higher. You can see a lot more of the area."

Nick took a dozen or so steps, "Oh I see what you mean Steve."

"About a hundred years ago, this region was a major logging industry. Giant white pines grew through this whole area, covering the north shore of Lake Huron. About a dozen towns sprung up along it, like Espanola over there," Steve pointed. "Going west is Webbwood, Massey, Spanish, Spragge, and Blind River just to name a few. Out of a dozen or so towns, all the way to the US border."

Nick's eyes roamed the landscape, taken by its size. "Just this area alone is bigger than most European countries," said Nick in awe.

"Now where you see those narrows down there on our lake, well that's Birch Creek. Lumberjacks would cut the trees in winter. During the spring run off, they would float the logs down to where it connected into the Spanish River to your southwest. Then it emptied into Lake Huron at the town of Spanish. Large sawmills would cut and dry the lumber before it was shipped to the States by schooners. This region played a big part in the restoration of Chicago after the great fire."

"Is that the one that was started by a cow kicking over a lantern?"

"Yes Nick. That's the one. How do you know that?"

"I was forced to take a little American history in my younger years. During the Cold War, our government felt that it was a wise way to learn who we were dealing with."

"I'll say. That was a smart move, because history can tell us a lot about places and people. Being up on our history, can greatly help your army plan wise strategy."

"You got that right Steve. Thank you, for the early Canadian history lesson."

"You're quite welcome. The next class will be on the great fur trade," Steve laughed.

"Well enough bullshit for now. Let's make tracks. Our trail runs downhill from here to the pond, then loops back uphill past the tree stand to another high ridge. We do have an old trail that connects to this one that will take you around to the south end of that pond. We only use that one during hunting season. So it's all downhill from here Nick. I'll stop at the place where I set that minnow trap."

"How about we just put our bikes in neutral and coast down with our engines off, just riding our brakes?"

"Smart thinking Nick. They won't hear us approaching at all. I'll have to remember that trick for hunting season."

"Do you have a round in your chamber?"

Steve reached over his handlebars and slid his pump action on his rifle back and forth, making a click-click sound. "I do now!" he replied feeling embarrassed that Nick had to prompt him.

"Okay then, lead the way."

Steve quietly coasted down the trail with Nick close on his tail as he approached the opening entrance to the pond. His heart rate increased, with the expectation of a confrontation with those babysitters guarding the pond. Remembering how they could shred a tractor tire with one chop of their claws, still played on his mind. His head swiveled from side to side, looking for any imperfection on the calm water. He glanced back at Nick still close behind him. The bikes came to a stop at that very spot where Steve had set his trap. Steve climbed off his bike. He removed his rifle from the rack, holding it in a ready position. With his rifle, he pointed in the direction of where the deer were slain. "It was just over there, by that deadfall, where those deer got it," he whispered. "And right beside that stump was where I set the minnow trap."

With his rifle strap slung over his shoulder, Nick unscrewed the top off the test kit bottle. As he crouched down to get a water sample, suddenly that loud and deep moan echoed over the still water of the pond. The same gory sound, which Steve had heard before, sent the hairs on his neck standing on end. Nick nodded his head slowly up and down, while capping the water sample. "Yes, that is one of them," he whispered. At the corner of his eye, Nick spotted, just under the water, a large wake heading in their direction. "It is using that old beaver house as a place to stand guard." Nick quickly took a few pictures. "Well Steve, I think it is time to go," he urged, as the wake got progressively closer.

"I agree. That looks like some big torpedo," Steve said, as they quickly climbed onto their bikes. Steve started his bike but Nick was having trouble. "Hurry up!" said Steve anxiously.

"It does not want to start!" replied Nick turning his key off and on.

"It's the button below your left thumb!" Steve shouted, as this huge gruesome creature sprung up to the edge of the pond. Steve brought his rifle up to his shoulder ready to fire, when Nick finally started his bike and pulled ahead of him. Steve followed with his rifle swung-out from his left hip, while applying the throttle, and steering with his right hand as they drove farther down to a safer spot. They could now observe the creature fully out of the water, waving its giant claws in the air in a vicious way, as they watched in wonder.

"I am sorry, but today is not your day!" said Nick towards the creature, as he took a few more pictures. "And that was quite the show Steve. You handled yourself just like John Wayne."

"Like I wanted to. I can't believe that it was in here all this time pilgrim!"

"You mean, THEY," said Nick...

"THEY?"

"Yes, THEY," he said. "There has to be a second one for a pond this size. I had two in Russia, and that pond was not as large. Maybe we should drive back, and try to lure it out," he said with a smile.

"Well, you can go screw yourself! I can think of better ways for entertainment," said Steve, as he put his rifle back on the rack. "That tree stand is just up here a ways. I think we deserve a coffee break..."

"I feel a little safer up here in this tree house," said Steve pouring them coffee from his thermos. "Over there, in that plastic box is a bottle of brandy. Pass it over, Nick." He shook the bottle with a surprised look. "Holy shit! It's almost empty!"

"I am sorry Steve. But when I spent that night here, I had a few sips."

"I'll say. No wonder you didn't hear me drive up that morning." While doctoring up their coffees, he squinted his eyebrows, and sniffed the air. "Do you smell something funny, like a little foul, Nick?"

"Now that you mention it Steve. I thought maybe you dropped something in your pants back at the pond," smirked Nick.

"No, really Nick. Don't you smell something?"

"I do pick up some kind of odor. A little like rotting fish."

"I'm glad I'm not just imagining it." Just then, his radio started beeping.

" Go ahead."

"How do you read me Steve?"

"Loud and clear Mary. I'm up in the tree stand with Nick."

"Do you two plan on being back soon?"

"Yeah. In about thirty minutes from now."

"I'll have breakfast ready then. Over and out..."

"Over and out. Well, I'm sure glad she's come around."

"We say in Russia. You can't live with them, and you can't live without them!"

"That's funny Nick, because we have

that same saying here too."

"But we sure as hell can live without those freak shows back at the pond."

"Thank God, me and the guys weren't ambushed the other day Nick."

"I'm surprised too Steve. Because after their warning sounds, they always converge."

"This is why I believe there should be at least two of them," said Nick shrugging his shoulders.

"The guys are gonna really shit when they see those pictures," remarked Steve in a troubled tone.

Nick could feel Steve's stress. "So is anything bothering you?" inquired Nick.

"Sure I'm bothered Nick," replied Steve with a stone face. Like how much, and how far do we, or the I.A.W. let those aliens go on for? What about the repercussions if we terminate their crop, and those NYANYA creatures? As intelligent as those aliens are, do you believe they will put their tails between their legs and hit the galaxy?"

"Nick took the last sip of coffee from this cup. Then tapped it against the window ledge cleaning out a few coffee grains, while in deep thought over Steve's concern. "Steve, your thoughts on this matter are no different than that of the I.A.W. I can tickle your ears by telling you that NORAD—the Aerospace Defense Command in North Bay—is closely monitoring this location with all the high-tech fighting arms in the world. But maybe it would be just as effective to the aliens as a fly on a cow's ass."

Steve stood up and patted Nick's shoulder and looked him straight in the eye. "Thank you Nick, for being real and shooting from the hip. I think it's time to start heading back.

Driving up the incline, Steve picked up the scent again. This time it was more evident. Stopping his bike, he told Nick to turn his off.

"I can really smell it now," said Nick.

"Yes, it's coming from upwind." All of a sudden, Steve heard the sounds of ravens cackling and squawking. He knew that some dead animal was close by.

They got off their bikes with rifles in hand. Not having taken many steps, they couldn't help but see the dead and

cracked-open shell of one of those creatures at the bottom of the cliff. "Holy
shit!" he said, looking back at Nick, who
was taking pictures.

"One for you!" he said. "That must be
the one that couldn't hang on to your
tracker tire. You're just going to have to
slow down a little Steve!"

"I knew I had a whiff of something the
other day."

"Well Steve, your nose wasn't lying,"
Nick said as they make their way back to
their bikes.

Upon arriving back at the woodshed,
they could see Mary and Brenda in the
gazebo.

"Well, that explains why she was so
nice on radio. But how in the hell did
Brenda get here?" said Steve.

Slinging their rifles over their shoulders, they proceeded down to join the
girls.

"Remember Steve, be nice!"

"Sure I'll be!" he chuckled.

"It's really strange to see you two carrying rifles in the summer," said Mary.

"Well, the ministry opened a new season on lobsters. They had to compensate us for taking away the spring bear hunt. It's just a little hard getting use to. And the fact that no one sells lobster decoys or lobster calls."

"Funny boy!" said Brenda.

"Nick got some good shots!"

"You did?" remarked Brenda with a shocking look.

"Yes, but with his camera."

"Well I'm not up to reviewing any of those gory pictures with you girls," said Nick, "but I would like to have Mike email them out, as soon as possible."

"Oh Nick, don't forget to see if they sent those satellite aerials of this area. I'm anxious to see them," reminded Steve.

"So am I Steve," responded Nick.

"So Brenda, how did you manage to make it over here?" asked Steve.

"It's been a few years since I used my canoe. And it was a perfect morning for a paddle."

"You must have worked up quite an appetite," said Steve.

"That's for sure," she replied.

"I think you guys should get those rifles put away," suggested Mary.

"Sure Mary."

"And that reminds me Steve. Sarah called a little earlier."

"Oh shit!" he looked down, not wanting to face or deal with Sarah, at this particular time. Steve inhaled deeply, "Well, give me the lowdown."

"Don't worry. I handled it well," confirmed Mary. "Sarah and Tom are getting a little impatient with that professor from the university. Tom is getting credit for discovering the creature, although, he's just stalling him on that study that he wanted to do out here."

"Well, thank God for that!" said Steve. "We have our hands full as it is."

"If I could borrow your cell phone for just one minute Steve? I think I can get them a little more recognition than that. I have to touch ground with the general anyway. I will join you guys at the table in a few minutes," Nick said, handing his rifle to Steve.

"Did everything go okay?" Steve asked Nick as he joined them for breakfast.

"Oh yes, very well," he replied with an ear-to-ear smile, sitting down next to

Brenda. "The aerial photos have just been sent out to Mike this morning. They got some great shots because the sky was free of clouds, here and in Latvia. And they were really impressed with the ones we sent them. Just wait 'til they see what their playing with here in Canada!"

"Yes," said Steve. "Those pictures should raise a few eyebrows in Ottawa."

"They were surprised that the coordinates we gave them, were taken from your bike's GPS."

"Well then, that was a good plug for Honda. We should get Honda to supply us with a few more bikes for marketing," he laughed.

"Stop it Steve! You're not in sales anymore," remarked Mary.

"And by the way," Nick continued, "your daughter and her friend will be chauffeured to Ottawa tomorrow, to give the science community a little briefing on that creature. It's a set up to keep them preoccupied, and a chance for them to rub shoulders with some big name scientists from around the world."

"Well, that should help Tom get his science degree," responded Steve.

"So be expecting a phone call anytime soon, and sound surprised for them."

"Oh, don't worry about that Nick. Playing dumb is what Steve does best," mocked Mary. "Well thanks a lot for taking care of that for us Nick. We really appreciate it!"

"No problem. We are all a team."

With breakfast over, Brenda and Nick were leaving the dock in her pontoon boat.

"We'll see you guys later," said Mary, standing on the dock with Steve.

"And don't forget to tell them about our seven o'clock meeting tonight!" yelled out Steve.

"I hear you!" responded Nick.

chapter 9

the meeting

"Oh yes," said Mary, "you should have heard Sarah! Apparently, her and Tom will be staying in a top notch hotel in Ottawa, with all expenses paid!"

"Well finally, I'll see a bit of my tax dollars coming back for my family," remarked Steve. Everyone knew how much he resented many of the government expenditures.

"Oh Steve!" she said as she elbowed him in the chest. "It's the fact that this will be a trip they'll always remember."

"You're probably right."

"Well, I have a treat for you guys," said Mike as he opened a brown folder on the table. "Well, here they are folks! This is what we look like from a satellite at two thousand feet, and at five thousand feet."

"Holy shit! These are great shots!" said Steve. "It even shows you the date, and time it was taken.

"Talk about a good ETA," he said with a proud look.

"ETA?" asked Mary.

"Yes," said Mike. "That means the estimated time of arrival."

"I told Mike to watch for Nick and I on his monitor around that time," said Steve, with a big smile.

"Oh shit! Here we go with the army lingo," she said.

"That's really something. You can even tell what type of bikes you're driving," said Bob. "Too bad we can't use this service during deer season."

"Are you guys crazy? You use enough of that high-tech equipment for hunting as it is. Do you think you're in the army or something?" asked Carol.

"Well, it's just a thought," joked Bob.

"Oh look here," said Mike. "You can tell who Steve is by the bald spot on top of his head!"

"You're really funny!" said Steve, with

everyone laughing. "Well, thank God I wasn't going for a piss at that time."

"Oh well, you don't have to worry there Steve. I don't think that satellite telescope can zoom in that close to your miniscule floppy. This photo here is something else," said Mike, as he placed it on top of the others. "If you look carefully, you can make out the rings under those crossed logs."

"You mean, the aliens' landing site?" asked Nick. "Oh by the way. Would you like to know what Steve and I were laughing about up on the plateau, when you guys radioed us? It was about the fact that the ETs were always using that exact spot to land their saucer. So, when they attempted to land there the other night, their saucer went out of control for a while. When this happened, the spacecraft door was opening and closing like an elevator door. When it opened again, one of those logs jarred the door open. That is when I ploughed my way through those yellow-eyed freaks. I squeezed through that door, and ran like hell! So, it was your log pile that really screwed them up."

"Okay. Now I see where you find the humor in this." responded Mike.

"So why didn't you guys want anyone to see what you thought at the time to be Indian drawings in the rock, anyway?" asked Brenda.

"Because if it was discovered by some archaeologist, we would have our hunting area closed off in a heartbeat," said Steve. "The First Nations might claim it as a place of worship, or something like that. Not that I would blame them, after all, they were here first. I'm sorry Nick, but did I say something that bothered you? Because I know sometimes I talk too much."

"No. Not at all Steve. But there is just one other thing I want you guys to know about those ETs."

"You mean the ones in the pond?" asked Steve.

"No. The ones that abducted me in that spaceship."

"What about them?"

"That night, when I was in the spacecraft, and I took those pictures of the aliens. It was quite dark inside there. So dark, that it caused the flash to go off. The flash made them close their big yellow eyes for about three or four seconds. So I used these valuable seconds to my advantage. When the door of the UFO was ajar with that log. I hit the camera shutter button and I ran like hell for the doorway, buying just enough time to slip past them."

"Smart maneuverings Nick. But, are you trying to tell us that you think the alien eyes are light sensitive?" asked Steve.

"Like I said. It was only for a few seconds after the flash."

"Well, that's interesting to know," said Bob. "You did say that it was really dark in that spaceship, right Nick?"

"I couldn't even see my hand in front of my face."

"I wonder if that's the reason why their eyes are so large? Their planet could have a low light level. Or maybe they're active at night only. It seems, that it's the only time we've encountered them."

"But I was abducted during daylight in Latvia."

"You did say that the bright light from the flash stunned them for a few seconds.

I just wonder if the light was consistent. Would you be able to walk up to them and kick their asses?" suggested Bob with a chuckle.

"Oh, now you're talking crazy!" said Mike.

"Am I? It's no different from the way poachers used to jacklight deer at night. They would drive around those farmer's fields and use a big spotlight to shine into their eyes. That light would blind them, making for an easy target."

"Are you suggesting that we jacklight the ETs?" asked Steve.

"No. I'm just trying to prove a point."

"Thank God for that! Oh, your Honor, I was just trying to jacklight ETs. That would go over real good in court!" chuckled Steve.

"Okay you two!" said Nick, "I am sure Steve is joking with you. But you made a good point there Bob."

"Thank-you Nick."

"It's really something how we can apply things we learnt years ago, to help us now," said Steve. "Like when you were wandering through the dark up there on the plateau, after your escape. By identifying the cry of a common loon, it told you two things. Number one, you were close to a body of water. And number two, you were in North America. All because you had studied water birds."

"Correction Steve. There are three things."

"There's a third?"

"Yes Steve. Knowing their diet told me there were fish in this lake. That's why I told you I was here on a fishing trip," he smiled.

"You bugger. You really played me."

"Holy shit Nick! You don't have any loons in Russia?" asked Bob.

"Not now."

"Not now?" repeated Bob.

"Yes. It is the red-throated loon that only exists in the Canadian Yukon and Alaska. It is considerably smaller than your common loon. It has a red patch on the throat and red stripes running down the back of the head. Unlike your common loon's cry, it makes a quacking sound. So if you remember your history, Alaska was once a part of Russia until we sold it to the US after the Second World War."

"Now, that's exactly what I mean," said Steve. "Sometimes even knowing a bit of history can help us."

"That's interesting Nick," said Janis. "So how many types of loons are there anyway?"

"There are four. Arctic, red-throated, yellow billed, and your common loon. And loons belong to their own distinct order, they are not related to other water fowl, like ducks, or geese."

"Well, so much for this loony conversation," said Steve. "Mike is there any way that your computer can warn you. Or beep if we have company on that plateau?"

"If you mean like a motion detector, the answer is no. It only monitors in a time-lapse mode. I have to keep playing it back and delete or backup the old stuff."

"What are you thinking Steve?" asked Nick.

"Well, if the ETs come back, do you think they'll try to land on those logs again? Because that's where we have them monitored. If they choose another spot, we can miss them altogether."

"You mean, they can land on the opposite side of the pond?" asked Nick.

"That's exactly my point. I think we should get our asses up there, and remove those logs that are obstructing their landing strip."

"Good idea!" said Nick.

"Thank-you, but I'm not finished yet. Those radios we use have a built-in pager. Like when Mary called me this morning in the tree stand. It just beeped to let me know she wanted to talk to me."

"Yes Steve, we're still with you," said Mike.

"Well, what if we keep one radio up on the plateau with a trip wire stretched across their landing area. When they land, it will compress the radio button and alarm all of us."

"Holy shit Steve! I'm going to have to start calling you MacGyver," said Mike.

"MacGyver?" asked Nick.

"Yes, it was a TV series of an agent who always improvised with different gadgets he created out of simple things. It helped him fight crime and different shit like that."

"Let's get to it, before it gets too late," urged Steve. "I'll need a couple of minutes to find a roll of wire, and some other knick-knacks to act as a base to secure the radio. Mary, I'll need a radio with new batteries. As well as one of those plastic zip lock bags, in case it rains on it."

"MacGyver is on a roll," exclaimed Mike.

"Just be ready to leave from the wood-shed in fifteen minutes," said Steve. "Nick, do you mind grabbing the rifles off the gun rack?"

"No problem Steve."

"Well, that should just about do it," remarked Steve, as he tied the opposite end of the wire around a big rock. "Now press down on that wire just a little Bob."

Within seconds, Mary called them on the radio. "Is that you Steve?"

"It's okay Mary. It works. Over and out."

"Steve, you son of a bitch. I have to admit, I didn't think it would work," said Mike.

"Why not? All we have to do is compress the button."

"We know your good at pressing buttons Steve," chuckled Bob.

"Ha, ha," responded Steve. "Well, we

just need to add UFOs. So let's get back and join the girls for a cold one. Removing those logs sure as hell made me thirsty."

Back at Steve's cottage, the guys were finishing a cold drink with the girls. "Those are some mean cuts that predator made in your grooming tire, Steve. I really think you girls should go up behind the shed and check it out. It's just so you'll know what we're dealing with," said Mike.

"No way," said Mary. "Didn't you understand Janis? We're grossed out enough over this shit!"

"Okay. Okay then, I'm sorry."

"Well, thanks for your hospitality, Mary and Steve," said Bob and Janis.

"That goes for us too," said Mike.

"No problem," said Steve. "You know, in one way, those ETs just brought us closer."

"Yes," responded Mike. "But my grandchildren are waiting to visit me. And it's hard to keep putting them off."

"I don't think this shit will last too much longer," said Nick.

"Well so far. It's one of the longest shits

I ever had," replied Mike.

"But I'm sure you still have a little more in you. Not insinuating that you're full of shit, you bugger!" jested Bob, as they all laughed.

"Are they this way all the time, Brenda?" asked Nick shaking his head with a smile.

"No. Not when they're sleeping."

"So, I would like everyone over to my place for dinner tomorrow," said Brenda.

"Oh great, perogies!" said Steve.

"No freakin' way!" exclaimed Brenda. "The last time, I ended up wearing them."

"But that was your perogie princess crown," said Steve.

"Sorry, not this time."

"I would have loved to have seen that," responded Nick, as he patted her shoulder.

"Maybe in your next life Nick," she replied.

"Well, we better get going now before my son gets suspicious of why we've been gone so long. He's phoning us back to find out when it would be best to come and visit us," said Mike.

"Oh, just tell him that you had to help your buddies clear out a landing strip so the ETs could land their flying saucer. And later tonight, you're going back out to jacklight them," joked Steve, as everyone laughed.

"I heard that part about jacklighting ETs," said Bob. "What are you going to tell Sarah? That you've taken up lobster hunting?"

"Okay, okay! You got me back Bob," he answered. Everyone then started departing from the gazebo.

Brenda stayed back up in the gazebo with Nick while Steve and Mary went down to the dock to see their guests off.

"So you and Mary drop by tomorrow."

"Sure Mike."

"Mary and I plan on going trolling. To catch a few sunrays or maybe a few trout. We'll probably drop by for a cold one. Oh yes, don't forget to keep your radios on. We just might get some unexpected company, if you know what I mean."

"We'll see you guys tomorrow," said Mike, as they departed from the dock.

Steve and Mary entered the gazebo to find Nick and Brenda looking over both satellite photos. They were comparing their pond to the one in Russia. "Well Brenda, there must be a common denominator with those two ponds, or others for that matter. What in the hell attracted those aliens?" said Steve.

"We should have that water test result back from Ottawa by tomorrow," said Brenda.

"Yes. I'm sure anxious to see how close their readings are to each other if any," said Nick.

"Don't look too hard," said Steve. "Sometimes, we can't see the forest for the trees. Let's just plant that thought and relax. The answer to that missing link, my guess is, will probably come to us when we least expect it."

"Good thought Steve."

"Nick is coming over to my place to help me finish off a meatloaf. This way, you and Mary can have some time together."

"Are you kidding me? We've had twenty-eight years together. You mean so you and Nick can have some time together. Well if I need his help, he's as close as my phone. You two have fun now, and don't drink and drive that boat."

"No Steve. I'll make sure it's anchored!"

"That's my line!"

"Sorry Steve, but I stole it," said Brenda, as she headed down to the dock with Nick. "We'll probably see you two out on the water tomorrow. If not, supper at my place."

"Sure, have fun and goodnight," said Mary, waving them off. She looked back at Steve as he was studying the aerial photos on the table. "Hey you there, practice what you preach."

"Sorry sweetheart. It's just driving me crazy! I'd like to know what those aliens are up to, stocking those little critters in that pond."

"Will it drive you crazy if I want to go skinny dipping later tonight dear?" she responded in a sexy voice.

"Well, I guess this alien stuff can wait. I found something else that's out of this world," he said, jumping up from his chair.

"Do you have hydro here?" Nick asked Brenda as they walked up the dock to her cottage.

"Oh yes, and phone service. It's also road accessible, which makes it a little more convenient. Not to say Steve and Mary's isn't. Although they do have their privacy."

"If you want yours. You just have to drive your boat to Passion Bay."

"That's right too," she said laughing, knowing full well what he meant. They entered the cottage.

"Wow. You have a real nice view of the lake from here!"

"Well thank you. It seems that every cottage on this lake has it's own nice view. Did I say that right Nick?"

"It sounds right by me."

"Are you cabin crazy?" she asked.

"What do you mean Brenda?"

"Well, we can go to town and catch this late night buffet in Espanola. It's only a fifteen minute drive from here."

"I would like to get out with you and have a change of pace. Except, I am afraid I will have to take you up on this some other time."

"You mean a rain check?" she asked.

"A rain check? That's a new word for me."

"Well, it means to do it some other time."

"Okay, I will take a rain check then. It is just my luck that, I will be away from the lake. And sure as hell, it will be the time when those aliens show up."

"Over here, we call that Murphy's Law."

"Murphy's Law certainly applies to me then. The one time that I ever fell asleep on a stakeout, was the same day my partner took advantage of an opportunity to do some investigating of his own. The rest is history."

"Well then, I can say that Murphy's Law worked in my favor because I wouldn't have met you." She looked deeply into his eyes with a warm smile.

"Now that you put it that way, I will have to agree with you." He responded, by giving her a warm embrace, and gentle kiss.

"So would you like to join me for a glass of wine?"

"Sure."

She returned a few minutes later with two large goblets filled with red wine. Handing one to him, she said, "Dieboursia!"

"Yes!" he agreed. "Now you're talking my language! Dieboursia," as they toasted.

"I'd better get that meatloaf warming before we get plastered. Is there any type of vegetables you don't care for Nick?"

"No, I am not fussy."

"Well, you're really easy to entertain."

"Thanks, because you are a good entertainer!"

"Don't count your chickens before they're hatched," she replied, as she topped off his wine glass. "Just excuse me for a few minutes. While I throw that meatloaf in the oven, and chop up a few vegetables."

"Care for an extra hand in the kitchen?"

"Thanks anyway Nick. Not this time."

"You mean, take a rain check?"

"You catch on quick!"

"By the way, chickens are already hatched. You must of meant eggs," he remarked.

"I'm sorry Nick. But that one, we'll have to leave for later," she hollered from the kitchen. " Otherwise it could take us to what came first, the chicken or the egg?"

While he was waiting in her living room, he noticed a computer in the corner. "Can you go online with that computer?" he hollered.

"Sure," she replied, as she walked back from the kitchen.

"We will be able to tap into Mike's telescope, twenty-four seven as well."

"That's right Nick."

"Do you mind if we email him and set this up?"

"I can do that right now, before dinner."

"That will be great," he said, as she sat down in front of the computer.

"I'll email him first to let him know what you want while you top off our glasses."

"I won't say no to that," he replied. "At the same time, can you ask him to send us those aerial photos of Russia, and here as well?"

"Russia?" she questioned. She stopped typing, and swivelled her chair to face him.

"Oh come on! I'm sorry Brenda. It's hard for me as an older Russian soldier, to think of Latvia, Estonia, or the Ukraine for that matter, as each being its own country, independent from the Russian Federation. And I am happy for them, with their own government, and independence. I know how hard your people had it under Russian rule," he sympathized. I remember it like it was yesterday, back in the spring of nineteen eighty-six. My unit was called into the Ukraine during the Chernobyl disaster to help with the evacuation of one-hundred and thirty-five thousand people from a thirty kilometer radius exclusion zone."

"Oh my God. You were there," exclaimed Brenda with a curious look about her.

"Yes," he said. He was tapping his wine glass on the table in front of him, with a serious look. "The actual death toll was hard to determine. Greenpeace Ukraine had estimated it at thirty-two thousand. But since then, the rate of thyroid cancer in children has increased two-hundred fold."

"Fuck off!" She blurted in a low tone. She was taken by his first hand knowledge of the disaster.

"We had to wait for at least ten fuckin' days before the fire at reactor four eventually extinguished itself. The radioactivity released was estimated to be about two hundred times that of the combined releases in the bombing of Hiroshima and Nagasaki. Millions of people were exposed."

"That's just too much to imagine," she responded.

"The scary thing of it all is that the remains of reactor four is encased in a concrete slab, still heating up, waiting to explode." As he expressed himself, a tear broke away from his left eye, and rolled down his face.

Brenda could sense that there was something still hurting him. There was something deep down inside of him that he was holding back. It needed to come out. She put her hand on top of his. "What is it Nick?"

"It's," he mumbled, as he had trouble

speaking. A heavy flow of tears ran down his cheeks and she handed him some tissues to wipe them. "It was a little girl that I carried out from a home. She was only five or six. Her skin was burnt beyond help. Like it was yesterday, I can still remember her mother crying out for someone to find her little girl."

"Oh, no," responded Brenda with a concerned look. "Well, did she see her daughter?"

"I approached her from behind and cried out to her that I'd found her. She then turned around to face me with both eyes burnt out by the radiation." He grieved, while sobbing on Brenda's shoulder. It was a door he couldn't close.

She embraced him as he let out deep emotional sobs with his chin on her shoulder. "It's okay Nick. I can see how this would bring down even the strongest person. God knows I couldn't handle half of that."

"No, I am sorry Brenda. It was complete chaos. The station's emergency cooling system was a big fuckin' joke! All because the Russians had no safety plans for this sort of thing and they didn't want to even try to implement any such safety measures. After all, they were only Ukrainians working in Chernobyl and just a few Russians. In the name of humanity," he said sobbing, "I am so sorry Brenda!" He then embraced her. "Thank God the UN got wind of that disaster. Our government didn't want the world to know what really happened on that day. It was the general himself that leaked it out to the UN. He informed them that the disaster was out of our control and that we desperately needed their help. This was one of the main reasons why the UN unanimously chose him to head the I.A.W.

"It all makes sense to me now." Seeing his tears only confirmed his innocence to her. "You're right, it's history. It doesn't matter whether it's the Germans, Russians, Americans, or Japanese."

"I just hope the world can be a better place to live in, by learning from our mistakes and forgiving the past. Now we have another battle on our hands."

"You're right Nick. So let's get to work and kick some ass!" she said. If only our ancestors could see us now!"

"Yes, USA, Russia, Canada, Ukraine and Latvia. All these countries now working together. Now that is a miracle!" he remarked, as they embraced each other.

"Well, lookie here. We have mail," she said looking back at her monitor. "Looks like Mike has some stuff for you Nick. Let's bring it up." Brenda pulled it out from the printer. "Hmm, it looks like the water test taken from that pond in Latvia. Well the ph is at seven. That's a neutral reading according to your friends. The conductivity is in the right range. The total dissolved solids are in a good balance. And the bio-oxygen demand is at a good level as well. The reading taken from that pond is in the same range as all other ponds in the general area. They're waiting for any further instructions from you Nick."

"Could I have a copy of that for my records?"

"Sure, Nick. Just give me a minute or so. I'll download everything on a disc."

"Good thinking Brenda. Can we email them back thanking them for their quick response to this matter. And that I will be getting back to them soon."

"Sure Nick. Only if you pour me more wine."

"You're the cheapest secretary I ever had. You work for a glass of wine every hour. Come to think of it, you wouldn't be able to put in a very long shift."

"Tell me about it. I would be bombed by noon," she laughed. "Oh, here are your maps now," she said, as she printed them out for him.

chapter 10

ufo sighting

Halfway through the night, Brenda woke up to use the washroom. Nick was not in bed with her. Walking down the hallway, she noticed her desk light on, with him looking over the photos. "It's hard to think with a tired mind," she said, kissing him on the side of his forehead.

"They say a picture is worth a thousand words. I can only get one out of this picture, and that is 'pond.'"

"What is this in the middle of the pond," she said pointing to a pile of old branches.

"Oh, that's just an old abandoned beaver house. So I wonder, why did they pick beaver ponds?" he pondered.

"You mean you have beavers in Russia as well?"

"That's right Brenda, even in Latvia!" he chuckled.

"Oh shit, I'm tired and you just made me eat crow!"

"That's okay, now at least it's not a pond anymore. It's a beaver pond. It just went from one word to two words. We only need nine hundred and ninety-eight more."

"Pardon me?" she said half asleep.

"Yes, I told you a picture is worth a thousand words."

"Oh you nut, let's get back to bed!" she said, tugging on his arm.

"You're right." He didn't resist and followed her back to bed.

The next morning, Nick woke up to the aroma of fresh brewed coffee and Canadian bacon. Making his way to the kitchen, her back was to him wearing his camo army shirt, just covering the cheeks of her buttocks.

"Well, did you get enough sleep?"

"Yes, and how did you know I was behind you?"

"Oh, you can hear those Russians com-ing a mile away. But in your case, it's a kilometer," not revealing that she saw his reflection on the stove clock, "Can I pour you a coffee?"

"Sure." Sitting down on the stool behind an island that divided her kitchen. "I could smell it at the other end of your cottage. What's that other good smell?"

"Oh, that's just bacon."

"Our bacon doesn't smell that good."

"That's just one of the things Canada is renowned for, eh," she said while pour-ing his coffee, "as well as our rye whiskey, beer and maple syrup. We also have sev-enty-five percent of the world's fresh water supply. In Ontario alone, if you fished in a different lake every day of your life, you'd have to live to well over three hundred years old."

"Holy shit! That does give you bragging rights," he exclaimed.

"Speaking of fishing, what do you say we try our luck after breakfast?"

"Sounds good to me, but what about a fishing license?"

"Oh that? Don't worry. I'm allowed two lines. If I catch one, I'll let you reel it in, that's if you promise to behave yourself."

"Well, it would be really hard. Especially if you plan on wearing my shirt on the boat."

"What do you mean by hard?" she smiled.

"Hard to resist you," he commented smiling back.

"Oh, you men are all alike. No matter where you're from!"

"What?" he gestured, holding his hands out so innocently. "You know what I mean."

"Sure, sure. Good comeback!" she said with a chuckle. Serving their plates on the island counter, she sat across from him. "That just reminded me why Canadian men are not susceptible to mad cow disease."

"They're not?" remarked Nick with a surprised look.

"No. It's because they're all fuckin' pigs!" she chuckled.

"You got me good!" he said, raising his coffee cup up to toast.

"That's it, that's it. Keep reeling, and keep

that rod tip pointing up!" she urged.

"Oh my God! It is a nice one!"

"Yes, now just hold it right there while I get the net."

"Please hurry," Nick said in an excited voice, noticing a boat approaching them. "Brenda, I think we have company."

"Oh shit! It's a C.O."

"A C.O.?"

"Yes, a conservation officer. That's just great!" Making a sweeping pass with the landing net into the water, she hauled up a large lake trout.

"Nice fish," said the C.O. He pulled up along side their boat. "Good morning Brenda."

"Good morning John. Nick, this is John. He's a local conservation officer around these parts."

"Pleased to meet you John," he said in his Russian accent.

John knew at this point that he was likely a non-resident. "So, have you guys been out long?" as he intently observed Nick.

"No John, we just got our lines out." Realizing her mistake, she quickly retracted her story. "I mean I just put my lines out John." Lifting the lid off the live well, she instructed, "Okay Nick, drop him in." She shook his hand. "Good work Nick."

"Well, would you mind showing me your fishing licenses?"

"Sure." She opened a small hatch next to the steering wheel. "Here you go John," as she handed it over.

After looking it over for a few seconds, he handed it back. "It's okay, but it expires at the end of the month."

"Oh, I'll have to remember to reapply for a new one then."

"That's right, if you want to continue fishing. Now Nick, can you show me yours?"

"Ah John, he's just visiting us from Russia."

"Well then. Show me a non-resident license."

"But those are my fishing lines. And I'm allowed to troll with two."

"That's right. But he can't participate in reeling in a fish. That's called fishing."

"You are right John. Here's my photo I.D. sir. Now if you radio this in to your authorities, I don't think there'll be any problem."

"Well thank you sir for your coopera-
tion." Ignoring Nick's instructions, John
pulled out his ticket book. They were
both shocked by his course of action.

"What are you doing?" Brenda asked
in an angry tone.

John could see that she was really
upset over his actions, as he proceeded to
firmly enforce his authority. "Under
Ontario's fish and game act, it's against
that law to fish without a license."

"Yes, we know that. Before you charge
him with that offence, I strongly advise
you to radio your area supervisor like
Nick suggested," she urged.

"That's not our policy."

"Believe me John, this is going to be the
one time you won't be sorry for not following the book. Please call your area
supervisor like he suggested."

He studied his Russian military photo
I.D. Then peered at them with a doubtful
smirk. "I hope you're not wasting the
Ministry's time on this one."

"No John. Your district supervisor
should have the low down on Nick."

"Okay then," he said with a bothered
look. "This should only take a minute

or two."

"Take your time John. After all, isn't that what M.N.R. stands for: Must Not Rush?"

"Oh that's real nice Brenda. Now John won't give us the time of day!"

"Oh yes he will Nick. He's a good sport, aren't you John?" She gave him a warm smile.

"That's okay Brenda. Now just let me put this call to rest." He brought out his cell phone and pushed a speed-dial button. "Hi Nicky, it's John. No, I'm not taking any sun," he replied to the receptionist. Embarrassed that they were listening in with smiles on their faces, "can you put Ken on the line for me. Okay then...Good morning Ken. Oh, just fine thank you...Yes sir, on Birch Lake. By any chance, did you receive any info on a Russian officer by the name of a Nicholas Trechrack visiting this area?...Yes sir, he's right here."

John now looked rather confused. Handing his phone to Nick he said, "Ahhh... he wants to speak to you sir."

"Hello...and it is sure nice talking to you as well sir...No, no, your officer is cooperating quite well. You sure have a beautiful country here...As a matter of fact, I just caught one...Sure, sure, maybe later...Yes, it is top secret and it's great that our countries can work together...Oh well, thank you very much then sir...Okay Ken, then just call me Nick...Sure I will try to squeeze in a fishing trip and don't worry if it is Canadian beer, I will drink anything...Sure Ken, okay, bye for now. Here he is," said Nick, as he handed John back his phone.

"Hello...Well I was going to Lake Agnew this afternoon...You mean for his full duration? But what about the other lakes?...Okay then...Oh, no sir. No, I have no problem with that...Okay, I'll do that. Yes sir. Bye for now," said John.

Folding his phone, and tucking it back into his pocket. Peering up into Nick's eyes, "I don't know what the nature of your business is sir, but I have strict orders to help you with anything you need from our ministry and all of its departments. By the way, this order was handed down to my boss from the minister himself. Sir, I've got to say, you must have big friends in high places."

"Oh, and by the way, here's your ID and my card with my cell, and office number. You can reach us twenty-four seven. I'll be working on this lake 'til your business is complete here. I'll try to keep out of your way sir."

"Oh, that's okay John." He reached out to shake his hand. "It's really nice to know that we can count on you, and your ministry for help at anytime. Thank you very much!"

"Like I said, If you need anything at anytime, just call me. So bye for now, and enjoy your stay sir." They both felt his sincerity as he drove off.

"Holy shit! Can you believe that? He went from Johnny, to Johnny-be-good within sixty seconds of that phone call," she laughed.

"Well, I guess this is our morning Brenda. It looks like more company."

A boat approached them from behind. "Oh, that's Steve and Mary. Go and lift up your fish for them to see Nick," she said as Steve's boat got closer.

"Well, I'll be a son of a bitch," said Steve, looking at the fish hanging from Nick's hand.

"It's my first fish ever!" he said with a big smile. Admiring his catch, Steve and Mary could see his pride and were happy for him.

"Put it back into the live well Nick."

"We'll include it into tonight's dinner. Was that John our friendly C.O. that just left here?" Steve asked sarcastically.

"You mean Johnny-be-good!"

"Johnny-be-good?" repeated Steve.

"Yes! He now has to serve our team!" exclaimed Brenda.

"Bullshit!"

Nick nodded. "It's true Steve!"

"Well, Mary and I are heading over to Mike's. Why don't you two meet us there. I'll give anything to hear this story about John...or Johnny-be-good," laughed Steve. "And congratulations Nick. We're going to have to toast your first fish. How about emailing a picture of you and that fish back to Russia? This way, your comrades can see how well you're doing in Canada."

"Are you kidding me? They will all walk out to that pond in Latvia and pray to get abducted by those aliens," laughed Nick. "Or haul my ass back to the Russia, big time!"

"Big time?" said Steve.

"Yes, big freakin' time!" laughed Nick with Steve and Mary departing.

"Nick, you have to let me make you a drink of your choice. So we can toast to that nice trout."

"Thank you Mike."

"Well what will it be?"

"I'll have one of those Black Russians."

"You see what I mean?" remarked Steve.

"Oh, don't say it dear," responded Mary, as she slapped Steve's arm.

"And Brenda, you helped Nick land that monster. So what's your poison gonna be? A Black Russian as well?" asked Mike.

"That's going to be a hard call," she replied looking at Nick. "Because right now, I have my hands full with a white Russian!" she remarked with everyone laughing. "Just make it a beer please."

"So Nick, I heard you had a visit from a C.O. this morning," said Bob.

"You mean Johnny-be-good!" replied Brenda.

"Yes, he paid us a visit. And to make a long story short, he asked to see my fishing license. All I had to show him was my military I.D. At the same time, I asked him to run a check on me with his supervisor."

"No shit!" said Brenda. "John already had his fine book out of his pocket. Sure wasn't easy getting him to make that call. When he finally spoke to him, it was like Dr. Jekyll and Mr. Hyde. His supervisor immediately asked to speak to Nick, insisting that Nick address him by his first name only. Now Johnny-be-good has to stay on this lake to be on standby, to assist Nick in every way. This was an order from the minister himself. I'm telling you guys! After that phone call, Nick could have made John clean his fish," she said, as everyone laughed.

"Yes, I would have loved to have seen that. From show me your fishing license, to how would you like your fish cleaned sir?" smiled Mike.

"The way I see it, he's just doing his job. It's a blessing in disguise. They're here to help us twenty-four seven. Big plus. So here's a toast to John-be-good."

"That's Johnny-be-good Nick," corrected Brenda.

"Oh good or bad, just as long as he turns out to be good for us," responded Nick.

"I'll drink to that," said Mike. "Cheers!"

"You mean dieboursia!" said Brenda with a smile

Later that evening at Brenda's for dinner Steve held his plate out over the table with a few drinks under his belt. "Sure Brenda. I'll have one more of those patties. With a little more gravy on top, if you don't mind."

"Steve you're overdoing it," said Mary worried over his health.

"What do you mean dear? I have an extra big appetite from chasing those extra terrestrials, or is it extra testicles, like three balls?"

"I'm sorry, he's drunk," said Mary, with everyone laughing. Finding his remarks to be somewhat humorous, she had a half smile on her face. "Steve, it's just that the doctor wants you to watch your shape."

"Well, isn't round a shape?" he asked while patting his stomach, with everyone laughing again.

"The next time I'm in the bush with Steve, I'll really keep my distance. Now that I know he's after testicles," smirked Bob.

"Oh come on now Bobby buddy." Steve put one hand on Bob's knee. "You know you can trust me!"

"Get that hand off me!" Bob squealed, as he slapped Steve's hand off, with everyone now having a good laugh.

Just when no one is expecting it, three radio beepers go off at once. "Holy shit! They're here!" hollered Nick, as he jumped up.

"Oh my God!" said Mary. "Please give us wisdom!"

"Brenda, can you link into Mike's site?" asked Nick with everyone in turmoil.

"It's already on," she replied, as everyone rushed into her living room. They couldn't believe their eyes. Everyone was paralyzed in total silence. They saw an opening at the side of the UFO get larger and larger, until it stopped. A huge human-like figure with a large oval head and big yellow eyes appeared. Slowly walking from the craft, it was carrying some kind of thick, gray briefcase-like container in each of his long fingered hands. Then, suddenly, two more aliens appeared from the craft, carrying a case in each hand as well. Without warning, the monitor went black.

"Quick Brenda, turn it back on," said Nick.

"It is on!"

"According to the monitor, it's their lights that went out! That's really great," said Mike. "They're up there doing God only knows what while we're here filling our faces!"

"Now, what in the hell do you mean by that!" said Steve in a harsh tone.

"Just what I said. We're here sitting on our asses, while they're up on that plateau doing whatever. We're down here in the freakin' dark!" Mike blurted in turmoil, wearing an expression of weariness.

"I thought you were insinuating the fact that we're a bunch of lard asses that don't give a shit!"

"Okay guys, that is enough," urged

Nick trying to keep peace. "Brenda, do you mind playing that back for me."

"Oh shit! I'm sorry Nick. I don't have the monitor in record mode. I'm really sorry."

"That's okay," said Mike. "I'll be able to play it back at my end."

"Yes of course, that's the main terminal," remarked Nick. "Now everybody be cool. It's unfortunate that we don't know what those aliens are up to, with those cases up there on that plateau. Maybe they're heading down to the pond to release more of those freaky things. They could be picking some up for market, like Bob said. Or they could be feeding them some high protein diet. One thing is certain. Their timing seems to be consistent. Every three nights: same place, same time. Compare this with the Russian pond. Consider the factor in our time difference. And I'm sure we'll find some kind of pattern. We'll all have to meet tomorrow afternoon at Steve's cottage, if that's okay?"

"No problem," said Steve.

"During that meeting, do you mind staying back at your cottage Carol, to watch that monitor? We can start a twenty-four hour visual, between your monitor and Brenda's, by altering shifts every three hours. Mike, if you don't mind me going back to your place, so I can send the latest data to Ottawa and Russia.

"Sure, that's okay Nick. I can do that."

"Just in case they want to talk to me Mike."

"Oh I see."

"And Steve, you and I should take a run back up that hill tomorrow morning. I want to know how those aliens are getting down to that pond. And we should reset that radio," instructed Nick.

"Providing those aliens aren't there and my radio isn't fried," replied Steve in a calmer tone.

"We'll know if they're still there in half an hour from now, when we get to Mike's."

"Nick, what about a couple of us camping out up there on that plateau?" asked Bob.

"Bob, you are one step ahead of me. That is one of the things I want to cover tomorrow at Steve's. Tonight has been an eye-opener for all of us, so let's call it a night. Let's get a good night's sleep, so we can do some serious planning tomorrow," suggested Nick. "I'm really taken by the courage you've all demonstrated, with no training for this sort of thing. Here you are fighting for your country and the world. Just hang in there."

"Are you kidding me? A good nights sleep Nick? After watching that freak show, with real aliens up on that hill across from my cottage, and not knowing what in the world they're up to, with those little creatures in that pond, guarded by those so called NYANYAS or babysitters. Oh, I guess I'll have a real good night's sleep. And to think I was worried when our teenage son had our car out after one am."

"I'm looking forward to seeing what tomorrow brings," said Steve.

"You sure as hell can't get bored around this lake," remarked Janis.

chapter 11

strategy

Steve and Mary were jerked awake by a loud and deep pulsating sound. Scrambling out of bed, Steve shouted, "What the hell?" gaping out the bedroom window surprised to see Nick and Brenda standing in the backyard. Nick was signaling to an army helicopter that was lowering a huge green container. "He certainly caught us by surprise."

"He obviously has big plans dear," said Mary now standing at his side.

"I just got to see what he's up to Mary," as he threw his clothes on.

"Sure, I'll join you in a few minutes."

Nick was unhitching a large hook from the container by the time Steve approached. He then signaled to the pilot with both thumbs up, nodding his head at the same time. The empty load line was winched up and the helicopter departed.

"So, what's in the surprise package?"

"If I told you, then it wouldn't be a surprise."

"Oh come on Nick. Don't be like that."

"You'll see, after the meeting."

"You bastard!" he said with a big smile.

"What the heck is it?" asked Mary, approaching them in her housecoat.

"Let's just say that Santa came a little early this year."

"I guess it's a mystery 'til after the meeting Mary."

"Sorry for the early rude awakening. We're trying not to attract much attention here."

"That's okay Nick. Something tells me, that what's in that container more than compensates for your rudeness."

"You're right there Steve. So do you have a couple of pry bars for later?"

"No problem. I'll get them right now," he replied, in an anxious voice.

"Come on in. I'll put coffee on," said Mary, watching Steve run to the tool shed. "He forgets that he shouldn't run," worrying about his condition. "I give up trying to remind him."

Brenda and Nick could understand her concern but choose not to intervene, as they followed her into the cottage.

"You two didn't have much sleep," as she put coffee cups on the table.

"Maybe six hours," replied Brenda. "We emailed Russia that late night attraction. But it gets better. When we first arrived at Mike's cottage, he received the same email from Russia about one hour earlier. Those aliens in Latvia are the same ones, by the looks of them."

"What do you mean by same aliens?" asked Steve, entering in through the screen door.

"We probably all look the same to them too," remarked Brenda.

"Good point," said Nick. "But I think we should leave this conversation for our meeting."

"I'm sorry," replied Brenda, respecting his wishes.

"That's okay," said Nick, with a warm smile. "I see you are really caught up in this."

"Well, do you blame me?"

"Not at all!" putting his hand on top of hers. Steve and Mary smiled at each other over their romantic gestures.

"So Nick, should we have our coffee here, or take it with us?"

"Holy shit Steve! You're in a real hurry.

Steve was somewhat upset that Nick's relationship stood in the way of their progress. "It's just that we're supposed to check out that bluff, and reset that radio, if it isn't fried from the UFO. Then we should loop around the pond before breakfast."

"Oh, just slow down dear. Enjoy your coffee first. You need to learn to have patience," as she started filling his cup.

He looked up. "Mary, if I wanted patients, I would've been a doctor."

"Now that's the Steve we know," smiled Mary.

"Don't forget we're going fishing after the meeting," reminded Brenda. "That's only if I don't have monitor duty this afternoon."

"If you girls would like to see us off at the woodshed, be ready in about ten minutes," indicated Nick.

About ten minutes later, the two girls walked to the woodshed, each with a coffee in hand. The guys were ready to depart, sitting on their bikes with rifles secured.

"We thought you weren't going to see us off," said Nick. They both turned their heads at the same time, looking back at the girls. Their faces were completely covered with black chimney soot for camouflage.

"Oh my God," chuckled Mary.

Brenda spat out her coffee, laughing uncontrollably.

Mary stopped laughing and gave Steve a big kiss. The girls could feel the tension, knowing the dangerous situation the boys were now faced with.

"Now what was that for?" he said trying to play macho in front of Nick.

"Just for good luck. I see that you're making good use of your duck hunting camo as well."

"I can't let you get off so easily Nick," said Brenda. She gave him a big kiss, taking him by surprise.

"I'm sure I have the hang of this bike now Steve."

"I sure as hell hope so," he replied, remembering the pond incident.

"Do you mind if I lead?" Nick asked.

"Go ahead, you're the trail boss. We plan on being back around nineish for breakfast. And don't forget to clean your faces off!" Steve chuckled as they departed.

"Oh shit!" she said laughing after seeing Brenda's face with soot on it.

"Don't tell me," realizing that she picked up some soot herself off of Steve's face. "So you and Nick seem to have really hit if off."

"Yes," Brenda replied, her arms crossed in front of her, still watching them drive away. "I really hope that this will come to an end soon. I know this is hard on Nick. He's trying to be really considerate," she said, speaking in a soft tone.

"I know that Brenda. That's why he wanted to lead. After all, that's what he's trained for."

Driving up the side of the hill close to the plateau, suddenly Nick brought his bike to a stop. "Is everything okay?" asked Steve.

"Yes," he replied. Lifting his rifle from the rifle rack, he held it in the ready position, with his forefinger just outside the trigger guard. "I just thought it would be a little quieter if we walk in the rest of the way. And if you don't mind, if we have to talk, then whisper. Now just let me walk in ahead of you, to give us space."

"Sure go ahead," he whispered, respecting Nick's decision. Grabbing his rifle, he followed him up towards the plateau. Wondering to himself, "Why was he suddenly being so cautious in this area?"

He finally reached the plateau and then waved Steve on to join him. "Look here," he whispered, pointing off to the side of the trail with his rifle barrel, as it brushed the morning dew off the ferns. "You see where those ferns are bent over. Well that's their travel way."

"Holy shit, right on," he answered, whispering. He could now clearly see the outline of the trail heading down to the pond. "I'm surprised I never noticed it before."

"Let's check out your radio." After walking just a dozen more steps toward the landing area, they were bewildered that the radio and trip wire were still intact.

"Well, how in hell is that possible for that UFO to have landed here? Not to have broken the wire, or have fried my radio?"

"You've got me there, Steve," he whispered. "Our scientists figure it's some kind of magnetic field that propels them. That's why we get a lot of crop rings, with no crops starting on fire."

"And all this time, I thought those crop rings were a hoax."

"Not all of them," he whispered smiling.

"Okay then, here goes nothing!" he whispered, resetting the radio, and pushing the pager beeper button.

"Good morning boys," said Mike. "We've been monitoring you two for a while. And yes, your pager works good at this end."

"That's a big ten-four at this end as well, good buddies," said Mary.

"Is that bacon I smell?' whispered Steve.

"You're a little early," she said.

"Just razzing ya Mary. Bye for now," he whispered. "Hey Mike, do you still have your ears on?"

"Go ahead."

"Yeah, those tourists left a path going down to that pond."

"Steve, tell them I'm going scouting down that path. I should be back in about forty minutes or so."

"Nick said he's going to follow that path down to the pond. He should be back in about forty minutes or so. I'll just wait up here, over and out," he whispered. Looking at Nick, Steve feared what he might have to encounter. "Be careful."

"Don't worry. I won't do anything stupid," he whispered back while he cautiously proceeded down towards the pond. His camouflage fatigues blended well with the background and he disappeared out of Steve's sight.

Steve picked a spot up on a rock, next to a clump of cedars that made for good observation.

Nick reached a spot where he started to make out parts of the pond. He was being ever so careful not to break a branch or step on any dry limbs, staying just inside the tree line when a loud knocking sound came out from the pond area. It sounded like someone striking two pieces of wood together about six times. Then it stopped. "Now what could those NYANYAS be up to?" he thought.

Slowly making his way closer, he tried to get a visual. When that loud knocking sound started again, lasting much longer this time, it seemed to be coming from a little further down. He came to a small opening between two cedar trees, where he could view most of the pond. As that knocking sound started up again, he then realized that it came from one of the dead trees standing out from the water. He picked up a small red flash up high on the side of the tree. He suddenly realized that it was the red head of a large pileated woodpecker, that he had only before seen in bird books. He watched it briefly peck away, then fly off to another tree.

Below in the foreground, he was shocked to see two huge NYANYAS lying half out of the water on the old beaver house in the middle of the pond. The woodpecker began to peck on a tree close to them. It kept the NYANYAS' attention, while at the same time muffling out any other sound, as he started taking pictures. As he zoomed in for a closer picture, the woodpecker suddenly stopped. Taking his finger off the zoom button, the camera still ran for a second more, making a buzzing noise. A loud moaning sound emanated from the water. Nick knew that noise too well to overlook it. Glancing back at the beaver house, he could see that the two NYANYAS were alarmed by the warning noise from their buddy. They were heading straight in his direction, causing large wakes.

Nick realized that it was time to leave. He heard a large splash to the right of him, behind a cedar tree line. "Was that another NYANYA? That was too close for comfort!" he thought to himself. Quickly vacating, he heard another deep bellowing sound coming from just behind him.

At the top of the plateau, Steve was feeling paranoid, hearing the deep bellowing sounds echoing from the pond. He swiveled his head every second or so with his finger on the trigger. Then, a ghostly silence fell over the whole area. The only sound that Steve could hear was the pounding of his heart. He wondered what was happening to Nick. Should he stay, or should he go? Each minute felt like an hour. Suddenly, he was startled by his radio pager going off. He took a deep breath to calm himself down.

"Come in Steve, come in Steve!" Mike said in a frantic tone.

"Yes, go ahead Mike."

"Is Nick back with you yet?"

"No, why?"

"Well, Ottawa just sent us another satellite picture of our pond, and it's not a pretty one."

"What's wrong?" asked Brenda cutting into the conversation.

"Oh Brenda, is that you?" asked Mike in a surprised tone.

"Yes. So what the fuck is wrong Mike?"

"Well, your gonna have to see these pictures. You know, those NYANYA things that guard that pond."

"Yes," she replied.

"Well, there are now three of them, and they've doubled in size!"

"Oh my God! Steve, can you go down

to the pond right now and warn him?"

"It's okay Brenda," said Nick from Steve's radio. "Yes, the aliens have doubled up on their babysitters. More and bigger...more bigger targets," he said chuckling.

"That's not funny Nick!" responded Brenda.

"I guess Steve's humor is starting to rub off on him," remarked Mike.

"Ha, ha," said Brenda sarcastically.

"Well, I don't think his jokes are that good!" remarked Steve. "Get breakfast on Mary, we're heading back."

"Oh yes Mike, don't forget to bring those satellite pictures to the meeting."

"Ten-four Steve."

"Over and out Mike."

"'Bigger targets,' now that's being optimistic Nick," Steve said as they started walking back to their bikes.

"So did you hear one of the NYANYAS make that warring call?" Nick asked.

"Can you smell shit?"

"Well, we can always learn something after a mission," jested Nick.

"Right Nick. It taught me to wear a

fuckin' diaper when I'm on a stakeout with you!" remarked Steve smiling.

After breakfast, the crew assembled behind Steve and Mary's cottage. Nick was sitting high up on the green container, with arms crossed in front of him, lightly bouncing his army boot heels on the container. "Well ladies and gentlemen. After last night's episode, I think that you guys would agree with me, that we really have to pull up our socks and get serious. You've all had some time to see what we're dealing with here. And I'm privileged that the I.A.W. has granted me this much authority. I could've had all of you temporarily removed from this lake, and could've had it cordoned off, until this matter was over. But I chose to keep you guys on as the main players. Not because you are good people, and are a lot of fun," he chuckled.

"It was a combination of factors. Like how much you guys know this whole area and its history. Like my first morning here, when Steve showed me his topographical map with every point of interest marked out on it. Even the coordinates that he got off his bike's GPS. The fact that Bob and Mike know this area like the back of their hand is such a bonus. And you guys already caught one of those creature things that inhabit your pond. Accidentally discovering that UFO landing area is another thing. It would've been just a matter of time until this whole area would've been overcome with military and government forces. Especially when that university professor brought that creature to Ottawa. If the I.A.W. removed all the cottagers off this lake, it would've tipped off the aliens that we were on to them. The I.A.W. intelligence now has strong evidence that there are aliens in human form living among us.

"This is another point on your side. The fact that you guys are a tight knit group means you can easily pick out someone new on the lake, or any outsider to try and penetrate in. Just remember to keep your ears and eyes open at all times. And go on as if nothing is wrong out here."

"So Nick, what I get is that you want us to connive for those carnivorous things," said Steve. Everyone groaned, while Nick shook his head.

"Now if anyone around this lake is asking questions or gossiping, then just play dumb and tell us at our next meeting. Take note of the date, time, what they look like and what they are wearing. Also, what type of boat they are driving and their boat numbers. With this information, we can have them checked out."

"Well Nick, now that you've said that, I heard that our friendly C.O. Johnny-be-good is asking a lot of questions around the lake," said Janis.

"Is that so?"

"Yes Nick. Apparently he's really curious about Arnold Schwarzenegger and all your pull with the government. He wants to know what the hell you're up to here? That's what the lodge owner's wife asked me when I bought a loaf of bread there yesterday," remarked Janis.

"Well, for a woman that doesn't talk much, I thank you for sharing this with Arnold Schwarzenegger," he said chuckling. "This is exactly what I am talking about. Now I can follow up on him, so he can stop asking questions."

"So are you going to terminate him?" shouted Steve.

"I will deal with him my way."

"Oh shit, this should be fun!" said Bob.

"I have more interesting news," Nick continued. "Last night in Latvia, the aliens pulled off the same shit over there. Within a time period of about two hours difference, three of them carried two cases each and headed towards that pond. They were monitored before their lights went out. The same occurrences happened here, which leads us to believe it's the same alien crew, but we can't prove it. They all look the same and so do their UFOs. So far, we're just assuming this. They also beefed-up their security, or babysitters to bigger ones."

"That only means bigger targets, right Nick," said Steve playing on Nick's earlier comment.

"So when you say 'same aliens,' do you mean from the same planet Nick?"

"Yes Janis, but how many of them are there? And how many space crafts are we dealing with? For the aliens to go to all that work to protect those ponds only tells me that they are up to something big. Up to now, there has been no other alien activity anywhere else in the world, according to the I.A.W."

"I was wondering why you were being extra cautious this morning Nick," said Steve. "Like when you wanted to lead and insisted we whisper."

"Well, after all that alien activity going on up there, I just had this gut feeling that they were up to something. If you all look at your aerial photos, you can see one NYANYA on the north shore of the pond. I was only ten meters from that one, when I was taking pictures of the others. At the same time, this big woodpecker was pecking away close to where they were. It helped muffle the sound of the camera. When it stopped pecking, the noise of the electronic zoom alerted that NYANYA."

"Oh you mean that giant redheaded woodpecker? He always hangs around there," responded Mike.

"No, actually it's a pileated male woodpecker," replied Nick.

"You keep forgetting Mike, Nick knows his birds like you know your shit!" remarked Steve.

"Well, to tell you the truth Steve, it was the first time that I'd ever heard or even had the privilege of actually seeing one."

"Yes, that was the picture I received at the same time you were there Nick," said Mike.

"So why don't we get them to cover our ass with an aerial photo, every five minutes or so, when we're out on maneuvers?"

"Good point Steve," confirmed Nick. "Can you make a note of that Janis?"

"Sure, I have it in the minutes."

"And make sure to tell them that it's a new picture every five minutes. So Mike, you, or Brenda can monitor our every move. Now, that also depends on if we have an overcast sky that day," informed Nick. "After last night's encounter, I called your I.A.W. in Ottawa, to put in a requisition for some supplies to help us with our situation here. So as you can see, their courier service didn't waste any time."

"Thank God they didn't use Canada Post. The contents of that container would've been obsolete by the time we would've received it," mocked Bob.

"Okay now, except for a few items in this container–like the hand-held, heat-sensor rocket launcher, and the quick-point infrared rifles with explosive tip ammo–we'll have to keep them out of sight, if you know what I mean," instructed Nick.

"Sure," agreed Steve. "We can hide them in the tool shed, up on the rafters where we can get at them quick."

"Well, I don't mean to pry," jested Nick holding up a pry bar in each hand. "But who would like the honors?"

"I'll take one," responded Mike.

"Me too," replied Bob. Each of them had an excited look on their face. Like two young boys on Christmas morning, holding a joystick, about to play the latest action computer game.

"While you guys are busy prying off that lid, I'll get us some cold ones," said Steve.

"I won't say no to that," responded Bob.

"Something tells me that it's going to be Christmas in June for some big boys," remarked Janis. She watched Bob working hard at prying off the wooded straps.

"Yes," added Mary. "Even if they've been naughty or nice..."

"What do you mean?" questioned Bob,

stopping to wipe sweat off his forehead. "Sometimes naughty is nice!"

Steve returned with a cooler. "So there's everything from bottled water, to beer in that cooler. Just help yourselves guys."

"All right, watch yourselves now, while we get this top off," warned Bob. He and Mike set the lid down, behind the container on the ground.

"I'll go and get a trash bag for all that packing," said Mary.

"Holy shit!" exclaimed Mike, as he pulled out some packing. "All of this stuff is brand new!"

"Excuse me," said Nick, as he picked up one of the four rifles that was form-fitted in it's own part of the container. "Yes, you are absolutely right Steve. You men will be one of the first in the world to use this type of weapon. It can shoot thirty rounds a second," he remarked, as he held it up high for the boys to see. "But I had them set the action to semi-auto, like your sporting rifles. Just so none of you would get carried away, if you know what I mean."

"Oh shit! I was hoping it could replace

my chainsaw, for slashing out new trails!" jested Steve.

"Just one shot with this explosive tip ammo, and I think you will change that thought," he said smiling. "So if you guys can pull out this insert with these rifles, we will be able to get at the rest of the goodies. Just set it over there. As you can see, that section also acts as a gun rack for easy storage."

Steve pulled up a smaller container, and put it down next to the large one.

"Now be very careful, to handle that one like eggs," he cautioned.

Being curious to what Nick said, Steve opened the lid to this dark green container. "Holy shit! They look like eggs. If they weren't green, I'd try to crack one open." Everyone looked at dark green egg-shaped things, packed in a foam-padded container.

"No, they look more like kiwis to me," remarked Mary.

"And twenty-four of them to boot. What is with the pins with the loops sticking out from them?" inquired Janis.

"Again, these are also the latest in weaponry," informed Nick, as he grabbed one out of the container. "Unlike eggs, these have no expiry date. This is a grenade and landmine combo," as he showed it to everyone. "And this little dial on the side here, is a sensitivity control. They have already been preset and like a land mine, it also has a built-in smart sensor. It will detonate if anything over three pounds in weight compresses it. And these two little black devices there," as he picked one out of the box, "are remotes. They act like a remote car starter, from up to a kilometer away, on, or off land mine. Just one of these babies can take out the biggest army tank ever made. So if we plant them around key areas, at the pond, we wouldn't have to worry about being stalked by one of those babysitters. Now please keep them out of the reach of children, if you know what I mean."

"Don't worry about that Nick. None of this stuff will be visible after this meeting," reassured Steve.

Nick looked up, "But it is you that I am worried about," he replied with everyone laughing. "Now for this baby, the grand finale of all our weapons," as he opened a plastic molded case.

"Holy shit Nick. The only time I ever saw one of those was in a movie.

"Well Bob," Nick smiled. "This here is the mother of all hand-held rocket launchers." Picking it up, he placed it tight to his right shoulder. "The max heat trailer range is seven thousand meters. This side-mounted variable scope makes it easy to I.D. your target."

"That's another thing you'll have to hide from Steve," remarked Mary. "He's still pissed off at Air Canada for losing his luggage, when we visited Cuba last winter."

"I will try to remember that Mary," laughed Nick.

"No, it would work better from Mike's deck. He has a clear view of that UFO landing pad," said Steve.

"Now in this box are four sets of night vision glasses. I sure as hell wish I had them that night I escaped. They should come in handy."

"Yes, they'll be great for night fishing," said Mike.

"Well, that's not exactly what I had in mind," said Nick. "But you're right. Make good use of them. I also ordered camo fatigues for you guys. I hope I got your sizes right. There are also some extra clothes in there for me. Any underwear and socks that you find are mine. Oh, and those freeze-dried army rations will make for great hunting food for you guys in the fall. Look at it as a donation for your hunt camp."

"Right on Nick, but I think you overdid it with the rocket launcher," remarked Steve, as everyone laughed.

"Wow!" exclaimed Bob. "You got us some nice threads all right," as he held up a camo shirt.

"You should come to the camo vests soon Bob. The pockets are loaded with goodies as well. There should also be a box of six long-range mini two-way radios, good for about fifty kilometers."

"Fifty kilometers, you're shitting me!" said Mike. "The CRTC would freak if they knew we possessed these!"

"What is that?" asked Nick.

"Oh, we have laws governing radio transmissions," said Mike.

"Well not to worry, those radios are on their own private frequencies. If they catch you, have them call your I.A.W."

"Oh shit, that's right. I keep forgetting!" said Mike. "We're actually fighting for the world!"

"Right on!" said Steve, as he clanged his beer with the others.

"Well, since you boys are so caught up in your toys, me and the girls are going into town to do a little shopping. We should only be a few hours," said Brenda.

"I thought you wanted to go fishing."

"Oh frigg. I forgot."

"That's okay. I'll take a rain check then," said Nick.

"You learnt our lingo quick," replied Brenda with a smile.

"Oh Mary, don't forget our list, and add an extra case of beer to it. This is going down too easy."

"You mean an extra case of bottled water. You're getting a beer belly."

"The extra beer is for company."

"Sure, sure! And Mike, do you and Carol need anything in town?"

"No I don't think so, but call her anyway. Sure Mike. It's just too bad she got stuck monitoring this morning," said Mary, as she walked away with the girls.

"Well guys. Let's get this stuff put away, so we can go out on the lake, and plan some more alien strategy. We can catch a few more trout for tonight's dinner," said Steve.

"Now, that sounds good to me," agreed Mike.

"Oh shit! I told Janis I would have the grass cut today," said Bob.

"Well then, just pour a beer on it," suggested Steve.

"Are you nuts!" replied Bob.

"No. You see then, this way, it'll be half cut by tonight!"

"Funny boy!" remarked Bob.

"Oh Bob, just tell Janis that Nick wanted to continue the meeting out on the lake. She'll understand."

"Yes, remember, it's a humanitarian effort," jested Mike.

"Yeah, she'll sure as hell eat that one up!" agreed Steve. Patting Bob on the back, he clanged his beer bottle against his.

chapter 12

ufo oversight

"Holy shit! Is this beginners luck or what!" exclaimed Mike.

"Tell me about it. He must have freakin' horseshoes up his ass. It's his third one in twenty minutes," said Bob.

"Now just take your time Nick. I have the net ready," said Steve, standing close to his side.

"Oh, look over there to your right guys. It's Johnny-be-good. He's checking us out with his field glasses," remarked Bob.

"Wave him over here," said Nick while reeling in his fish.

"Are you sure?" questioned Steve.

"Yes, remember I have a bone to pick with him."

"Oh yeah," replied Bob with a big smirk on his face. Curious to see how Nick was going to deal with him, as he waved him over.

"Yeah, he's on his way. Oh shit, this should be fun!" said Mike.

"It's a beauty!" said Steve, as he netted Nick's fish.

John's boat pulled up alongside Mike's. "Nice fish Nick," said John. "Does he have horseshoes up his ass or what? I couldn't help but notice that Nick is the only one catching fish."

"I said the same thing a minute ago," remarked Bob.

"Now, don't rub it in John," said Steve. He was working hard with a pair of pliers trying to remove a hook from the trout's jaw. "There's no way, that this one was getting away!"

"Yes, I saw you waving. Is there something you need Nick?"

"Well, in a way John. It's like this. I'm trying to keep a low profile around here. And I don't want any publicity either."

"I don't think I understand what you mean Nick."

"Well, back in Russia, I have a TV fishing show. Like the one you have over here with Bob Izumi. I'm learning how to fish this lake. If this lake proves to be good, then Bob Izumi and I will be doing a fishing show here next month. Then, he'll go over to Russia, to do one with me."

"Wow, that should make for great viewing!" replied John, all pumped up.

"So you can be a great help to me if anyone asks any questions about this new guy on the lake. Do you know what I mean?"

"Yes I do," said John. "Don't worry. I'll do my best to keep this low-key. And by the way Nick, in what I've seen in the last half hour, Bob Izumi couldn't hold a candle to you!"

"Well, thank you John," he replied, "and have a good afternoon." They all waved to John as he drove off.

"Well holy shit Nick! You played him like a violin!" said Steve laughing out loud.

"Yeah, Johnny-be-good was the fourth fish Nick caught today!" said Bob.

"I'll say! Hook, line and sinker! So how do you know about Bob Izumi?" asked Mike.

"You don't think we have TV in Russia?" answered Nick. All the guys laughed at the way it came out.

"Well, let's head back. These three lakers are going to make for a great supper. We'll have everything ready for when the girls get back. Fresh fish, and fresh-cut fries," said Steve. "As long as I can get a volunteer to peel the potatoes."

"What about that Russian Bob Izumi? He must have experience in peeling potatoes in the army," said Mike.

"Yes I do."

"Oh, so you fucked up a couple of times, did you now?" asked Steve with a big curious smile, while glancing at Mike and Bob. "Care to tell us the story Nick."

"Let us just say, I was a lot younger," he smiled.

"Let me guess. You were young and dumb and full of cum, and you really thought you knew it all," jested Bob, as everyone laughed.

"Ya, something like that," replied Nick with a smirk. "Ya, it was something like that all right."

"But now he's old and bold and full of mold!" joked Steve, as they all laughed.

Back at Steve and Mary's cottage, Mike held up a large bowl of peeled, cut potatoes, "So Steve, what's up with the brownie points?"

"Just set them down on the table and open us another beer. I wonder what's taking Bob so long just to fillet three trout," remarked Steve.

" Ah, he's probably teaching Nick at the same time."

"Oh shit! Be prepared to eat fish bones then. I should have made him peel the potatoes," said Steve.

"What is this about fish bones?" asked Bob as he and Nick entered the cottage.

"Mike mentioned that you might be teaching Nick how to fillet fish."

"No, not this time Steve. Nick showed me a whole new technique on filleting fish."

"Bullshit!" said Steve.

"No shit." responded Bob

"Yes, I cleaned fish for a whole summer, when I stayed with my uncle, back in Russia. But, the first time I ever caught one was with Brenda, here in Canada."

"Well now, that's a switch, cleaning before catching," said Steve. "Just set that

bowl on the counter Bob, and help yourselves to a cold one. Mike and I will join
you two in the gazebo in a couple of minutes. Oh, and thanks for your help.
Everything else is ready to cook. We'll just
have a cold one and wait for the girls to
arrive."

"Holy shit!" said Bob. "The girls are
going to like you."

"I said the same thing to him earlier. So,
what's with the brownie points?" asked
Mike.

"Okay guys, it's called getting into
scoring position, like a sacrifice fly in
baseball."

"Bullshit Steve," responded Mike.

"I told you before. I know pussy-
whipped," said Steve.

"Well then, if the shoe fits..."

"Don't try to lecture me on being
pussy-whipped. You don't want to go
there Mike!"

"Okay, okay, let's change the subject,"
said Bob. He sensed the conversation
could lead to an argument.

The girls entered Brenda's cottage with
supplies from town in their hands. "I'll

just bring these cases of beer right to your boat Brenda," said Mary.

"Oh, let me help you with that," urged Janis.

"I'll pour you girls a cold cocktail for the front deck. We have time for at least one before we head back to the boys," remarked Brenda.

"Sure, I think they're big enough to take care of themselves by now," said Janis. "Oh yes, we have to remember to call Carol, before we leave to give her a few minutes to get ready for dinner. I'm sorry you have to monitor this afternoon Brenda."

"It's only fair. Carol put her shift in today."

Back at Steve's cottage, the boys were sharing jokes. "So now you have these two boobs hanging way down from this eighty-year-old lady. And one boob says to the other one, if we don't get some support around here soon, we'll be nuts."

"Oh Steve, that's almost as crazy as the two bald guys who put their heads together and made an ass of themselves," added Bob.

Everyone laughed, except for Nick. He was focusing over two aerial photos on the round table in the centre of the gazebo.

"I see Nick didn't get your humor," remarked Bob.

"Oh, I'm sure he did," said Steve. "He's still looking for some so called common denominator, between the pond in Latvia and the one here."

"Well, they both have those little feisty freaks, which are guarded by those NYANYAS, as Nick calls them," said Mike, now a little intoxicated.

"No, I heard Steve's joke," said Nick with a smile, while still studying the photos. I am sorry guys, but I am sure there is something right under our noses, and we can't see the forest for the trees. It's just a matter of time, until one of us stumbles onto it. And I sure as hell hope that time is on our side," now looking up at them with a poker face.

Just then, Steve's cell phone rang. "Hello. Oh, Sarah, how did everything go in Ottawa?...Oh, that's great. So you and Tom are back in Sudbury...Oh, okay...No, your mother is over at Brenda's with the girls...Yes, they went to town for supplies and things...No, not now, I mean we're dealing with some issues right now...I'll get her to call you when she gets back from Brenda's, if it's not too late...No, sweetheart, we're not fighting," he replied with a chuckle. "I'm glad you and Tom had a good trip to Ottawa. I'm looking forward to seeing you...Yes, and the university should let you know soon...That's good...Okay, I love you too," said Steve.

He slowly placed the cell phone back on the table, and lowered his head without saying a word. The guys could sense his emotion. They all knew how much Steve loved Sarah and how hard it was to keep his distance from her while dealing with the dilemma at hand.

After a long shift of watching the monitor, Carol was starry-eyed. She casually sat back with her feet crossed up on the desk. Listening to a tune on the radio, she tapped her thumbs along the brim of an empty coffee mug sitting on her lap. Startled by the ringing of the telephone on the wall behind her, she left the comfort of her chair. "Hello...Oh sweetheart, it's you!" Distracted, Carol talked to her son with her back to the monitor. The computer monitor showed a saucer appearing up on the plateau. The alien activity continued while she engaged in a lengthy conversation with her son.

"Excuse me, but I think that, my drink contained vitamin-p," said Janis, as she stood up. She entered the cottage and stopped dead in her tracks, puzzled by what she saw on Brenda's computer monitor. "Brenda, is that the image from the other night?" she shouted.

"What do you mean?" asked Brenda, with a curious look. She got up to take a look at what Janis was talking about. "Holy shit! That's them! They're back!" exclaimed Brenda frantically running to her phone as Mary joined Janis at the monitor.

"Hello," answered Steve.

"Steve, those things are back!" she said frantically.

He asked sternly. "What things?" realizing it was Brenda.

"Those spacemen. They're fuckin' here!"

"The aliens are at your place?" The guys jumped to their feet, startled by what they heard.

"No, no, up on the hill! We can see them on the monitor."

"Okay, I understand now. Hold on." He looked at the guys with a terrified look. "The aliens are back up on the plateau!"

"Look Brenda, they're going back into the saucer," said Mary.

"Steve, Steve," said Brenda.

He exclaimed, "Yes, I overheard Mary. They're now entering the saucer!" looking over at Nick.

"The door is now closing," said Brenda.

"She said the door is closing Nick."
Nick shouted. "Those son of a bitches!" He slapped his hand on the table in anger. "Do you see what I mean? Just when we thought they had a pattern."

"Well, what can we do Nick?" asked Steve.

"There is fuck all we can do but go over to Mike's and review this freak show. How come Carol did not notify us sooner?'

"Oh my God! That's right. She didn't call us!" exclaimed Brenda.

Steve said. "Nick and Mike will be at Carol's in about ten minutes. In the meantime, phone Carol and tell her they're on their way. And confirm with us immediately that everything is okay with her."

"The girls will be heading over to your place after they pick up Carol. And I'll continue to monitor from here," said Brenda.

"We'll let Nick review the video. He'll probably want to call the general afterwards."

"That sounds good Steve," replied Brenda in a calmer tone.

"Can you put Mary on?"

"Sure Steve."

"Hi Mary. I just wanted to let you know that Sarah called and I'll fill you in later. Okay dear, see you soon. Bye for now." Steve turned off his cell phone. It was quite evident to them that Nick was dismayed.

Steve said. "Well Nick, we have them monitored now," trying to pick up his mood.

"Yes, we should be up for company next weekend...I love you too," Carol said as she hung up the phone. She turned around to face the monitor. Traumatized by the spaceship that was in full view on her screen, she just stood there in shock. Her coffee mug fell from her finger shattering on the floor. Once again startled by the telephone ringing behind her. She quickly answered, "Yes, hello!" while at the same time watching the spaceship depart.

"Is everything okay Carol?" asked Brenda in a concerned tone.

She cried. "I'm sorry Brenda. I was on the phone, with my back to the monitor."

"That's okay," comforted Brenda. "Mike and Nick should be arriving at your place any minute. Mary and the girls will be picking you up shortly. I'll take over monitoring from this end."

"Well some help I was!" replied Carol feeling distraught.

"Don't worry Carol. That's a part of being human. We all make mistakes."

Brenda's call helped, but Carol still felt flustered, missing the alien encounter.

"You're right about that Steve," said

Nick. At least we have something to send to the I.A.W. Even though we didn't first detect their arrival."

"Yes Nick. "I'd like to go up there and find out what in the hell went wrong with our radio alarm system."

"Just hold on Steve, we should check out that monitor first. I'm curious to see what in the hell those aliens were up to. And I'll be talking to the general within the next fifteen minutes."

Steve suggested. "Well Mike, the quicker you and Nick leave, the quicker you'll be back. If there is anything you want me to know right away. I'll be as close as my phone."

"Right on." He finished the last swig of beer. Then crushed the can with his hand, and dropped it down with a real attitude. "I'll be back!" Nick said firmly.

"Okay, now I see why Johnny-be-good thinks you're like Arnold Schwarzenegger."

"What do you mean?"

"You just said, 'I'll be back,'" said Steve, trying to amuse him, as Bob and Mike nervously chuckled.

"You're nuts!" said Nick shaking his head with a smile. He left the gazebo with

Mike behind him, smiling back at the boys on how Steve's humor lightened him up a little.

Steve shouted. "I'll have that trout cooked just right. So send those girls back pronto."

Everyone except Brenda assembled at Steve and Mary's cottage for dinner. Steve said. "Well, I'm sure glad to hear that everything went well with the general, Nick."

"Yes, but we still have a few more wrinkles to iron out. And I'm sure we will" responded Nick with a content look.

"Well Steve, since this is your spread, you should have the honors of saying grace," said Mike.

Mike never encouraged anyone to say grace. This surprised Steve and everyone else. They all realized how serious things were now getting in regards to the aliens.

They all joined hands around the table. "Oh Heavenly Father, we give you thanks for this meal. And we ask you to give us wisdom and protection in dealing with these unearthly creatures who are among us. In Jesus's name. Amen."

"Yes, a big time amen to that prayer!" said Bob. Everyone was very responsive to Steve's prayer.

"All right folks. Let's dig in," said Steve.

Nick said. "Carol, are you okay?" Seeming to be somewhat distant.

"Oh yes Nick, I'm sorry, I just never felt this way before."

"What way?" asked Mike.

"Oh, I just feel so close to all of you...a little emotional...and yet grateful in my spirit...as if this is our last supper or something."

"Holy shit! Don't say that!" said Bob. He reached over and patted Carol on her shoulder. "But just in case. I'll have another piece of that trout," as everyone chuckled.

"Speaking of which. This is the best fish and chips I have ever eaten Steve," remarked Nick.

"Don't forget. It was the Russian Bob Izumi that caught them," jested Steve. The guys all chuckled out loud.

"Is there something we girls missed?" asked Mary.

"Oh yes, Nick had fun with Johnny-be-good out on the lake today," said Bob. "Nick led John to believe that he had his own fishing TV program in Russia and that he and Bob Izumi would be doing a show together on this lake sometime soon. And that John could help him in keeping a low profile on the lake."

"This must have made John feel ten feet taller. The fact that he could help Nick in his situation," said Mary.

"Oh, I see how that worked well," responded Janis.

Nick said. "That's right. I used that as ammunition when playing him. I remember his boss wanted to join me on a day's fishing."

"Yes, and not to mention the fact that, Nick caught these three trout within thirty minutes. Now if that wasn't bullshit enough!" remarked Mike.

"What do you mean, bullshit?" remarked Nick. Everyone laughed out loud.

"Hey, bullshit or skill, they all taste the same to me," said Bob with his plate out. "So pass them over Steve."

After dinner, everyone was seated around

a campfire enjoying a coffee. "Yes Steve. We'll go back up to that plateau first thing tomorrow morning to see why your radio didn't trip," said Nick. "And I'm curious to know what in the hell those aliens were up to with those briefcases. They sure as hell don't need any more babysitters."

"Maybe it's some kind of feed for those little critters in the pond. A growth accelerator or protein additive," suggested Bob, gazing into the fire.

Steve jested. "Yeah, maybe Crappy Tire had a sale on Miracle Grow!" Everyone chuckled. Nick, didn't understand the joke.

"Well, it's no different from fish farming where they feed them liver pellets," remarked Mike, stoking the fire with a long pole.

"So what are these things in the middle of these ponds?" asked Janis. Looking over the two aerial photos on her lap.

"Beaver houses," answered Nick.

"You mean you actually have beavers in Latvia?" asked Janis with a curious look.

"Oh yes, we have all kinds, even throughout the Russian Federation!"

"And do your beavers have legs?" asked Bob. Everyone laughed.

"What do you mean? Do they have legs?" Nick asked with a confused look.

Steve said. "Well, to some people, beaver means something else. And Bob's next question is probably, have you ever eaten beaver before Nick?"

"Oh yes, it actually tastes really good," he answered with a straight face. Still unaware of what Steve was referring to as everyone laughed even louder.

"I do not quite understand what you guys are laughing at," inquired Nick.

"This is what we sometimes call beaver," gestured Bob. He attempted to grab Janis's crotch, now a little intoxicated.

"Keep your hands to yourself," she responded, with an upset look.

"Okay. Okay now I get it!" he said with a red embarrassing smile.

"And you said you ate it Nick?" inquired Mike.

"Well, he wouldn't be a man if he didn't!" replied Steve, coming to his rescue.

"Yes. Breakfast of champions is what we call it in Canada, eh," said Bob. "So, are you a champion Nick?"

"Well, I am working on it."

"Now to be fair. I really think we should phone Brenda for her input on this matter."

Janis slapped Bob on the back of the head, while still studying the photos. "Sorry to interrupt this intelligent conversation boys, but for sure, these are two beaver ponds?"

"Yes, abandoned beaver ponds," answered Steve. "Because those lobsters or alien things like to eat beaver as well."

"Holy shit. Think of those ETs fly all around the galaxy in search of strange beaver to eat," blurted Mike.

"I bet they have a lineup for that job," responded Bob.

"Oh yes. And you'd probably be the first in line," said Janis. Looking up at him from her photo, with a disgusted look.

"That sounds like a Rod Stewart's song. 'Some Guys Have All The Luck,'" jested Steve.

"Okay guys. Let's get your minds out of the gutter for a minute and think about this situation here," urged Janis still studying the photos. "Now, do each of these beaver ponds have a beaver dam?'

"Well, the one in Latvia does," said Nick.

Janis asked. "Would it be possible to see a wider photo of this area Nick?"

"Sure," said Steve. "I'll get them in the cottage. Our pond has a beaver dam as well. On the east end of it."

"Steve, can you get the higher elevation for that one as well?" asked Nick.

"Sure Nick," said Steve. "We should view them in the gazebo, now that it's getting dark. Steve brought out the photos and laid them open on the gazebo table. They were all curious to see what Janis had in mind.

"All right Nick," said Janis with the two higher elevation photos in front of her. "Can you point out to me exactly where that beaver dam is located, on this pond in Latvia?"

"Yes, right about here," he said, as he pointed on the photo. "So if that beaver dam broke, my guess is that the water would flow down that creek and empty into that main river over here, which looks like only a half a kilometer away."

"Yes Janis, that's the Daugava River,"

Nick said.

"So where does this Daugava River run?"

"Oh my God," he said with a poker face. "It runs into the Baltic Sea close to Riga."

"So Steve, if our beaver dam was open. Where would that water run?" Janis asked.

"Well, it would run into Birch creek. You can see here where it connects into the Spanish River. Then it flows into Lake Huron."

"Holy shit, if those freakin' things get into the Great Lakes or the Baltic Sea, it would be catastrophic. Especially if they get to be as big as their babysitters. The world would be history," said Bob.

"Well it's funny that those aliens are using our waterways to their advantage. Almost the same way our early loggers did."

"Well Holy shit. That has to be their fuckin' plan then. To take the world by water. And let these creatures kill us off!" remarked Bob.

"Big time! Those creatures will do all the dirty work. Then they'll move right into a non-populated planet instead of nuking us, or any other destructive force. They chose a non-polluted, smart environmentally-friendly way of taking us out," said Steve.

"Big time, and Greenpeace would probably support their cause," responded Bob.

"Well Janis. I'm sure that's the common denominator, or the missing link Nick was looking for," said Steve.

"Thank God for that," said Mary.

"Yes," said Steve. "Our prayers were answered."

"That they were," confirmed Janis.

"I don't believe it," said Nick, rubbing his neck, starring at the photos. "All this time and we couldn't see it. Steve, I have to use your phone."

"Sure Nick. And ask the I.A.W. if they can pick up this month's phone bill too."

"Are you kidding? After I explain our theory to them. They'll shit their pants!" exclaimed Nick. He grabbed the cell phone, and quickly left the gazebo to make the call.

"Yes," said Janis. "It's just like those zebra mussels. They made their way up the St. Lawrence Seaway, then into the Great Lakes in Canada and the US. The aliens are doing the same, but in reverse."

"Yes," confirmed Mike. "But they'll spread even quicker because they're working their way down stream."

"Well, the government won't be worried about zebra mussels, if those creatures get into the waterways. That gun law eliminated over seventy-five percent of our firearms in this country. So how can we defend ourselves against those predators? And the I.A.W. believes that there are aliens living among us in human form. Well, my guess is, they're probably all working in government positions in Ottawa. That's why the aliens started that shit here. Because they must have heard that our military sucks."

Nick returned to the gazebo. "Well guys, the I.A.W. is now having an emergency conference call. They should be calling us back within an hour. Oh and Bob, the next time Janis speaks, just try listening to her." He smiled, as everyone laughed.

chapter 13

big time preparation

Sarah and Tom were back from Ottawa and in their apartment, both lying on their backs in bed, staring at the ceiling. "That was quite the time we had in Ottawa," said Sarah. "And it was really nice of your professor to have wined and dined us at such a high-class hotel."

"Yes, I'm really grateful for that. Especially, meeting scientists from all over the world. But it doesn't make sense to me. What's taking the professor so freakin' long to let me get started on my research? At this rate, it'll take me the whole summer to complete it. I'll lose my term!" Tom felt downhearted over the whole scenario.

Sarah could feel Tom's disappointment and knew how much this research meant to him. "Well, my parents aren't up for company, but we can still use the spare boat at the public dock and go around by water to a spot I know. We can easily access that pond over another ridge that my dad showed me years ago. We can tie up the boat, climb over the ridge and collect one more critter from that pond," she suggested.

"You don't mind?" said Tom, all fired up now.

"No, not at all. And we can have a picnic at Passion Bay afterwards."

"Oh shit Sarah! That would be just great. Because I'm going bonkers."

"I know. You're driving me fuckin' bonkers just listening to you."

"Oh shit. I can't thank you enough." He gave her a big hug and kiss.

"Yes, now that's the Tom I like to see. Now, promise me, that right after we get one of those critters, we're gonna have a picnic at Passion Bay before coming home."

"Right on Sarah! And you can wear that string bikini for me."

"Well, we'll see."

"'We'll see means yes, right? Yes, a double hitter. I get my specimen and I get to see a sexy specimen all in the same day!"

"Sorry Tom, but I don't like to be referred to as a specimen. As if I'm being studied under a microscope."

"No. I'll only be looking at you through my sunglasses." He hugged her then gently kissed her on the forehead.

"Well like I said, I'll pack it. But it'll depend on how well you behave, if I choose to wear it or not."

"Well Sarah. You are like sweet candy to me. Whether you choose to wear a wrapper or not. Although nice packaging does enhance the looks of sweet candy."

"Okay. That's enough Tom. Quit, while you're ahead!"

On a beautiful Birch Lake evening, the group of friends were waiting for their attack plans from the I.A.W. "So Nick. Did they ask you for your advice on the matter?"

"Yes Mike. I advised them on the fact that the aliens can break those dams at anytime. And that we should move on it now by first taking out all the babysitters over here and in Latvia. I feel that every time we knock off a babysitter, it somehow alarms the aliens. They have a tendency of showing up right after a kill. Maybe they have some kind of homing device built into them. That's the gut feeling I have. But like I said before, just when you think you have the son of a bitches figured out, they'll do the opposite. And as for my gut feeling. I think we should-"

Nick stopped speaking when the cell phone rang. "Oh probably that's the general," said Steve. He handed Nick the phone. "Here, go back up to the water tower for better reception."

Minutes went by without a word spoken. As the tension mounted, Steve broke the silence. "Well guys, I think this is going to be it. I'm going inside to grab us some cocktails."

"I'll help you," responded Bob. "I think I'll need one after Nick fills us in on his conversation with the general."

Minutes later, Steve and Bob returned with a large pitcher of some alcohol concoction. "Is Nick still on the phone?" asked Steve.

"No," said Mary. "I see him walking back now."

It was dead silence when Nick entered the gazebo. "Well friends, this is it." He laid the cell phone down on the table and sat down beside Steve. No one wanted to hear what his next words were going to be. There was no joking this time, as they all waited patiently for his news. "Well, it was unanimous with the I.A.W. In regards to disbursing those creatures into the world's waterways-first, they want to start by taking out all the babysitters, at the same time, in both countries."

"So, how do they plan on doing that Nick?" asked Steve.

"By bringing in an apache chopper."

"You've gotta be kidding Nick? There's no fuckin' way!" shouted Steve. "Don't they know? Just the heavy shock air-waves from their rotary blades alone would be enough to break that fragile beaver dam. Fuck that idea. I'll go in there alone. And pop those fuckers off by myself before I let some chopper jockey, who can't even I.D. a beaver dam from a hole in the ground. This is way too risky of a job for those kids."

"He's right Nick. And I'm with him a hundred percent!" remarked Bob. He reached over and patted Steve's back.

Mike looked up. "You can count on me too!"

Nick was stunned by the quick turn of events and stuck for words. "Well, I love all of you. And greatly respect your outdoor knowledge. But you have your loved ones to consider here."

"We are Nick. That's why we can't let those chopper jockeys fuck up. It's not only our families, it's the whole world we're talking about here," cautioned Steve. "And that beaver dam in Latvia would be just as fragile as ours. They're old and abandoned, which means they lack maintenance.

"Okay, point well taken then. All right, so we take out the babysitters!" said Nick. "Then how in the hell do we handle those frisky little creatures? And heaven forbid, if they are still not little!"

"With lime," said Steve.

"Lime?" asked Nick. "I don't understand what you mean."

"They must use lime in the making of concrete in Russia. It's used as an activator."

"Now that you mention it. I remember hearing something about lime in cement."

"Well, there's a little lake close to this one that was excellent for brook trout fishing. Until a type of fish called suckers took it over and out-numbered them five to one. So the natural resources department put lime in the water to raise it's ph level, which killed all the fish instantly. Within a year or so, the ph level came back down to it's proper level. Then they restocked it with fingerling trout. And within four to five years, that lake was rehabilitated big time!"

"This makes a lot of sense to me," agreed Nick. "But how would the ministry get this lime into that pond when there are no roads anywhere near there?"

"They could mix it into a liquid slurry. And use one of those water bombers that they use for forest fires to fly over that pond, and dump her in."

"Okay, I understand now Steve. That would be the smarter and easier route to go then."

"And it's also environmentally friendly," added Bob.

"Like I told the I.A.W. That is why you guys are best for this job," said Nick.

"Yes Nick. And remember what Johnny-be-good said. Anything, anytime," said Janis, with a sexy smile.

"Anything, anytime? Oh, I think Johnny likes you Nick," said Bob.

"Okay guys, you can knock it off now," he said with a smirk. "Now are you sure this is this the route you guys want to go?"

"Yes! said Steve.

"I'm in!" replied Mike.

"Me too!" agreed Bob

"Okay. Then we'll have to put a plan of attack together. I'll explain to the I.A.W. what you shared with me Steve about our plan here. I'll strongly recommend that they do the same in Latvia, using lime," confirmed Nick.

"I'm sure that our ministry can work with the Latvian and Russian biologists to assist them with the lime treatment, if they don't already know," recommended Steve.

"Okay then," said Nick, sitting down in front of the aerial maps. The girls silently observed them.   "This is going to be the plan. We need one man stationed here." He pointed to a higher position, just south of the beaver dam. It's just in case those aliens try to break the dam before we take them out."

"Okay Nick. That makes sense to me. But why not have him approach on the north side?" suggested Steve.

"Because the sun will be at his back that way. And won't be a blinding glare in his scope."

"Oh shit! I should of known better to ask a dumb question like that," said Steve. "Military fighting has always used the sun for advantage. Even in Roman times."

"Okay Steve, just let Nick explain the game plan first. Then we can ask questions later," said Mike.

"All right. I'm sorry," he said holding up his right hand. "But, just one more thing I'd like to add here. A guy can get there with a four-wheeler by driving around our old hunting trail that leads to where that dried-up creek enters into this lake. After that, it's not even a two-minute walk up to that spot. And he'll still have the sun behind him."

"Good thinking," nodded Nick.

"Yes Steve. I've pushed a few deer out to you from that end before," remarked Bob.

"So Bob. Would you mind then taking up that position?" asked Nick.

"No, not at all. There's a huge uprooted poplar, just to the right of that dam. It would give me good cover, but I would have to bring my bike over."

"Mike, since you are so up with that computer and telescope, how about monitoring our attack. Have the I.A.W. send us a satellite photo every five minutes so you can keep us up on any activity up on that plateau, or in the pond. And don't forget, we'll all have our radios," instructed Nick.

"Sure," said Mike. "So I guess only you three are going to have all the fun."

"Mike, for God's sake. We're all a team here," said Steve.

"So what in hell do us girls do then?" inquired Janis.

"What do they call those babysitters in

Russian again Nick?" asked Steve.

"We call them NYANYAS"

"Well, you girls can go to that general store in Webbwood and buy lots of butter and garlic, and wine. You've heard of a lobster fest? Well, we're gonna have the world's first NYANYA Fest," said Steve.

"Yes. And the taste should be out of this world!" punned Bob.

"You mean they're to die for!" jested Mike

"Whoa. Lets hope that it's not the way that sounds," remarked Steve.

"I don't believe what I'm hearing. You guys are about to take on real critical tasks and all you can do is joke about it," said Mary.

"I don't think Steve's joking," said Nick. "His gesture is a positive one. He's planning our victory party. Just like sport teams do before they leave their dressing room," remarked Nick. "You girls can be our communicating link. You will have a list of phone numbers for air and ground support."

"Now just hold on there for one minute Nick. Could you please fill us in a little more on this land and air backup stuff," said Carol

"Sure. Remember the I.A.W. brought in some high-tech combat aircraft in case we need some help?"

"Yes, but can you be a little more specific."

"Sure Carol. There are six US, F twenty-two Raptors, each carrying ten tons of ordnance. That is rockets included. As well as four apache choppers. With a response time of five minutes from here."

"Only five minutes away!" remarked Bob.

"Well, that is after take-off at a supersonic speed of 1,500 kilometers per hour. The ETA from that Elliot Lake airport would only be five minutes at most. Personally, I think they could have used a more medium combat aircraft like the Russian MIG twenty-seven."

"Now that's being specific," said Steve. "But Nick. I sense a little jealousy with those US Raptors."

"No. Not at all Steve."

"What I meant was that the Russian MIG twenty-seven has a dual role design. Outfitted for both air-to-ground, and air-to-air and possessing a greater resistance to hostile action."

Bob remarked. "Well it really sounds like Nick knows his planes," impressed over Nick's knowledge.

"So you mean to tell us that those fighter planes and choppers are sitting at the Elliot Lake airport as we speak? Not to say that it wasn't a smart choice since they're almost due west of us, as the crow flies. Elliot Lake became a retirement community after the mines closed so the air traffic must be next to none."

"That's why the I.A.W. chose it Bob. It seems that the biggest resistance that the I.A.W. or the UN got was from the mayor."

"The mayor?" asked Mike.

"No shit! I thought you guys were following this on the news," said Steve.

"Apparently his shorts are in a big knot over those heavily armed aircraft parked at his airport. He was playing with the media to his advantage, demanding an immediate explanation in regards to this matter, which sounds to me like a smart move on his part," remarked Nick.

"After all it is a municipal airport," said Mike.

"Oh, you're right. But just watch and see how fast the UN will charm those knotted shorts off of him!" jested Nick. "And let's not forget your natural resources ministry for air backup. We'll need them for that water bomber. As for the ground support, your army will strategically position a specialty task force around this lake."

"A specialty task force! I can just imagine!" said Steve.

"Oh, come on Steve! Lighten-up and give the one or two dozen troops a chance!" said Bob as they all laughed.

"So how about you working with Mike, Carol?" advised Nick. "That way, we will have a direct phone line."

"Not to say that the cell phone won't work," said Janis.

"Smart thinking again Janis. Not only serving as a back-up line, but we won't tie up the phone line," acknowledged Nick. "Remember Bob," he pointed his finger at him."

"Yes I'm listening to her," replied Bob with a smile.

"Now, I'm going to phone the I.A.W. and give them the low down," said Nick.

"And then, I would like to give Steve and Bob a crash course on firearms, up in the woodshed."

"Sure Nick, I'll get them ready," said Bob.

"Come to think of it. There are a few mice in there that we can use for practice."

"You're a real joker Steve!" said Nick, as he shook his head with a big smile, walking out to make the call.

"Here we go again. More deliberation," replied Bob.

"Well, we may as well just stay put, 'til we find out what the verdict is gonna be," suggested Mary.

After another lengthy phone call, Nick returned to the gazebo. Everyone was patiently waiting. "So what's the verdict?" asked Steve.

"Well, it took a lot of convincing for the I.A.W. to agree, since you guys are civilians. But you're in a strategic position. And they were impressed with a combination of things. Like Janis figuring out how the aliens were going to use the waterways, and Mike's surveillance and photos, also Steve's lime idea with the water bomber really impressed them. So they will be right on our heels tomorrow. If anything goes wrong, we can call them right away and that chopper jockey will be only five minutes away. In sixty minutes, the I.A.W. plans on striking the pond in Latvia. And we will follow the same plan here tomorrow morning. I will have their results in three hours from now."

"Holy shit! I forgot to take the time difference into consideration. So we'll know if we have to make any changes in our plan, pending their outcome," remarked Bob.

"That's right Bob. And things just might get a little crazy around here."

"What exactly do you mean by that?" asked Steve.

"Remember, those aliens seem to always show up right after one of their babysitters is terminated," Nick cautioned with everyone listening intently.

"Well then, let's go and set the stage for tomorrow's show!" urged Steve with excitement, as though it was the night before the opening of deer season.

Nick and the boys were in the woodshed.

While the guys were assembling their rifles, Nick was carefully looking through a Sports Illustrated swimsuit calendar above the tool bench. "Okay Nick. Stop checking out the chicks. And help us get the guns assembled," insisted Steve.

"I'm not checking out the chicks. I'm just seeing what day next month I'll be retiring."

"Sure, sure. Then, why in the hell are you looking at the month of November?" asked Steve.

"Oh Nick, you naughty boy! I'm afraid Steve has caught you with your hand in the cookie jar," said Mike.

"That's Steve's menu you're looking at," remarked Bob.

"Menu?" asked Nick with a curious look.

Bob said. "Yes, Mary lets him check out that menu every now and then. But he has to come home to eat," as the guys chuckled.

"Ha, ha!" said Steve in a sarcastic tone. "And that's why hunters make better lovers."

"We go into the bush deeper!" said Mike.

"Okay Nick. I think I got this scope on right."

"That's right Steve. Now bring that rifle up to your shoulder. And point it at Miss June."

"Holy shit! This scope has a built-in auto focus," said Steve.

"Now you see that dot in the middle?"

"You mean her navel?"

"No, you idiot! I mean on the scope!" said Nick.

"Oh, I'm just kidding," replied Steve.

"Well, that dot is sighted right on. Up to two kilometers."

"You've got to be kidding me!" said Bob.

"No, that gun has no trajectory. That power head bullet, or projectile flies flat, and straight as a laser. And at night, that dot projects a red laser beam as well."

"Yes, it's similar to a quick point scope that some hunters use up here," indicated Bob now pointing his rifle.

"And talk about balance! " remarked Bob. "I bet this puppy kicks like a mule. It would probably take my shoulder off!"

"That's not so," said Nick chuckling. "Its recoil is not anymore than one of your thirty caliber sporting rifles."

"Holy shit! If we can eliminate those explosive tips off the bullets. This would make for one hell of a deer rifle!" said Bob.

"Yes. The governments are keeping these prototypes low key. They are worried about terrorists getting their hands on them," indicated Nick.

"I can see why!" said Steve. "I would have felt a hell of a lot safer having the company of this puppy earlier on the plateau.

"I hear you Steve. But I was given strict orders. That these guns were not to be used without proper instruction. How do you think I felt down at the pond?"

"Now can we carry this rocket launcher out on the front rack of your bike Steve?"

"Sure. It could sit sideways, right beside the gun rack with a couple of those heavy-duty bungee cords to hold her down. And those extra rockets should fit nicely inside that storage compartment, behind the passenger seat. Well guys, it would be a real joke just to see the expression on a conservation officer's face if he decided to stop us, being equipped like this," said Steve. "So, are you guys thinking what I'm thinking?"

"Yeah," answered Mike. "Maybe after all this shit is over with. Poor Johnny-be-good would just shit his pants!"

"That's right," said Bob. "And his boss would never believe his story. And I don't think we would ever see his ass around Birch Lake again! That sounds like a plan."

"Okay guys. Put a lid on it for a while. Now pay close attention," instructed Nick. He opened a plastic molded case carrying the rocket launcher. "Now this is loaded in the same way, like a single shot shotgun. Watch closely," he demonstrated, as he picked it out from the case. "Now you just push this little lever here. Just in front of the trigger guard. It will now allow you to break open the action. You slide one of these mini rockets down this cylinder like this. And you close the action. Bring it up to your shoulder. Then aim and fire away. And if your target puts out any kind of heat at all, then, these warheads have a built in heat sensor. And it will follow that target, halfway around the world, at the speed of six thousand meters per second. Now does that help you to understand what you are playing with fellows?"

"Yes Nick, big time!" exclaimed Steve.

"Other than the radios, I don't think we need to bring along anything else," advised Nick.

"Not even a few grenades?" asked Bob.

"No," said Nick. "I think we have enough fire power. You may as well take a radio now Mike. You'll need it for tomorrow when you are monitoring us."

"Right on Nick. Well okay then. Let's go back to the gazebo and join the girls."

"I am sure they are missing us," said Nick.

"Like a sore ass!" replied Steve.

"It sure sounds like you boys were having a good time up there," said Mary.

"We just had to educate Nick on a few things regarding women," said Steve.

"Ha!" remarked Mary with a big smile. "I think you got that the other way around!"

"Okay. Let's not go there," said Steve.

"Looks like the stage is all set now. And we should all be back here celebrating around eleven a.m. tomorrow," said Steve.

"Well, I don't want to sound negative, but the weather will also play a big part in tomorrow's outcome. We'll need clear skies for our aerial photos," said Nick.

"Well, in World War Two, the US third army had been driving back the Nazis, until fog and rain forced the troops to stop. General George Patton phoned a chaplain to ask if he had a good prayer for weather. This prayer was printed and distributed to the quarter-million soldiers under his command directing them to pray for clear weather," said Steve. He stood up from his chair. "And now for our battle. Would you guys mind if I lead us in a prayer?"

Everyone knew how serious Steve was at this moment. And they also understood how important it was. To all bond as one.

"You couldn't have picked a better time," said Nick standing up with the others.

"Dear Heavenly Father. You know what we're up against at this time. And we ask that you give us clear skies, strength, and wisdom on how to terminate these unearthly things from our planet. And we thank you for answering our last prayer. In Jesus's name. Amen."

"Amen to that!" answered Bob in a loud positive tone.

"Well then. Let's have a toast to the Lord," said Mike holding his glass up high.

"How do you say that toast in Russian?" asked Steve.

"Dieboursia," replied Nick.

"Okay. Dieboursia!" said everyone, as they all toasted together.

"I feel like I'm at the last supper, when Jesus raised his cup to his Father in heaven," said Bob.

"Well, it was a little different. But we are sacrificing ourselves in this battle with those aliens, for all our fellow man," said Steve.

"You know, it's amazing how history has a way of repeating itself. And that was a real inspiring story about General Patton, Steve," responded Mike. "Sometimes I find it hard to believe that you're a believer."

"Well Mike, we're all sinners. But it's what's in our hearts, that the Big Guy sees."

"I have to admit it Steve, you do have a big, loving heart. That's for sure," said Bob, patting Steve on the shoulder.

"Now just hold on there Bob. I never said I loved you. But I do like you now and then. Especially when you open me a cold beer," jested Steve, as everyone chuckled.

"I'd like to call it an early night. Because tomorrow's a big day," said Mike.

"Are you sure? Because I'm going to bring out some munchies," said Mary.

"No Mary, don't bother. We'll have to do the same," said Bob.

"I guess that goes for all of us," said Mary.

"Now, that is the spirit!" remarked Nick. He picked up his glass to finish the last of his drink.

"Would anyone like one more for the road?"

"No thanks Steve," said Bob. "But you should've offered us one for the lake instead. Just to be politically correct."

"Politically correct my ass then Bob!" blurted Steve.

"No way. That would be way too much

politics," said Bob.

"So Bob, I will meet you and Janis here tomorrow morning at six-thirty, when you bring your bike over. And don't forget your rifle and radio in the woodshed next to the tool bench."

"And try not to sleep in Bob!" teased Steve.

"Are you kidding me? I wouldn't miss this for the world!" said Bob with a smile.

"Oh, that reminds me, can you girls take shifts on monitoring that UFO landing spot tonight? Brenda at her computer, and Janis, can you share with Carol?" asked Nick.

"Sure, I'm game for that," answered Janis. "And I'll take any shift."

"And feel free to phone us if we have to make any last minute change of plans Nick."

"Let's hope not. So everybody can get a good night's rest. And hopefully, all this shit will be behind us."

"Are you kidding me Nick? It's this kind of shit that keeps us motivated. There's always something happening at Birch Lake," indicated Steve.

"That's for sure!" said Bob.

"Only at Birch Lake!" said the guys, all at the same time.

"So Bob, don't forget to wear your camouflage army fatigues tomorrow," advised Steve.

"Don't worry Steve. I'll put them out for him," said Janis.

"Why do you embarrass me in front of my friends, Janis?"

"Well, it's true. I have to be like a mother for you!"

"Okay. Okay, that's enough!" he said. Everybody laughed, while leaving the gazebo. They all headed down to the dock.

"Wow!" expressed Steve. "Those northern lights are out again."

"Like we talked about before," said Mike, "people travel from hundreds of miles away, just to see them."

"Yes, and even other galaxies," remarked Bob.

"Unfortunately, I don't think we want to share what we have with those aliens," remarked Nick, as he untied Brenda's boat.

"Well, good night guys," said Janis, Carol and Mike, as Bob started up their outboard.

Bob said. "So thanks again. We had a great time. We'll see you in the morning," departing with his crew.

"And that goes for me too," said Nick, as he departed.

Steve and Mary stood hand in hand at the end of their dock, appreciating this time they had together as they watched their friends drive off at a distance. Each thinking, "Could this be their last time together!"

"Steve, tell me the truth. How have you been feeling lately?"

"Good Mary."

"Well, that was a dumb question I asked you. Because I know that even if you were getting more chest pains, you would deny it just so you could tend to more important matters, like saving this world," she said as large tears began to run down her face.

Steve took her in his arms to comfort her. Then, gently patted her on the back, while he gazed up at the stars. "No sweetheart. They won't be handing us a Nobel Peace Prize for this event. And it won't be recorded in history. But one thing is for sure, we'll be able to look at ourselves in the mirror each morning. And thank the Lord for what we have done here to make this planet a safer place for everyone to live. And our biggest acknowledgement will be from Him." He embraced and kissed her as if it was their last evening together.

Standing on the dock, in each other's arms, they remained lost in that moment. The sound of loons could be heard crying from a distance over the calm water.

chapter 14

john's shift begins

At five-thirty a.m., John headed to work hauling his boat behind his half-ton. Like every workday morning, he had the ritual of picking up a coffee at a local highway drive through. Approaching the coffee shop, he couldn't help but notice a military convoy parked in front. He pulled up to the drive through window. A cheery young woman held out his coffee, "You're quick this morning," said John, reaching out. "With all those soldiers, I didn't think you would have any coffee left. Or that it would be a battle just to get served."

"That's a good pun John," she smiled. "They just showed up out of the blue.

Apparently, they are on some kind of training north of Webbwood. Isn't that where you're stationed?"

"Yes," replied John, glancing back in his rear-view mirror. He was confused and surprised as to why his office failed to inform him of military training going on in his area. Or could she be mistaken? "Hmm," he said as he grabbed his coffee and paid.

"Well, have a good day John. Don't get too much sun today!"

"Oh no, not you too!" he replied smiling, while driving away. With his window still down, he pulled up and parked behind one of the army trucks. A dozen or so soldiers stood around. Some stretched while others sipped their coffee and had a smoke break. "And I thought we were the only ones working this early," commented a soldier.

"Are you kidding? We have our share of long shifts as well," replied John, "but from the looks of your toys, your jobs seems a little more comfortable."

"Oh yeah?" remarked another soldier sitting on the tailgate. "Our jobs take us through thick-wooded areas with tons of black flies and mosquitoes. Not to mention wading up to our necks in leech-infested, loon-shit swamps while you cruise around a lake in a boat checking out chicks in string bikinis taking sun."

"Sure, sure!" responded John with a smile. "I get that story every day. I guess the grass would appear somewhat greener from where you're coming from. Believe me, those fringe benefits of chicks in strings don't come along too often."

"You mean not often enough," joked another soldier stepping forward and placing his coffee on the hood of John's half-ton. He lit up a cigarette.

"So I understand that you guys are on some kind of training just northwest of here."

"Training?" remarked the soldier. "More like some kind of weird standby. Who knows?" He shrugged his shoulders, taking a drag from his cigarette. John couldn't help but notice his ammo belt loaded with live rounds.

"Excuse me sir," came a loud, stern voice approaching John from his side-view mirror. Suddenly, all the soldiers stood at attention. "Is there anything I can help you with sir?" said a tall, elderly soldier with a thick mustache and beady eyes.

John was certain that this had to be the warrant officer of this infantry unit. "It's not too often we have a convoy pass through this area."

"We're up here for some practice drills, like war games."

Judging by the officer's quick response and "by the book" approach, John knew he would never exchange any information. "Have a good day men!" He gave a small wave from his steering wheel and drove off. Glancing back in his rear-view mirror, John was surprised to see the officer intently watching him.

It was six a.m. when Nick and Brenda arrived at Steve's dock. "Glad to see you up," Nick said to Steve.

"Well, to tell you the truth, I've been up for the past two hours. I just couldn't sleep." He helped them tie the boat to the dock. "I topped off the bikes with fuel and got all the hardware ready."

"There's nothing wrong with being organized Steve. Remind me some time to share some old army stories with you about not being organized."

"I bet they're very embarrassing," he remarked.

"More than that," he said with a sly smirk.

"Just make sure that I'm around when you share these stories Nick," responded Brenda.

"Well, maybe for some of them."

"Oh, don't tell me that they have this guy thing going on in Russia as well!"

"Is that what they call it?" asked Nick still smiling. He reached over the boat railing to grab his satchel. "I plan on taking a dip this afternoon."

"I thought maybe you two would be power drinking tonight and you'd spend the night."

"Maybe after this assignment is over. That power drink will really sound good then," said Nick, throwing the satchel strap over his shoulder, making their way up the dock.

They entered the gazebo to find Mary waiting with a thermos of coffee, the radio on low, tuned to a local station. "Can I pour you two a coffee?"

" Yes thanks, Mary," answered Brenda,

as they sat around the table.

They heard a boat pulling up to the dock. "I see Bob and Janis are a few minutes early as well," remarked Steve.

"So did you guys sleep well?" asked Mary.

"I got a few hours. Janis took over the end of my monitoring shift, so I could join Nick over here today."

"Oh that was nice of her," she responded.

"Steve, you really look like a soldier in those camo fatigues," remarked Brenda.

"Yes," added Mary. "I like a man in uniform. I think it's sexy on him."

"Right. In that case I'll never take them off. As long as she doesn't call me "GI Joe" again," shaking his head with a big smirk, rolling back his eyes. Everyone chuckled at his comment and facial expression.

"It sounds to me like I missed a good funny," said Bob entering the gazebo with Janis.

"That you did Bob," said Brenda. "Thanks again Janis for relieving me on monitor duty."

"Oh it was nothing," said Janis, yawning. "Carol and Mike are monitoring now."

"It looks like we're all dressed to kill. And how is GI Joe this morning?" asked Bob looking down at Steve.

"Oh please. Don't you start now," urged Steve. "Or I'll call you GI mini-me," as everyone laughed again.

"Your timing was perfect Bob," said Mary pouring him a coffee.

"Well, I still have to unload by bike. But I'll have this coffee first," replied Bob, sitting down to join them. "I passed by our friendly C.O. just a few minutes ago on the lake, and he actually waved to me with a big smile."

"Oh shit Nick. You have to let him do a cameo on your fishing show," remarked Steve.

"Right. I was talking to his boss at around five a.m. They have the water bomber filled, and they're waiting for our call. Apparently, there is a large forest fire out of control north of us. They want it back ASAP. And they did give Latvia that formula to kill their little critters in their pond last night. It's called rotenone or something like that."

"So everything went well in Latvia last night Nick?" asked Steve.

"Oh yes! They've terminated the NYANYAS without a glitch."

"That's good news," said Mary.

"Yes, too good. There has been no resistance from those aliens so far."

"That's great Nick. And it's nice of those aliens to let us have the night off," remarked Steve.

"Yes, maybe they're on their days off back at their planet. Or their boss doesn't want to pay them overtime," added Bob.

"Well guys, this is the plan," instructed Nick. He pulled out an aerial photo from his satchel and rolled it out on the table. "Bob. We'll give you a fifteen minute head start, in front of our departure time to get to this location," pointing to the high spot, just to the right of the beaver dam.

"Thanks for the advance time. There will likely be some windfall trees crossing that old trail that I'll have to drive around.

"And Steve, I would like you to drive around to the north-easterly end, over here."

"Okay then. I'll have to drive up to that

plateau, close to where those aliens landed and walk down to the pond from their
trail. It's a lot shorter."

"That's right," confirmed Nick. "Not
too far from the UFO landing area, then
Mike will be able to have a visual on you
as well."

"Smart thinking Nick," said Steve.

"That's why the Russian army pays
him the big bucks," remarked Bob.

"Big bucks?" he responded, with a
smirk. "I wish. So Steve, your position on
that pond should be right here, just inside
the tree line, yet high enough to get a
good shot. And I'll drive to the tree stand
and walk down that ridge to the pond at
this end," he said, pointing it out with the
handle of a teaspoon.

"It sounds to me, like where you're
going to be is where those NYANYAS or
babysitters seem to hang around. It'll be
just be like shooting fish in a barrel,"
remarked Steve."

"I'm sure Nick will get the lion's share.
And I see he also has us at a higher contour."

"Well Bob, he has to make sure that we
civilians keep out of the crossfire," cau-

tioned Steve with a poker face.

"That is a good evaluation. I'm sorry Steve, but that's the way it has to be," Nick concluded.

"Don't be. After all, this is your job, and I'm honored to be out there with you."

"That goes for me too" said Bob toasting his coffee cup with them.

"That's the part that troubles me most," Nick revealed. "Having you guys doubt my tactics."

"Are you kidding? No problem Nick. After all, you're the veteran alien hunter. And we're just the greenhorns," answered Bob.

"When we get greenhorns hunting with us, we make them dog," said Steve.

"Dog?" Nick asked.

"Yes. We'd make them run through an area like that cedar swamp," said Steve. "And make them bark like a dog every minute or so, to move the deer in our direction."

"I get it," he replied, "but I wouldn't dare try that tactic with those NYANYAS."

"No. And I don't think you could get anyone who'd volunteer to dog for you either!" added Bob.

"No. Not unless they have some kind of death wish or something!" responded Steve, as they all chuckled. "Okay then. I have my rifle, and that rocket launcher loaded on my bike. And your rifle is on your bike Nick."

Just then, the seven o'clock news came over the radio and everyone quieted down. "In local news," said the announcer, "the UN will be training fighter pilots for practice on terrorist attacks. They have leased the Elliot Late airport for the next month. This information was received after the mayor and council demanded an explanation as to why the UN planes were ordered there..."

"You see what I mean? They have their ways of covering up. And now the mayor can feel more comfortable over this big ordeal," remarked Nick.

"You mean he can feel more comfortable with that big knot now out of his shorts!" jested Steve. Bob chocked on his coffee, trying to stop laughing as Janis patted his back.

"That's better," said Bob as he caught his breath. "Your jokes are gonna kill me

Steve!"

"Bob, don't forget when you leave, your rifle is leaning against my tool bench with a radio and fifty extra rounds. And your radio is on your bike seat Nick."

"Thanks Steve. Okay guys, let's synchronize our watches. I have seven-ten."

"I'm just off by two minutes," said Bob, making an adjustment.

Steve then took his radio out of his pocket and held it up to his mouth. "How about you Mickey Boy? Have you got your ears on?"

"Ten-four GI Joe," he answered, as everyone laughed.

"You bastards!" he said with a smile. "How in hell did he know?"

"That's our secret," answered Bob.

"Okay smart ass. My watch says seven-twelve. How does yours compare Mike?"

"That's a big ten-four good buddy!"

"Yes. I like good buddy better than GI Joe...Over"

"Whatever makes you happy Steve. And with that clear blue sky, I see that the Big Guy answered your prayers."

"You mean our prayers Mike."

"Yes. That's a big ten-four correction

there, good buddy."

"Okay motormouth. Bob will be departing soon. Just keep your ears on. Over and out. Holy shit. He's like a kid with a new toy!" said Steve to the others.

"Oh, lighten up a little! He's just having fun," said Mary.

"Yeah. You're probably right. I'm sorry, maybe I'm too tense."

"Yeah. I think we all are!" replied Bob. Tom and Sarah were in the process of crossing the lake, with Tom operating the outboard and Sarah guiding. "Is that your cottage over on that far shore?" Tom asked.

"Yes. And there's a couple of boats there."

"They must of partied last night and ended up crashing there," remarked Tom.

"You mean too much power drinking. But they're too busy to see me!" responded Sarah, in a bitter tone.

Tom could feel her emotions. He too had trouble understanding why her parents had been keeping their distance, considering their closeness. "Oh Sarah, don't think the worst. I know they really love you. They probably have a good reason."

"Well, I sure as hell hope so...Okay Tom, now stay along this shore. It's just up ahead," she said pointing her finger.

"Holy shit Sarah. You don't expect us to climb that hill?" remarked Tom. He was discouraged, gazing up at the steep bluff.

"No. But bring us closer to the right of that ridge." They followed the shoreline for another minute. "Okay now, slow down," she cautioned.

He slowed the boat down to a crawl close to the shoreline. It suddenly became very shallow. "Aren't you worried about the prop touching bottom?" He could only make out a foot or so of water under the boat.

"Okay. Turn it off now and tilt up the motor." she said in a quick tone, looking over the side into the clear calm water.

"Excuse me Sarah. But what in the hell are you looking for?" somewhat confused.

"Just be patient Tom! Okay, now look down."

Looking into the shallow clear water, he could see a bunch of heart shaped indentations on the bottom of the lake. All with the same type of pattern. "What in hell are those imprints from?"

"Deer tracks. This is where they enter and exit the lake, when they swim across over to that island. This is their escape route from the top of this ridge. My dad calls it the 'back door' because a lot of deer would sneak off on him when he hunted this high ridge. The deer trail starts here, and follows up along this hill, right up to the top."

"Wow. That's incredible Sarah! So how in the hell did your dad ever discover this?"

"It was really by accident. When my dad and I were fishing one day, we saw a deer swim over from that island, and cross over to here. He made me promise him that I would never tell anyone about this trail. Especially his hunting buddies."

"You're kidding me!"

"No," she remarked. "It's kind of like a card up his sleeve. It helps him to be the better hunter over Bob and Mike. I think it's a guy thing."

"Okay. I got you now Sarah. So, we tie the boat up here?"

"That's right. Now remember Tom, we are in and out of here!"

"Sure. I just need one of those crustacean things and I'll be more than happy," he reassured her, as he threw a small satchel over his shoulders.

"You're really going to like the view from up on the bluff," she remarked as she started walking ahead of him up the steep trail. He followed right behind her, checking out her ass in her short shorts.

"I'm already enjoying the view."

"Just remember. If you're a good boy, I'll wear my string on the beach."

"In that case, your wish is my command!"

Carol was pouring Mike a coffee as he sat in front of his monitor. Bringing it over to him, she noticed a flickering reflection on the lake, right in line with the high plateau above the area they were monitoring.

"Ah Mike... there's some kind of flickering glare on the lake. And it's right in line with our observation point," she said, as she set his coffee down beside him.

"I have another incoming aerial photo

from the I.A.W. And Nick wants us to keep him up-dated on them, if we see anything different. We have no action on the monitor. It's probably just the glare off an aluminum boat fishing there or something. But if it helps your curiosity, then bring that telescope down a few clicks and you'll have a full view."

"This one?" she asked, as she grabbed a locking knob.

"Yes, now just one turn counter-clockwise," he said, while sipping his coffee. Still sitting in front of the monitor, "now, you see that lever in front of you?"

"Yes."

"Pry it up gently until you can see your image. And I'll be able to see it on my monitor as well." As she brought the scope down to the water level, he could now make out an empty aluminum boat.

"Okay, hold it right there, Carol. Now, lock that first knob, one turn clockwise. Okay, come on over here, and join me with your coffee."

"All right, but let me top it off first."

"Sure Carol, take your time," he said, checking out his monitor. "The action won't start for another good hour. I'll just lower this contrast a little. Ha, that's funny!" he remarked.

"What do you mean?" she asked, pulling up a chair beside him with her coffee.

"Hmm. That's strange. No one's in the boat."

"Well, maybe they're lying on the bottom having a quickie," she said with a smile.

"No. Because you would see a wake on that calm water. Look how still it is with the motor tilted up and the bow rope tied to a tree."

"Maybe someone is berry picking," she suggested.

"Berries won't be ready for another five or six weeks. And besides, there's no way anyone can access that high ridge from there. Huh, come to think of it, it looks like one of Steve's boats. The one he keeps for Sarah at his dock at the public boat launch. Let me zoom in a little more. Okay. That's Steve's. Check out that sticker of that bass logo on the back of the transom. You see how it's half tore off. He did that backing up onto on our dock one night, a couple of years ago."

"Yes. The night you didn't have our dock light on. Well, are you going to radio him, and let him know?"

"Eh? I don't think we should bother them right now. Remember he called me a motormouth," he remarked feeling humble.

"Well, you were talking too long."

"Do you really think so?" he asked. He took another swig of his coffee, while staring at the monitor.

"Yes!"

"I'll make sure I'm not long-winded this time," he promised. He picked up his radio, and brought it up to his mouth. "Okay Carol, you're my witness," he insisted staring into her eyes.

"Okay Mike. If that's what it takes for you to make that call."

Everyone was down at Steve's dock to help Bob unload his bike. "I told you guys, if I can load it by myself, I can unload it just as easy," Bob said driving the bike off his boat and onto the dock.

"Okay Bob. But we came down just in case," replied Steve.

A call came over the radio. "Come in

GI Joe. Do you have your ears on?"

"Oh shit. Not him again." said Steve, with a disgusted look. He pulled the radio out of his pocket, and brought it up to his mouth. "Yes, go ahead."

"Well Steve, you might find this hard to believe. But one of your boats is tied up along the shoreline directly in line with that lookout bluff."

"Is that a positive ID Mike?"

"Yes Steve. Your half-ass, or half-bass sticker is on my monitor right now."

"How long has it been there Mike?"

"We don't know Steve."

"Carol noticed it there six minutes ago."

Steve stood there, deep in meditation, taking a few deep breaths. Everyone stared at him in wonder.

"Well Steve, do you read me...Over?"

"Ten-four Mike. Put your telescope back up on that plateau. And keep me posted. Do you read me?" speaking in a strong dominating tone.

"Ten-four," replied Mike.

"What is it Steve?" asked Mary, knowing quite well that something was wrong.

He couldn't hold back his emotions

anymore, fearing the worst for Sarah. Not moving a muscle, with the radio still held up to his mouth, he stood there as if to be in some kind of trance. "It's the back door," he said in a trembling voice. He tilted his head back, and muttered out, "Oh God, help us."

Confused and concerned over Steve's emotional state, she grabbed him by his wrist, and softly spoke. "Steve, what back door are you talking about?"

"The back door is a deer trail. That runs alongside that hill to get up to that plateau. It starts right where my boat is tied. And the only two people that know about it is me and Sarah."

"Oh my God!" shrieked Mary. She fell to her knees with her hands covering her face. "No! No! Not our Sarah!" she cried out. "They'll kill her...Please help her!"

"We're moving out now!" yelled Steve. He jumped on Bob's passenger seat. "Drop me off at my bike in the wood-shed!" he shouted in a frantic voice.

"Go Bob go! And I'll fill Mike in on my radio as to what has happened," replied Nick. He looked down at Mary weeping, as Brenda and Janis tried to comfort her.

"Brenda, get her up to the cottage. And keep your radio close," he instructed. Then he ran up the dock to join Steve in the woodshed.

By the time he got up to the woodshed, Steve was on his bike ready to go. Bob had already headed off on his bike at a fast pace, to get himself in position for the confrontation.

Nick knew that there was no stopping or slowing him down at this point. He just wanted to make sure that they could still carry out the mission. "Okay Steve. If your daughter is not up there yet, our plan is still on. Just give me one minute to notify the I.A.W. I'll be right behind you!"

"Okay Nick. See you there!" he yelled, as he speeded off on his bike.

Just then, a voice came over Nick's radio. "Come in Nick."

"Yes. Go ahead Mike."

"We have a visual. It's Steve's daughter up there. Wearing a yellow windbreaker. And her boyfriend Tom is carrying a pack. They just went over the plateau in the direction of the pond. We can just see a little of them now."

"Oh shit!" blurted Nick. "I have to

leave now. I'm sure Steve heard you Mike. His radio is on in his pocket. Steve and Bob, if you guys can hear me, I'm heading over to my position now!" as he climbed on his bike. He knew how critical every second was. His call to the I.A.W. would just have to wait.

Sarah and Tom were now up past the plateau, about twenty feet from the UFO landing area. "Yes Sarah. I can't believe the view from up here!" trying to catch his breath with his hands on his hips. "I'm sorry that I didn't bring my digital."

"There'll always be the next time," she replied.

"I hope we won't have to take that way up again!"

"Are you kidding? We'll take the bikes up this trail the next time."

"Now that's a pretty steep hill going down to that pond!"

"You city-slicker. It's a lot easier if we just stay on the bike trail."

"I can see that. I sure as hell wouldn't want to fall down there!" looking over the rock bluff towards the pond. "Aren't you hot with that windbreaker on?"

"Yeah, I think I'll take it off now. I guess you have no room in that knapsack?"

"Not really Sarah. Just leave your jacket here."

"You're right. We'll be back this way in thirty minutes or so," she said dropping her jacket on a large rock. "Is there any chance, I can get a drink from you?"

He turned his back to her, "Sure, I think it's in the bottom pocket."

After fidgeting with the zipper for a few seconds, "No it's only toilet paper."

"Oh shit!" he blurted out.

"Yes, that's what it's for," she replied with a big smirk. "But it's water that I'm craving."

"Funny girl! Like father, like daughter." he replied. "Okay. The next one up to the left then."

"Bingo!" she said, as she noticed another bottle beside it but it was empty. "And how come you didn't fill the other bottle?"

"Because that's the one that I'm putting our specimen in."

"Oh I see," she remarked.

He could hear her drinking heavily from the water bottle with his back still turned away, as he checked out the view. "So, did you save me some?"

"Oh shit! I'm sorry Tom." Now feeling quite selfish, as she handed him the nearly empty bottle.

"Well, I hope so!" he exclaimed. "I was hoping to have another water break. After walking back up from the pond."

"Frigg. I should have rationed better," said Sarah.

"Is that what you call rationing?" rubbing it in to her. "That's just real great. I'll just have to have a cold beer then." he said smiling.

"You bugger," she said. She slapped him on the shoulder, after seeing one in his hand. "And you had me feeling really guilty. I should have known that you always take a few beer with you, wherever you go."

"Okay then. Would you mind putting it back in?" he asked, handing her back the water bottle. "So, that pond is just down there?" he asked looking at the winding trail that headed downward.

"Yes. The pond will start to become visible, as we go further down that trail."

Minutes later, they arrived at the pond,

with the water as calm as glass. "Now, we don't want to get too close to the water. They might see our shadow and it could spook them," he whispered.

"How in the hell do you expect to catch one then?" she whispered back.

"I'll just use my brook trout tactics."

"Now this should be really entertaining!" she teased.

"All right boys, what are your locations?" Bob replied, "I'll be at my location in four more minutes Nick."

"I'm just going through that thick cedar area now. There are a lot of fallen trees across the trail."

"Okay Bob. Steve can you hear me? Ten-four."

"Nick, I'm up on the bluff. I have my bike parked just inside the tree line. And I'm going down to the pond by that alien trail as planned over."

"Any sign of Sarah?"

"Negative Nick. They probably took the bike trail down to the pond."

"That's a ten-four Steve," responded Mike. "We can only see up to where you stashed your bike."

"Ten-four Mike. Steve I'm almost at the pond now," said Nick. "Over and out."

Steve failed to see Sarah's yellow jacket lying only a few feet from where he was standing. He started to walk at a fast pace downhill, being cautious, but trying to get there as fast as he could, fearing the nightmare that Sarah and Tom were about to face. He would be their only chance of survival, as his heart pounded heavier.

As the girls sat around Mary's kitchen table awaiting news on the radio, she noticed Steve's nitro spray sitting on the window ledge. "Oh my God!" she said to Brenda. "He doesn't have his nitro."

"Oh Mary," Brenda responded. "I'm sure he won't overexert himself, knowing this," trying to keep her from panicking. She patted her back, "He'll do just fine. You watch and see."

Sarah stood back as Tom quietly lowered his pack from his back. He unzipped one of the longer side pockets, and pulled out a small green fishing rod and reel. "Now watch this," as pulled on the front eyelet.

His telescopic fishing rod was quite similar to the ones her father used, on their bike fishing trips.

She responded. "Oh how neat," leading him to believe she was impressed.

"Notice the wire leader I've tied to the line. Those critters won't be clipping my line. It's what I fasten to the leader that counts." She watched, as he pulled a small plastic box out of the same pocket. He then picked out a small silver lure with a black buck hair tail, and fastened it to his leader. Just then a loud and deep moaning sound echoed out over the whole area. They both looked all around to try and locate the source. "What in the fuck was that?" he whispered.

"I don't know," she replied. "But it's sure as hell sounded freaky to me! It gives me a real eerie feeling."

"It's probably a cow moose calling its calf. I'll just catch one of those critters. And we'll be on our way. " He took a few more steps closer to the water's edge.

"Right over there by that stump. That looks like a hot spot." Casting out his line, they both watched as the lure hit the calm water. At that split second, one of the critters came out from under a shaded log, attacked and hit his lure. He quickly started reeling it in To their surprise, it was followed by hundreds of other ones. It was as if they were waiting for their buddy to drop the lure, so they could indulge in it. "Holy shit. For it's little size, it's sure as hell is frisky!" His reel's drag screeched from the resistance of this hard fighting critter. "Hurry Sarah. Get that water bottle ready for me!"

"It's already done."

She stood right behind him as he lifted the critter out of the water. Squirming frantically, it let out a high-pitched cry, like that of a bat. Its wide mouth displayed rows of needle-like teeth. And it's scorpion tail with a fin at the end, swung intermittently from side to side.

"That tail must help to propel it, like a fish."

"A crayfish swims in reverse when threatened. These things don't seem to know danger. Okay drop it in."

"Are you crazy?" she exclaimed. "There's no fuckin' way I'm going anywhere near that thing!" She saw its claws opening and closing at a fast pace, remembering what one of them did to Tom's thumb.

"There's a pair of long nose pliers in that same pocket. Hurry, they're on the bottom."

She quickly brought them out, and handed them to him, being totally unaware of three NYANYAS stalking them from different parts of the pond, as their wakes were clearly visible.

"Hold still little fellow, while I unhitch your claw from this lure. There you go."

As the creature fell into the bottle, she quickly screwed the lid on. "Okay. Now let's hit the trail," she insisted while putting it into his pack.

"Just one more cast please," he urged.

"What the hell for! You got what you wanted."

"If I cast out further into deeper water. I just might catch its mother."

"Okay Tom. But promise me. Or you'll have a long swim back to your car!"

"You're on. I promise it's my last cast." He extended his right arm behind himself, and cast his line forward like a baseball pitcher. They watched his lure fly high in the air, landing way out into much deeper water. "I have to make this one count," he insisted smiling. He waited a few seconds for his lure to sink. "Okay mommy or daddy, where are you?"

Just then, the once mirror-calm water suddenly erupted with one of the NYANYA creatures being totally exposed to them. This sudden horrifying experience put them in a state of disoriented shock. His fishing rod fell from his hand and they just stood there frozen with their eyes wide open.

They watched this huge, engrossing creature that their minds could never have imagined, heading their way. Its claws were opening and closing simultaneously, with its large mouth revealing rows of long, sharp teeth. Glaring at them with crocodile-like eyes, swinging its tail back and forth, it crawled closer to them.

Tom grasped her trembling hand, as they slowly retreated taking a few steps backwards. He whispered, "we'll make a run for it in the count of three."

She whispered back. "I'm with you."

"Okay Steve. Can you take the shot?"
    "Yes Nick!" he shouted over the radio.

"I can't Nick. It's too risky," cautioned Bob, crouched down with his rifle lying across a fallen tree. "I have that creature in my sights. But Sarah and Tom are on the opposite side of it."

"Okay Bob. I'm in the same predicament. Steve, it's your shot," said Nick.

"Okay Nick. But I can't see Sarah and Tom."

"Don't worry. You're elevated high enough behind them," he said, knowing that time was of the essence. Just then, two more creatures emerged from the water just behind the first one. They just stayed stationary, treading water, waving their claws in the air, as if to intimidate. The closest one started to climb onto shore not even ten yards away.

"Hold on Steve."

"Bob, can you get a bead on the one closest to you?"

"Ten-four Nick."

"Okay then fellows. Just let me sight in on that third one. I have this branch in my way."

"Hurry then!" pressed Steve, as both he and Bob were ready to take the shot.

"All right one, two, three," said Tom, as the two turned and started up the trail. They took two strides. When the creature lunged out from the water, its head exploded as the other creature to the left of it did simultaneously. Tom was holding Sarah's hand as they glanced back to see what the explosion was. A shower of guts and body debris was scattered all about them on the ground and on tree limbs. Large pieces of reddish sticky goo landed on Tom's shoulder.

When Tom looked over his shoulder to remove the goo, he caught a glimpse of the third creature now totally out of the water. It was heading their way making that bellowing sound, as they ran for their lives.

Another loud explosion could be heard behind them. This time they didn't make the effort to look back. They just kept on running, putting as much distance as possible between them and that pond.

"Okay Steve. I got that third one as well!" said Bob over the radio.

"Thanks. And good shooting." said Steve. "Nick are you out there? Come in."

Disappointed in not being able to get

his sights on the third creature fast enough, Nick came over the radio. "Go ahead Steve."

"Sorry Nick. I had to make that call."

"Sorry my ass! With your daughter's life on the line, you made the best call!"

"So Steve. Where is Sarah and Tom now? Over," asked Mary on radio.

"They're headed back up to the trail to the plateau, over."

"Ten-four Steve. We'll be watching for them at this end," said Mike.

"Ten-four Mike, " said Steve.

chapter 15

nyanya fest

The loud booming sounds that came from the explosive tip bullets could be heard over to the next township. It even lured John, the conservation officer, over to that area of the lake.

While approaching, he just couldn't help but notice Steve's small aluminum boat pulled up and tied on the shoreline. He drove up closer for a better look, still curious about the loud explosions he'd heard. He got close enough to Steve's boat to make out its identification numbers. He stopped his boat, then pulled a black book out of his pocket, and began to log the numbers.

Mike was receiving another aerial photo, as Carol noticed John's boat up close to Steve's. She jumped out of her chair, and ran over to his telescope.

"What's wrong?" asked Mike.

"It looks like we have some more company." She lowered the telescope, while looking through it. "Oh that's just great Mike. It's our buddy, Johnny-be-good."

"I guess all that loud shooting got his curiosity. I just wonder what in the hell is going through that fucker's head about now?" he said. They both watched the drama on the monitor as John tilted his outboard up and positioned his boat right up alongside Steve's.

John scanned the general area around where the boat was tied. He then noticed the narrow deer path heading up the side of the steep hill. It looked rather intriguing to him. He wondered, "Why on earth would someone risk his or her life, climbing up that steep trail, to the top of that plateau? It's still too early for blueberry pickers."

He reached into one of his coat pockets, and took out what appeared to be a map.

After a brief look at it, he folded it back up, and put it back into his pocket. Then pulled out a cell phone, pushed some numbers, and brought it up to his ear, still scanning the hilltop. "Good morning Nicky. It's your favorite C.O. still stationed at Birch Lake. And yes, I do have suntan lotion and a swimsuit. All I'm missing is a cold beer!"

"Well John. I wish I could join you."

"Yes. Especially if you have that swimsuit you wore at last year's staff barbecue. The guys are still talking about it!"

"Sure, sure. You're just trying to flatter me as usual. So what is it this time?"

"I'm halfway up Birch Lake on the south shore. According to my map, over this high ridge is a large pond."

"You're right on John," replied Nicky. Confirming those coordinates on the large map on the wall, next to her desk. "That's real strange of you to inquire about that area. With all the weird things going on here this morning, your call doesn't surprise me at all."

"Surprise you?" he asked in a curious tone.

"Yes, because that very pond you just

inquired about, is on standby, ordered from head office as of five this morning. One of our twin otter water bombers was to drop some kind of rotenone concoction to poison whatever is in there. What's so strange is that they could really use that bomber up at that large fire just north of you. And get this, the person who's running the show is some Russian visiting Birch Lake. How can he have so much pull for something so bizarre? And it gets better. Four large army trucks loaded with troops stopped off at Tim Horton's parking lot earlier this morning. According to Sergeant Ross of the OPP detachment, they were fully armed with live rounds. And were to be on standby on some back road close to Birch Lake. What the heck is going on over there anyway John?"

Nicky's input shifted John's curiosity into high gear. Especially after he remembered seeing live rounds in the soldier's ammo belt earlier.

"Yes, I ran into that same convoy there earlier this morning. I really don't know what they're up to, but I'm about to find out. In the meantime, can you run a check

on this boat number that's tied up here?"
He gave her the series of letters and numbers. "I'm going off my radio now. I'll get
back to you soon by my cell phone only."

"Shouldn't you talk to Ken first?" cautioned Nicky.

"And get the run around," he said in a
bitter tone. "I'm tired of the ministry
treating me like a freakin' mushroom–
keeping me in the dark, and feeding me a
lot of shit. I'll get back to you shortly. Bye
for now." He put his phone back into his
pocket. "Bob Izumi my ass!" he muttered
as he started the steep climb.

"No John. You don't want to go there!"
uttered Mike, still watching John on his
monitor. "Oh shit! Don't tell me!" he
blurted out, as he shook his head. "Now
what?"

"Just call Nick," advised Carol calmly,
sipping her coffee.

"Come in. Come in Nick."

"Go ahead Mike."

"It looks like you guys are getting company. Johnny-be-good is climbing up that
trail to the plateau."

"Oh shit! That's all we need," replied

Nick, "Ten-four Mike!"

Tom and Sarah were now close to the top of the plateau. They were distracted by a loud humming from high above them. Stopping to catch their breath, they looked upward through the heavy cover of oak and branches. Through an opening in the branches, they could make out a silvery large saucer-shaped object, with a long circular base protruding from the bottom. It appeared to be making a landing just ahead of them, high above the plateau.

"Oh my God! Am I seeing things?" said Tom.

"I see the same thing too," she said. They stood there frightened and motionless, but intrigued over the UFO encounter. "We can exit out back on the same trail, and head to the cottage," she suggested.

"Okay, go ahead," Tom muttered.

Just then, Sarah saw a man in uniform suddenly appear up on the ridge close to where the saucer was landing. "Look!" she cried out pointing to the plateau. "Over there by the ridge, the man looks like a C.O." She ran out of the tree line cover towards him, with Tom right on her heals shouting out, "Officer! Officer! Help us!"

At the same time the large, dark shadow of the spaceship covered John. He just stood there in dismay. As the young couple ran to him seeking refuge, the spaceship slowly descended to the plateau.

Mike and Carol were watching their monitor in awe of what they were seeing. A UFO appeared just above the plateau. But they couldn't see John, Sarah or Tom, who were just out of their view, at a lower level.

"Holy shit! Talk about bad timing," muttered Mike.

Carol yelled out frantically, "Call Nick! Call Nick!"

Not wasting any time, Mike got on the radio, "Come in Nick! Come in Nick!"

"Yes, go ahead Mike."

"They're back! They're back! Up on the plateau!" Everyone assumed, that Mike was referring to Sarah and Tom.

"Yes Mike. I was expecting that they would appear about now. That's good!

It'll keep John busy until Steve gets there." Nick ended his transmission with a bit of a chuckle.

Mike and Carol's eyes made contact with each other. They were both surprised at how calmly Nick took the message. "Oh well. Nick did mention that he expected the aliens to return after they terminated those predators. I guess this is all kid's stuff to him."

Shifting their eyes back to the monitor, the top of John's head suddenly appeared. "Quick Carol, lower the camera." They could now make out Sarah and Tom at John's side just standing there bewildered. It was as if they were under some hypnotic trance. The saucer came to rest, not even twenty yards from where the three were standing.

Time seemed to switch to a slow motion mode, as seconds seemed like minutes. Suddenly an opening appeared along the side of the spacecraft, similar to an elevator. They watched a set of long human-like legs step down from the saucer, which led up to a tall larger frame. It was approximately seven feet tall with long arms and fingers on each hand.

The alien walked about ten feet from the saucer. It seemed to be preoccupied with something, not noticing or even detecting the presence of an audience. It suddenly stopped, and turned around to look back at the saucer. This time it looked over at the three earthlings, as it briefly stared them down with its large, yellow, cat-like eyes that protruded from its oval head.

Then totally ignoring them, it stared back at the opening of the saucer. Slowly raising its right arm towards the space-craft, it began to maneuver its long fingers. It seemed to be making some kind of hand signals. Mike's and Carol's eyes were glued to the monitor, as they set their coffee cups down.

A huge nightmarish creature crawled out from the saucer. It was more grue-some and larger, than the ones that they saw earlier in Nick's photos. It was mak-ing its way towards the alien, that was still signaling it. Mike picked up the radio.

"Come in Nick! Come in Nick!" shout-ed Mike frantically.

"Yes, go ahead Mike."

"I just want you to know that an ET has exited the spaceship. And it has one of those creatures with him. Sarah and Tom are up on the plateau with John as well, over."

Nick was stepping up onto the bike and couldn't understand how he misunderstood the earlier transmission. He knew that time was now a big factor for their survival. He picked up his radio, "Ten-four, I got you Mike. I'm on my way there now! I hope you got that message too Steve."

Steve was taking a few deep breaths as he took his radio out from his pocket, shocked by what he heard. "Ten-four Nick. I'll be up there shortly."

"Oh my God!" shouted Sarah trembling at the sight of such a gruesome thing. It quickly came to a halt after her loud outburst.

"Shhh! Keep it down!" said John grabbing her shoulder.

The creature turned to face them, then began to make a deep moaning sound. They were now faced with a critical dilemma. Close behind them was a high drop-off, down a cliff. The entrance to the trail was the only chance they had.

John unclipped the leather guard over his service pistol. He quickly analyzed the situation. The creature was now heading towards them, displaying its claws held high in the air. Greenish goo dripped from its large mouth, which displayed rows of long needle-sharp teeth.

John realized that the creature took commands from the ET, so it was wise to deal with it first. He drew his pistol out of its case and pointed it at the alien, "Okay, in the count of three, I'm going to open fire. Get ready to make a run for it back up that hill." Holding up his pistol with both hands, he took aim on the centre part of the alien. He quickly counted down "One, two, three," then fired three quick rounds into the alien's chest.

Sarah and Tom's timing was good. They ran to a higher level as they watched the alien being jolted backwards from the impact of John's bullets. Piercing its chest in a tight pattern, a light blue liquid oozed out from its wounds. John swung his pistol sights over to the creature, only ten yards away. Unexpectedly, the alien let out a loud shrieking noise, putting its hands on its chest. Those shrieking cries seemed to provoke the creature, making it much more aggressive. John quickly opened fire on the creature. But he realized his pistol was too small of a caliber to have any impact on its massive size.

Sarah and Tom stopped and looked back. They were surprised to see the alien still standing there observing the creature attacking John.

"Oh my God!" said Carol. As she saw the creature about to overtake John, "Please help him!" She wept as she watched helplessly.

John tried desperately to shoot the creature's eyes out but his bullets only ricocheted off its hard shell. It was too late.

The creature grasped both of John's arms just below his wrists in one of its claws, causing his pistol to fall, then hoisted him high off the ground. Loud horrifying cries of pain, continually blared from the top of his lungs, as he was yanked from side to side.

Sarah and Tom were still watching in shock. John suddenly fell to the ground.

The creature's claw had cut clean through his forearms like pruning shears. He just lay there moaning in agony, with blood gushing from his stubs, onto the flat bedrock. The creature clamped around John's abdominal area, its agile claw again lifting him up off the ground. His screams became muffled, due to large amounts of dark red blood gushing out from his mouth. It's razor sharp claws shredded John apart.

Tom and Sarah watched in horror, as it began to consume him. This horrifying confrontation between John and the creature, left Sarah and Tom disoriented, and frozen in fear.

Carol still kept her face covered with her hand, as Mike sat and watched the whole show, absorbing the horror as beads of sweat rolled down his forehead.

Mike watched the creature now heading in Sarah and Tom's direction. The alien still remained standing. The wounds on its chest had somehow congealed showing no sign of pain. It looked like a coach, proud of his team's performance.

Mike mumbled, gritting his teeth. "Come on you guys, get the fuck out of there!" watching helplessly, as the creature pursued its next prey.

Tom finally came to his senses and yanked Sarah's arm. They fled over the ridge, with the creature right on their tail. With its impressive speed, and maneuverability, Mike watched on feeling totally helpless. He pounded his fist on the desk, thinking they didn't have a chance, as a call came over his radio. "Come in. Come in Mike," radioed Nick.

"Yes. Go ahead Nick."

"Can you fill us in on the latest up there on the plateau?"

All choked-up over the gruesome events he just witnessed, he didn't know how to break the bad news to Nick, in fear of it being too much for Steve's heart to handle. Just then, as he looked up at the monitor, he saw the creature standing behind the alien, as they headed over the plateau in the direction of the pond. "Could this be the same one? Or did the alien call out another one from the saucer?" he wondered.

"It's all hell up there Nick! That alien,

and another one of those NYANYA creatures are following them down to the
pond. Right in Steve's direction!"

"Did you get that Steve?" asked Nick.

"Ten-four. I'm ready for them! And
what about Sarah and Tom?"

"Steve, I lost their visual over on the
plateau."

"Ten-four Mike," said Steve. Mike's
reply wasn't what he wanted to hear.

"Why didn't you tell us earlier that
they returned? Over," asked Nick.

"I did. Over," replied Mike.

Nick knew that their stories got mixed
up somewhere along the line, and that
this wasn't the time to iron it out. "Mike I
want you to call in for air and ground
support. And get back to me right away."

"Ten-four Nick! "

"Steve, I am driving around to join you
right now!" he insisted in a stern voice.
"Over and out!"

After hearing Nick's transmission,
Steve turned off his radio, fearing that
any sound now could tip-off the aliens to
his location. It was only his strong father-
ly love for Sarah in his heart that gave
him supernatural strength to carry on.

He was close to the plateau, when he heard a rustle on the trail heading in his direction. He knew full well what to expect after overhearing the radio transmission. He quickly brought up his rifle to his shoulder, with his finger on the trigger. The rustling got closer and closer as each second passed. Taking a couple of deep breaths to help calm down his heart, he waited quietly. He could hear his own heartbeat, and remembered his nitro spray was back at the cottage.

Like a ghost, the alien appeared and disappeared back into the foliage, like so many deer had done to him in past. "You son of a bitch!" He whispered.

Lowering his rifle, he could hear something else approaching. Something a whole lot louder. He had a good idea what it was, as he quickly brought his rifle back up to his shoulder. He could now clearly make out that horrific head of the creature in his sights. This time, with no hesitation, he squeezed the trigger. A loud explosion came from the creature. With blood and guts flying in every direction, bits of the debris landed and hung from him.

Turning his radio back on, he headed up the trail in an angry rage to hunt down the alien that had out-foxed him. His adrenaline rush kept him going, as he reached the plateau, when another call came over the radio,

"Come in Steve," said Mike in an exciting voice.

Steve knew that when Mike's voice was frantic like this, it was for a good reason. He reached for his radio while still in motion. "Yes, go ahead Mike."

"Yes Steve, that ET is now entering the UFO. And Nick, the air and ground support are moving in!"

"Ten-four Mike," Steve replied, in a quick manner not to waste any time. He dropped his radio back into his pocket, and proceeded to the plateau at a quick pace. Just then, Steve saw Sarah's yellow jacket lying down on a rock, amongst all the spilled blood on the trail. He remembered Mike's conversation on the radio with Nick about all the hell that happened up there.

Steve raised his head to see the saucer just ahead of him, with its elevator-type door slowly closing. All his wonder was now converted into extreme rage. "No fuckin' way!" he muttered. Steve quickly brought his rifle up to his shoulder, and squeezed the trigger with his sights fixed on the alien just inside the saucer's door. His timing was a fraction of a second too slow. The power head bullet only deflected off the spacecraft's door with a loud explosion. Quickly, he followed it up by firing another round, but the results were the same.

Steve hoped to at least cripple the spacecraft just enough, to keep it grounded, and wondered how much firepower he'd need. Then he remembered the rocket launcher that he had strapped to the front rack of his ATV. Running up to the tree line where his bike was hidden he quickly unhitched the bungee cords. Steve brought the rocket launcher up to his shoulder. After lining up the sights on the saucer, he squeezed the trigger, but nothing happened. He lowered it down from his shoulder to examine it, but couldn't see anything wrong. So he brought it back up to his shoulder again, and quickly aimed and squeezed the trigger, but it still didn't fire. A low humming sound started coming from the saucer. This only added more fuel to his rage, not wanting the aliens to escape. Steve placed the rocket launcher on the bike's rack, and started his bike.

Mike and Janis were watching this whole episode, as if they were watching an action-packed Hollywood movie. "What in God's name is he up to now?" said Mike. He watched him drive up to the UFO, like he was going to ram it or something.

Steve stopped just inches from the craft. Suddenly, the noise from the spaceship became more intense. He shifted the lever into low range, while muttering to himself, "Okay baby, you're in bull low four-by-four. Now do your thing," pinning the throttle lever to the handlebars. All four tires squealed and smoked on the bedrock. Then the bike started to shimmy. This motion acted like a jackhammer against the saucer.

    To his surprise, this impact action caused the UFO to slowly skid on the flat bedrock, towards the lookout area. For every foot the saucer advanced, the more the bedrock base sloped towards the cliff, as the UFO began to pick up speed. The rumbling sound from the saucer greatly increased. It was now skidding at a faster clip. Steve got the saucer right up to the edge of the cliff, and then hit the brakes. Watching the saucer topple over the edge, Steve could hear loud scraping noises.

Putting his park brake on, Steve jumped off his bike to look over the steep cliff to see the saucer wedged sideways down in a large crevice. It looked totally paralyzed like a fly caught between two panes of glass.

Just then, Nick came driving up to the plateau and parked beside his bike. He got off to stand next to Steve. Looking over the edge, he saw the saucer deeply wedged in the crevice. Then he couldn't help but notice the dents and scrapes on Steve's new bike.

Looking back at him with a big smile, they could hear the sound of a chopper approaching them from a distance. "Don't tell me!" exclaimed Nick. He shook his head still smiling, finding it quite humorous that Steve took out the saucer with his bike.

"Well, that thing you call a rocket launcher in my rack is a piece of shit!" he blurted out. He watched Nick pick it up, and carry it back to the edge of the cliff. Bringing it up to his shoulder, he aimed it at the UFO that was still humming, in the crevice. As he squeezed the trigger, the rocket shot out and struck the target with a gigantic boom that sent pieces of rock fragments flying out onto the water.

Just seconds later, the chopper came in to view and hovered just above them. The co-pilot noticed the UFO down in the crevice. "Nice work fellows!" he said, speaking over his P.A. holding his thumb up high.

Except for the humming sound that had now totally ceased, the saucer still remained fully intact, without a scratch, despite the tremendous hit from the rocket. Steve was somewhat frazzled over the rocket launcher only working for Nick.

"So what was the big deal Nick?"

"Nothing." Still holding it up to his shoulder, he turned sideways to Steve. You just didn't take the safety off," he indicated with his right hand index finger taping where it was located.

"Well, you son of a bitch!" Steve replied, as Nick took out his radio to make a call.

"Come in Mike."

"Yes, go ahead Nick."

"You can call off all military air and ground support units. We have the situation under control. Over."

"Ten-four Nick."

"Well Steve. It looks like we did it!" He patted Steve on the back.

"Did we, or will this just be a start of even bigger things to come?" replied Steve in a negative tone. Nick couldn't blame him for all the gory bloodshed that was all around them.

"Come in Nick."

"Yes. Go ahead Mike."

"I have the general on the line wanting to know how things are going?"

"Let him know that other than a few mishaps, we've had all the NYANYAS terminated. And as for the critters in the pond they will be dealt with shortly. We also have a souvenir for the I.A.W."

"Do you mean the UFO in the rock-cut Nick?"

"That's a big ten-four Mike!"

"I'm sorry Nick, but the general already saw it on a satellite photo."

"I guess nothing is a surprise anymore. Tell him I'll be getting back to him in a couple hours. After we get things cleaned up, over."

"Ten-four Nick."

"Come in Steve," said Brenda.

"Yes. Go ahead."

"I have a very important call for you."

He looked at Nick with a curious expression. "Go ahead."

"Dad would you mind bringing the boat back to the cottage for me? It's tied up down at the back door." There was a long pause as he lowered the radio and looked upward. Large tears appeared from his eyes and ran down his face. He mumbled out "Thank you, Lord."

With his radio silence, everyone could feel the deep emotion, that he was experiencing. Nick helped to comfort him by gently patting him on the back. He slowly brought up the radio to speak again and took a deep breath. "Yes sweetheart. I can do that for you. But there's just one thing."

"What's that Dad?"

"You'll have to cook me and the crew a big breakfast."

"You're on Dad!"

"Nick, come in... over."

"Yes Mike. Go ahead."

"It's that supervisor from the natural resource office. He said that their plane is up and ready to dump."

"Yes Mike. We can see it now," Nick said as the huge water bomber was approaching them from the southern sky. At the same time, Nick noticed a pistol lying on the bedrock in a large pool of blood. "Tell him to go ahead and dump. And let him know I'll be calling him back within the hour."

"Ten-four Nick."

Nick knew then that his next conversation with the supervisor wasn't going to be a pleasant one. Steve and Nick watched the water bomber as it dumped the concoction over the pond.

"I guess that should finish the job," commented Steve.

"Yes. I would say so," replied Nick.

"Now I'll take you up on that cold one!"

"I don't know how the rest of you feel, but because of what I experienced here today, I feel that no country should ever be independent from each other. Like the I.A.W., we are all that much stronger when we all work together. Whether it's aid or trade."

"Holy shit, Brenda! You sound like a true politician. I mean a true politician! You should be our ambassador!" stated Bob.

"She'll get her chance to say that in Russia," acknowledged Nick.

"How in hell will that ever be possible?" questioned Brenda.

"Well, I hope you'll be there next month for my military retirement party. And there are other countries close by that you might want to visit, like the Ukraine.

"Is that an invite?"

"It sure is!" declared Nick.

"Here's a toast to Nick's retirement. And to our new ambassador in Russia!" said Mike, as they all toasted.

"Well Nick, can we expect to see you back soon after that?" asked Janis.

"I heard tell of some sexy broad on this

lake, that needs some coaching on her fishing. And if your government will let me back in with a visa, there shouldn't be any problem."

"As if they'll give you any problems," responded Brenda, hugging Nick.

"I don't know about that Brenda? Right now, he is considered to be an alien. After all, he did enter into this country by way of a UFO. Get it, alien!" said Steve, as everyone groaned.

Three days later, everyone was sitting around picnic tables that were pulled together.

"Well, that was quite the turnout at John's funeral yesterday. It was just too bad that his family or colleagues will never know what really happened. Or how much of a hero he really was," sympathized Mary.

"Yes, this toast goes out to John for his heroic effort in saving Sarah and Tom," expressed Nick. "And slowing down those aliens so we could terminate them." They all toasted.

"I'm sure glad that they managed to get that saucer out from the crevice."

"Hell no Steve!" blurted Bob. "They should have left it right in place! It would have made for a good conversation piece for boaters passing by!"

"No Bob. I still think we could've sold it on eBay," suggested Steve.

"Yeah. And those were some big choppers that they used to pull that saucer out of there! I wonder where the I.A.W. lifted it to?" asked Tom with a curious look on his face, like he was trying to pump Nick in an indirect way.

"Well Tom. There are some questions that you sometimes will never get the answers to." Smiled Nick knowing full well that Tom just wanted to pick his brain. "And I understand Tom, that you'll be wrapping up your year at the university shortly. Well, if you're interested in working directly with the I.A.W. biology department, I just might have enough pull to get your resume in the front door."

"That would be totally cracked-out awesome. My utmost fantasy ever!" he replied in an exciting tone.

"Oh yes Tom. That reminds me," said Bob smiling over his remark. "We found your fishing rod, and backpack when we picked up these NYANYA claws at the north end of the pond. They're up on Steve's workbench in the woodshed."

"Thank you very much Bob," he replied. Sarah looked up at him seated across from her, and inhaled as though she was about to comment on the creature that they still had in their water bottle. But Tom, looking at her straight in the eye, shook his head slightly from side to side, indicating he wanted her to keep it hushed.

Steve sensed that she wanted to say something. "Do you want to say something Sarah?"

"Yes. This NYANYA fest is a great idea Bob. And the taste is out of this world!"

"You mean to die for!" said Brenda.

"Yes," replied Sarah. "Big time!"

"Well then," said Steve, standing up with his wine glass up high. "This is a toast to Nick and his comrades back in Russia who I understand are having a pig-out on NYANYA as well!"

Everyone else followed by saying, "Dieboursia!" as they stood under a homemade banner that read NYANYA FEST!

Photo taken by Reg Clark
Clark Photo, Blind River, Ontario
rclark4@sympatico.ca

about the author

Brian Horeck is a businessman and lives with his wife Shirley in Blind River, Ontario. This is his first novel, and he plans to release others in the near future.

Visit the author's website at:

www.minnowtrap.ca